Visions of Kerouac

a novel by

Ken McGoogan

Pottersfield Press, Lawrencetown Beach
Nova Scotia, Canada

Canadian Cataloguing in Publication
McGoogan, Kenneth, 1947 -
Visions of Kerouac
ISBN 0-919001-75-0
I. Title.
PS8575.G66V57 1993   C813'.54   C93-098526-5
PR9199.3.M34V57 1993

Published with the financial support of the Nova Scotia Department of Tourism and Culture, the Canada Council and the Department of Communications.

Cover illustration by Sheena McGoogan

Pottersfield Press
Lawrencetown Beach
R.R. 2, Porters Lake
Nova Scotia B0J 2S0

For Sheena, Carlin and Keriann

ACKNOWLEDGEMENTS

This is a work of fiction. All the characters are imaginary, but in creating "Jack Kerouac" I've adhered to the known facts about the real-life King of the Beats (1922-69).

For these facts I am indebted to many scholars and writers, among them Ann Charters, Gerald Nicosia, Tom Clark, Charles E. Jarvis, Dennis McNally, Barry Gifford and Lawrence Lee, Carolyn Cassady, Arthur and Kit Knight, Dave Moore, Joyce Johnson, John Montgomery, John Clellon Holmes and, of course, Kerouac himself. I am grateful to Lesley Choyce, the father of transcendental wood-splitting, for his sponsorship; to Kerouac aficionado Rod Anstee for his reading; to TVOntario's *Imprint* for inviting me to talk Beat; and to the *Calgary Herald* for allowing me to make a fictional hash of certain factual articles.

Thanks, finally, to Sheena McGoogan, my wife, for her front-cover illustration, back-cover photograph and million contributions to everything in between.

Walking on water wasn't built in a day.
Jack Kerouac

1

Mystical mumbo-jumbo was the only way to describe it. Repentances, confessions, solemn promises to avoid temptation — everything but dying to be born again. Besides, how often did I visit San Francisco? And with that I swung into Vesuvio's bar, where thirty years before, almost to the day, in the late summer of 1960, Jack Kerouac had taken a lethal first drink.

He lost control and couldn't stop drinking — was physically unable to stop — when what he really wanted to do was drive down the coast to visit Henry Miller. From this very bar, Vesuvio's, Kerouac telephoned the older writer every two hours to postpone, secretly believing he could drink himself back to sobriety, reach that remembered still point of controlled equilibrium. Ended up drinking until finally, disappointed, Miller told him no, Jack, it's too late, we'll do it another time.

Which, of course, they never did.

Though what I remembered that afternoon in 1990, as I swung into a padded seat on a bench against the wall, was subtly different: that Kerouac had chosen to drink himself blind that afternoon rather than visit and have Old Henry realize the truth about him — that he had become a drunk, an alcoholic bum. I believed Kerouac had done it on purpose, motivated by shame, and not that, having taken that first drink, he lost control.

I'm good at revising awkward facts.

A few days before, driving north up the California coast with my wife, Camille, and our two children, I'd spotted the Henry Miller Memorial Library and insisted on stopping. We were still forty miles south of Pacific Grove, where we'd reserved a room at a fancy bed-and-breakfast, and the kids wailed in protest. But no way I was going to miss this opportunity and Camille felt the same.

It wasn't until we were inside the library, really a frame house, looking at books and watercolors and pen-and-ink sketches, that I realized the place was also the home of Emil White, once Miller's best friend. Of course! This was where Miller, who for years had lived in a shack on a nearby ridge, had waited for Kerouac that long-ago evening and taken his painful telephone calls.

That's what I remembered, though later I discovered Miller had taken those calls at the house of another friend who lived further north — and mostly from Lawrence Ferlinghetti, phoning for Kerouac.

At revising awkward facts, make that VERY good.

So now, sitting in Vesuvio's, I told myself I'd closed a circle. And as my eyes adjusted to the relative darkness I savored the place, famously unchanged from the glory days of the fifties. A few seats away, three men my own age or a shade younger, late thirties, obviously regulars and drinking coffee, sat hunched over a chess board. A black-haired man stood at the bar, the far end, talking with a lanky bartender in sneakers and brown jeans, who glanced over while wiping the counter but made no move to serve me.

Soft jazz established a mood, sounded like Charlie Parker, and black-and-white photographs adorned the walls. Two were of Kerouac, one of them illustrating "The Jack Kerouac" under a list of Vesuvio Specials that included bohemian coffee, brandy amaretto with a twist of lemon and the J.K. itself: tequila, rum, orange juice, cranberry juice and a squeeze of lime, $3.

Carefully, I copied the hand-written sign into my notebook. Might become part of the travel article I was planning — though mainly this trip was a celebration. Back home in the heart of the Canadian Rockies — which is where I sit at this moment, surrounded by snow-capped mountains — Camille and the children had rejoined me after three endless months.

To mark the occasion we flew to Los Angeles. After four days at Disneyland, we rented a car and drove north up Highway One. We followed that twisting two-laner as it climbed and dove along the California coast, oohing and aahing over craggy bluffs and wind-blown trees and the Pacific Ocean crashing white-capped over black rocks — surely one of the world's great drives.

Besides the Memorial Library, the highway produced two moments. First, just north of the Esalen Institute, now closed to the public, I spotted an old fire road I remembered from the sixties. Back then, with a rucksack on my back and a girlfriend named Misty, I'd ignored a "Keep Out" sign, climbed a fence and hiked down the hill to camp beside a stream. Now the trees and shrubs looked different, tamer and browner, less green, but this was the place and no mistake. I ached to do it all again but contented myself with snapping photos from the highway.

Second, fourteen miles south of Monterey, I drove across Bixby Creek Bridge — sensational enough that it figures in tourist brochures — and swung right onto the Old Coast Road. No pavement now, just hard-packed dirt-road that wound steeply downhill and became a rutted track as it disappeared into a forest. The children were getting ratty, needed a play, so Camille took them out and I drove alone, thumping and banging, into the trees and across a tiny creek.

This was the road Kerouac had started down one night thirty years before. He'd taken an eight-dollar taxi ride from Monterey and got out at the bridge, the cabbie refusing to descend into the darkness. He was making for Ferlinghetti's cabin in the woods, destined to become the main setting for his novel *Big Sur*. But he'd been drinking, the night was dark and moonless and loud with crashing ocean and Kerouac lost his way, ended up bedding down in a meadow.

Ferlinghetti's cabin was still down here somewhere, I'd been told. But overwhelmed by trees and barricades and signs saying "Private Property" and "Keep Out," I couldn't find it. I decided it was magic to have come this close, backed the car along the rutted road for a couple of hundred yards and finally managed to turn around.

In San Francisco, we stayed a short slog from Union Square. First night in town, having dropped off the car, we went walking. In 1967 I'd worked here as a bicycle messenger, roared around downtown for up to ten hours a day. From memory I could still draw a map of streets and alleys and show you absolutely the quickest route from Grant and O'Farrell, say, to Battery and Jackson.

To Camille and the children, that first night, I proposed a shortcut: "Trust me, I know my way around this burg." But suddenly I was leading them past wigged-out crazies cutting dope deals and would-be prophets proclaiming the end of the world. And homeless people, so many homeless. Camille gave me a look.

"City has changed, what can I say?"

Next day, like many another vacationist, I shut a mental door on the homeless so I could revel in San Francisco. We visited the Coit Tower and stared out, wind-blown, at the Bay Bridge, long since repaired from the earthquake of the previous year. In Chinatown we crowded into shopping emporiums and bought San Francisco sweatshirts. We rode cable cars, visited Pier 39 and paid a street-artist to sketch the children.

From Fisherman's Wharf we took a boat cruise that brings you within howling distance of that gloomy island prison, now unused, Alcatraz. The cruise highlight comes a few moments later, when you're standing on deck in the wind and suddenly the sea gets rough and you look up at huge red girders and shiver to realize you're sailing under the Golden Gate Bridge, and yes, you're here again, this is it, you're back in San Francisco.

Next morning, Day Three, Camille took the children to the zoo and I rambled around the Haight-Ashbury. More on that later, the old haunts a story in themselves. By two-thirty I was back downtown, still on schedule and scrambling onto the running board of a Hyde Street cable car that was already standing-room-only.

We rattled up Jackson and turned onto Hyde, still climbing. I had my map out — this area unfamiliar, too steep for bicycles — and checked as we rumbled and clanged across Pacific Avenue, then Vallejo and Green. Suddenly there it was, Union Street, and as we crested the hill I jumped off and stepped smartly to the sidewalk, watched the cable car disappear down Hyde Street towards the waterfront, a sign on its back-end shouting "Meet me at the St. Francis," and the brakeman ringing out a crazy tune.

I registered the view of the Bay as spectacular, but mainly I stood savoring the knowledge that this was Russian Hill. This was where, walking one foggy night in 1952, Kerouac had chanced upon the actress Joan Crawford at work on a film. He'd gone back to the house to fetch Carolyn Cassady, then his mistress. But she hadn't wanted to leave the children untended, so he'd returned alone to watch and scribble notes for an eight-thousand-word tour-de-force called "Joan Rawshanks in the Fog."

Map in hand, I danced across Hyde Street through the afternoon traffic, swung back the way I'd just ridden and there it was: Russell Street. Half a block down Russell, and right up against the sidewalk, stood Number 29 — a tiny brown house with a false-brick front and a peaked roof. I stood surprised at having found it so easily.

Here Jack and Neal and Carolyn Cassady had lived out their ménage à trois. Here Jack had written *Visions of Cody* and entertained the Cassady children with an early cartoon version of *Dr. Sax*. Uptairs, in an attic room behind that window and those drawn blinds, he'd worked and made love with Carolyn, lain with her listening to the pitter-pat of rain on the roof.

Strangely moved by this thought, so textured it was almost a memory, I snapped photos of the tiny house. I wanted to see the place from the rear, and also the court yard, but could find no alley, no way to get around back. I walked up and down out front, trying not to look suspicious. Then, enough. I wheeled and emerged onto Hyde Street, strode uphill past barbershops and laundromats and beauty parlours. At Union I swung downhill towards City Lights and Vesuvio's bar, enjoying the sunshine, buoyed by the knowledge that Kerouac must have hiked this route many times.

In Vesuvio's, having realized finally that the bartender had no intention of serving me on the padded bench, I'd moved to the bar. Now I sipped coke through a straw. Upstairs, on the balcony level, I'd discovered more photos and funky folk art and copied signs into my notebook: "If you drink to forget/ please pay in advance." And this sexist quotation from W.C. Fields, Kerouac's old favorite lush: "T'was a woman who drove me to drink... and I never had the decency to write and thank her."

I found myself thinking that, unlike my own generation, the so-called Flower Children, the Beats had made their mark on this city. A seeker could still drink coffee at the Café Trieste, as Kerouac had, and Spec's bar, where I figured to go next, doubled as a Beat museum. City Lights Bookstore — where I'd just bought a copy of Kerouac's *Safe In Heaven Dead* — boasted a whole Beat Literature section, with books not only by Kerouac but by Allen Ginsberg, Gregory Corso, Bob Kaufman and, of course, City Lights owner Lawrence Ferlinghetti.

But now the lanky bartender, who'd left off talking with the black-haired guy at the end of the bar to mix up some fruity concoction, slid a chimney glass in front of me.

"What's this?"

"Courtesy of that gentleman," he said, nodding down the bar. "It's a Jack Kerouac Special."

The black-haired stranger made like he was tipping an imaginary hat. I grinned and did the same. The chimney glass was frosty. Kerouac would have preferred a double bourbon and gingerale — though a quick sniff told me The Special packed wallop. My whole body shuddered. Hell, one drink wouldn't hurt. I picked up the glass, glanced again down the bar — and saw something strange.

Maybe I'd done too much hatless walking in the sunshine. Maybe I'd wrestled too many heavyweight memories, both Kerouac's and my own, but as I stared at the black-haired stranger, I saw his face change. Ridiculous, I knew — but for an instant I thought I was staring at Jack Kerouac himself. Near the end.

But I see I must start further back.

2

This obsession with Jack Kerouac? It's rooted in Montreal where I came of age, goes back what? More than a quarter century. December, 1965. See me standing in a basement bookstore in a blue-pinstripe suit, shirt-and-tied, my overcoat open, leafing through a paperback copy of *On The Road*. I'm eighteen years old, tall, dark and intense. Yes, and handsome, too, why not declare it? Slim and fit, no hint of a beer belly. In high school I'd been an athlete.

Kerouac I knew only by reputation, as King of the Beats: a wild-man writer in the tradition of Jack London and Thomas Wolfe, two of my father's old favorites. This last had made me leery, but recently I'd resolved to bury the past and so I took out my wallet.

Nine o'clock that night, set to read for twenty minutes, I picked up *On The Road*. Didn't put it down until two in the morning, having finished it. Impossible then to sleep. The novel had hit me like the fulfillment of some half-forgotten prophecy.

I swung out of bed, pulled on blue jeans and bulky sweater, overshoes and duffle coat. Then plunged into the winter night. The cold didn't hurt, though I could see my breath as I strode through empty, snow-banked streets, waving my arms and talking to myself. I ended up at Ben's Delicatessen, where I downed a lean smoked-meat sandwich on rye, dill pickle on the side. And decided to take the next day off.

I was working at a personnel agency as a "vocational counsellor," really a glorified salesclerk, but I phoned in sick, spent the day hunting Kerouac in bookstores. As Christmas came and went, slowed only by party-season binges, I pounded through *The Dharma Bums* and *The Subterraneans*, through *Big Sur* and *Dr. Sax* and even *The Town and The City*. Early in the new year, when

Desolation Angels turned up in hardcover, I celebrated my nineteenth birthday by staying home from the agency and reading about life on a fire lookout.

What was it about Kerouac that entranced me?

Certainly his poor-boy biases and French-Canadian cadences rang familiar. But above all I relished his youthful exuberance, his wild, shouting joy at being alive. Six months before, I'd tracked Henry Miller to The Four Horsemen of his Apocalypse, among them Dostoevsky and Nietzsche. From there I'd plunged into Sartre and Camus, into Kierkegaard and Heidegger and Walter Kaufmann, and can you imagine trying to wend without guidance through these existentialist halls?

Kerouac showed me that I'd lost myself in a maze of God-is-deadness designed by middle-aged Europeans. Reminded me that I was young and North American. In his celebration of experience I found a thread I hadn't known I was seeking. That was it! To become a writer I needed experience.

This put me on the road to Psychedelic San Francisco, that road winding through the Do-It-Or-Back-Down Game and a North Dakota jail cell, through a fiasco in New York City and a rainy night in Boston when ... but I'm getting ahead of myself.

A few months after I discovered Kerouac, and while still socking away funds for my Great Escape, I got fired from my job at the agency. I'd met an ex-job-seeker, a gorgeous red-head, at a down-and-dirty bar and imagined — such was my naiveté — that she'd appreciate my ferreting out her old application, her height and weight and where she'd gone to high school.

The firing plunged me early into my new life, though psychologically I was overdue. No thought of looking for a new job. Instead, with a ne'er-do-well friend named Duggins, a fellow would-be writer, I hitchhiked to Toronto. Covered the distance, three hundred and forty-odd miles, in three rides, nothing to it, and went to see Dixon, an old basketball buddy.

A couple of years before, Dixon had dropped out of high school and moved to Toronto to live with his sister. Trouble with his father. Recently he'd answered an advertisement to share a one-bedroom apartment with an "older guy" named Charles, who was all of twenty-eight. The place was on Jameson Avenue in the west end, on the fourteenth floor of a highrise. Hardwood floors, fridge and stove, a small balcony — it was perfect. Dixon said we could crash as long as we liked. Party time.

Two weeks into this arrangement, tired of the juvenile carousing, Charles moved out, just disappeared one afternoon, taking his furniture with him. An old record player and a couple of Dylan albums belonged to Dixon, and those he left behind. Also a few dog-eared paperbacks.

Who cared? The hide-a-bed we missed, and the table and chairs, because now we had no place to sit. The only real problem, though, was the rent. Dixon was struggling to pay off his new sports car, a Triumph TR-3, while working as a stock-control clerk. To get the job he'd lied, claimed he'd graduated from high school. Lately his boss had been asking to see written proof. Dixon kept insisting that he'd sent for the records. And hung on.

Every morning he'd crawl out of his sleeping bag and bang around the apartment getting dressed. Duggins would open one eye and complain: "Jesus, Dixon! Show some consideration."

Duggins kept promising to borrow big bucks from his father, a management consultant who lived here in T.O. But he never got around to it. In the secret pocket of his houndstooth jacket he'd stashed fifteen dollars, thought nobody knew. Instead of spending it, though, he mooched.

As for me, before leaving Montreal I'd applied for unemployment insurance. A friend who'd sublet my bachelor pad had promised to forward all cheques, but as yet he'd sent nothing.

Finally I decided Canada Manpower was the answer, get some temporary work. The hard part was reaching the centre before six in the morning, when the dispatcher doled out jobs. Duggins kept promising to join me in the crush, but never got out of his sleeping bag.

One day I loaded cartons of tomatoes onto trucks. Another I spent out front of a factory using a pike-like tool to pick up paper, cardboard and banana peels. Then I almost crippled myself emptying a warehouse of car parts — bumpers and steering wheels and boxes full of seat belts — and decided I was too gung-ho. Took a break.

Back on Jameson Avenue, cooped up on the fourteenth floor, no money to go anywhere, Duggins and I developed our own vocabulary, a private language of macho posturing whose key phrase was "Do It Or Back Down." The trick was to be as patronizing and disdainful as possible. We started with large assertions — with Duggins declaring that soon he'd be drinking rum in Jamaica, mon, or me boasting that I'd publish The Great Canadian Novel before I was twenty.

Gradually, we worked our way to smaller issues, until finally one of us would say, "I'm going to make a peanut-butter sandwich," or, "I think I'll take a shower," and instantly the other would challenge him: "Go ahead, talker. Do it or back down."

Then, if you didn't do it, whatever It was, you were a coward, a craven milksop, a whey-faced poltroon, or maybe a spineless sniveller whose balled-up courage would look like BB shot rolling down a four-lane highway.

Probably you had to be there.

But Dixon got the idea and we all three began to push it, this Do-It-Or-Back-Down Game. One evening, as we sat against various walls in the living room eating spaghetti covered with ketchup, Dixon said, "This tastes awful."

Duggins said, "You'll eat it, talker, and like it."

Dixon looked up in mock astonishment. He was the strongest of us, a muscular six-three, though Duggins was heavier. "Duggins, I don't like your attitude."

It didn't take a genius to see where this was going. "Now wait a minute, guys," I said. "This is the only food in the house."

This Duggins ignored: "What are you going to do about it?"

The point of no return. Dixon looked at the ceiling: "I'm going to shove this plate of spaghetti into your face, that's what."

"Go ahead, talker. Do it or back down."

That's how the free-for-all began. As Dixon made good, Duggins didn't even flinch. Calmly, deliberately, his face and sweater dripping spaghetti, he strode to the stove. He took the remaining noodles, added the rest of the ketchup, then wheeled and ran across the room. Dixon ducked. The spaghetti landed in my lap and suddenly there we were, three overgrown five-year-olds in a highrise apartment, flinging food and battling for water taps.

Dixon was emerging as undisputed king until Duggins grabbed the broom and began swinging it like a staff, yelling, "Make way for the mighty! Stand aside and let the better man pass!"

Dixon took a few shots in the shoulder but managed to grab the broom. The two of them crashed against the balcony door before tumbling onto the floor, wrestling and punching in earnest.

"What's going on in there?" This from the front door, where somebody was hammering: "Hey! Open up!"

We froze. I called, "Who is it?"

"The superintendent! Open up or I'll call the cops."

I went to the door, opened it a crack and explained that we'd been practising jujitsu. That we weren't properly dressed and couldn't invite him inside. "But if we're bothering our fellow tenants, we'll stop right away."

The usual adolescent arrogance. But the red-faced super didn't want trouble. He growled that next time he'd call the cops and strode away down the hall. I closed the door and leaned against it: "That's it for me, jokers. I'm pulling a Kerouac."

"Do it, talker," came the derisive chorus. "Do it or back down."

3

When you die you're transformed, transmogrified — especially your mind. Death is the Great Transmogrifier. You come out the other side but you're not the same person, not exactly. The body is the least of it. This I was realizing in August of 1970, ten months after I'd finished drinking myself to death, as I slogged up a mountain in the Canadian Rockies. My memories were intact but my rhythms were different, the way I thought and used language. Also certain attitudes, though I didn't know why.

Earlier that day I'd awoken disoriented, found myself standing on a two-lane highway surrounded by spectacular mountain peaks, my rucksack beside me in the dirt. I was still blinking when a top-down Lincoln Continental, a cinnamon-red convertible, roared around the corner and squealed to a halt. Behind the wheel sat an ethereal blonde in a white bikini. A cosmic joke, this, because a famous editor had once wanted me to cut just such an incident: "Unbelievable," he said. "Doesn't matter if it happened."

Grinning madly, chortling even, I swung my pack into the back seat and hopped over the door into the front.

Like the original, this dynamite blonde was maybe twenty-two years old, but she spoke English with a French accent — a lovely twist. Said her name was Camille and, with a wave of her hand, identified the mountains around us: "Les Rocheuses." We tooled west along the Trans-Canada and then north up Highway 93, the Banff-Jasper Highway, with me oohing and aahing at the scenery and the crisp, clean air, at the elk and horned sheep roaming wild.

Camille told me I was on my way to visit a fire lookout stationed on Mount Jubilation, halfway between Banff and Jasper. "Frankie's a long-time fan, early twenties, your basic rucksack warrior. He spent a year in San Francisco, watched the Haight go bad. Hails from Montreal."

16

"He's French?"

"Half and half — *comme toi.*" She pronounced it *"tway,"* *à la Québécoise.* "His father's half-French and his mother partly Acadian. *Sa langue maternelle, c'est l'anglais.* But he grew up in a French town: Ste. Thérèse Sur-le-lac?"

"I remember now!" A fragment came back. "This is the guy I've bet on!"

"Frankie's your kick at the can, Jack." She pulled over onto the shoulder. "Today's August thirty-first. You've got three days."

Camille let me out at a sign saying "Jubilation Lookout, 4.5 miles," then waved and zoomed off up the highway, gone from me forever. I shouldered my pack and followed a rutted road into the pine-smelling forest. In a few minutes I came to a wooden bridge, leaned over the railing and watched an angry river twist and roar through a steep-walled canyon. By now the sun was high in the blue sky, so I took off my shirt and stuffed it into my rucksack.

For the next hour I climbed through a forest of fir, spruce and lodgepole pine, enjoying the feeling of being alive, even the buzz of the black flies and the stink of bear droppings. I stopped by a stream that tumbled across the trail, sat on a rock and ate peanut butter sandwiches. Then I started hiking again. The trail grew steeper, switched back and forth, and I huffed and puffed and talked to myself about the Great Transmogrifier.

The air grew thin, the white-barked pines less bushy. Painted rocks lined the trail. I kept climbing, thought I heard a voice and then, yes, someone up ahead was strumming a guitar and singing. Thirty yards more and I could make out the words: "Don't know why there's no sun up in the sky, stormy weather. Since my gal and I ain't together, it's raining all the time."

Sounded like Frank Sinatra — the early Sinatra, but with what a sense of desolation. And that's when the first rush hit me, triggered by the singing, and I realized that in transformation I'd lost plenty, but also I'd gained. Images and scenes rushed at me, fragments and chunks out of Frankie's past, and I hiked the last stretch of trail in time to the music: "Life is bare, gloom and misery everywhere, stormy weather. Just can't get my poor old self together. I'm weary all the time."

I rounded a final corner, emerged from the evergreens and stood looking up at a wooden fire tower straight out of the 1940s. An octagonal office, all eight windows open, perched thirty feet above me on four gigantic telephone poles.

Still I couldn't see Frankie, but as he hit the bridge his voice made me shiver: "When she went away the blues walked in and met me. If she stays away that old rocking chair gonna get me."

I strode towards the tower, still lugging my pack, and couldn't help joining in: "All I do is pray the Lord above will let me walk in the sun once more."

Frankie didn't miss a beat. He stepped over to the window on my side and looked down, still strumming. Now the rushes came thick and fast, whole vistas of experience, but we finished the song as a duet: "Can't go on, everything I had is gone, stormy weather. Since my gal and I ain't together. Keeps raining all the time, the time. Keeps raining all the time."

We held that last note a long time.

"Stormy weather?" I waved my hand at the sunshine, the cloudless sky, and broke into another standard: "Blue skies smiling at me/ Nothing but blue skies do I see."

"I don't believe it!" Frankie slapped the window ledge. "In this day and age? A fellow Sinatra fan?"

I dropped my pack on the ground, wiped my brow with my arm, then stood savoring the picture-postcard panorama: green trees, blue sky, jagged mountain peaks and, far below, a turquoise river winding through a shadowed valley.

Frankie called, "Come on up and check the view from here."

I climbed the wooden ladder that ran up one side of the tower to a platform. Frankie opened a trap door and I went up a second, shorter ladder into his office.

Here, besides the guitar, an old Harmony Sovereign leaning against one wall, he had a hardback chair, a wastebasket full of crumpled paper and a fold-out table that held a typewriter, a dictionary and a typewritten manuscript. Everything from the waist up was open windows. I looked out: "This is incredible."

"Here, try these." He handed me binoculars. "Put the cord around your neck."

Frankie was half a head taller than me, and slimmer, but we had the same coal-black hair, the same blue eyes, and we were both struck by the physical resemblance. The rushes were coming so fast I could barely register them.

My unexpected arrival at this, the most isolated fire lookout in the Rockies, had raised Frankie's spirits. And as I peered through the binoculars, focusing with difficulty because of the rushes, he blathered: "Directly opposite, that's Mount Murchison. Local Indians used to think it was the tallest mountain in the world. There's the highway — that necklace in the forest. And see where the Saskatchewan River meets the Howse? That's Saskatchewan River Crossing. The early fur traders used to travel through that pass. But, hey, you must be thirsty."

Frankie handed me a thermos of water.

I said thanks and took a swig. "How high are we, anyway?"

"Seven thousand feet."

"And the mountains around us?"

"Most are ten-six or ten-seven. The one we're on, Jubilation, is ten-nine."

"Look, mountain goats!" I peered again through the glasses. "This reminds me of my own days as a fire lookout."

"You were a lookout?"

"Down in Washington. The Cascades. I was on Desolation Peak."

"You're kidding! That's where Kerouac was. When were you there?"

"Let's see. Must have been 1956."

"Wow! You don't look that old! I forget when Kerouac was there, exactly, but it was in the fifties. Ever run into him? Jack Kerouac?"

"Maybe I should introduce myself." I let the binoculars fall to my chest and held out my hand. "I'm Jack Kerouac."

"Hey, that's not bad." Frankie laughed and took my hand. "Jack? I'm Friedrich Nietzsche."

"No, you're not. You're Frankie McCracken."

"Ha! This gets better and better! Come to think of it, you do resemble the King of the Beats. But haven't you heard? Kerouac died last October."

"Drank myself to death," I said, turning again to stare through the binoculars. "Not to worry, though. As you can see, I'm still on the road."

"Uncle!" Frankie clutched his head and did a little dance. "Uncle! Uncle!"

4

A bizarre series of accidents and misadventures, I called it in
Winnipeg. An unpredictable sequence of mishaps, setbacks and reversals. In this I included the Chicago flophouse, the
North Dakota jail cell and the looming betrayal of Duggins,
entirely foreseeable, as yet unacknowledged.

But even a modest road tale, a fragment of highway saga,
cries out for linear treatment, so take it from Toronto, where the
Existing Plan had the three of us heading West. Vancouver, San
Francisco, Mexico City — ultimately, we'd hit South America.

After the childish free-for-all, and my declared intention to
pull a Kerouac, I laid out a Revised Version. Dixon would drive
me to Detroit, get me across the border, and from there I'd
hitchhike. I'd travel via Winnipeg, set up a base in Vancouver.
Duggins and Dixon would follow and together we'd embark on
phase two of our journey.

Money was the challenge. Still, I had thirty dollars and
Duggins owed me forty. He'd spent his secret stash but had also
visited his father. The man, obviously no fool, had refused to
lend him a cent, but had phoned around and located a furniture-
moving job.

On Monday, Duggins would start work. Wednesday, he'd
receive his first pay cheque. Thursday, I'd arrive in Winnipeg —
and Duggins would wire me twenty dollars. The remaining
twenty he'd send to Vancouver the following week, care of
General Delivery, along with any unemployment cheques forwarded from Montreal. "How's it sound?"

"Do it or back down."

The expedition started well enough. Sunday morning, the
three of us roped my giant black duffle into the trunk of the TR-3.
At ten o'clock, jammed into bucket seats, we pulled out. And five

hours later, having lied at the U.S. border about the purpose of our visit, we rolled into Detroit City. We drove around downtown, joked about visiting a strip joint and ended up in a greasy spoon eating club sandwiches.

Late afternoon found me on the ramp to Highway 94, a high-flying interstate, alone with my monster duffle bag. My head was still spinning with the sudden-ness of goodbye when two sailors pulled over in a Rambler. They'd seen my black duffle, regulation American Navy, and figured I was one of them. By the time they knew better, I'd settled into the back seat.

The sailors drove me to Gary, Indiana, just outside Chicago, talking together while, entranced, I watched the miles roll away: Ann Arbor, Battle Creek, Kalamazoo. This hitchhiking was fantastic. I piled out at a train station, caught a commuter special and found myself rattling towards Chicago, clickety-clack, my giant duffle in the seat beside me, staring out, my face against the window, clickety-clack, clickety-clack, thinking of Thomas Wolfe crossing America this way, with Jack Kerouac hot on his heels and then, well, what can I say? clickety-clack, clickety-clack, clickety-clickety clack.

Maybe hubris was a factor?

Certainly, Chicago was a city of surprises. On arrival, I discovered the first of them: train tracks wound through downtown on a trestle high above street level. This made an impression, I know, because months later I dreamed a variation. Now I lugged my kitbag down wooden stairs to the sidewalk.

The area was deserted. The air was cool, maybe forty degrees Farenheit, but no problem, I was wearing my red-and-black hunting jacket. It was after midnight. No sense wasting money on a room. I staggered the streets, my kitbag on my shoulder, seeking an all-night restaurant. A couple of seedy bars were open, but they looked tough and might run into money.

Finally, I spotted a bus depot enclosed by frosted windows. A place to crash? Through the door I went and surprise: fifteen or twenty down-and-outers had already claimed the place. Most were snoring peacefully, jammed against each other, but two guys eyed me and exchanged a look.

I lugged my duffle back into the street, glancing over my shoulder. Half a block away, I noticed a sign: "Rooms, 55 cents. Deluxe, 65 cents." At those prices, how could I miss? I climbed the battered stairs to a counter top and pounded on a bell. A red-eyed man, unshaven, dressed in baggy trousers and an undershirt, shuffled out from behind a curtain. I told him I wanted a room.

"Plain or Deluxe?"

"What the hell?" I handed him a five. "Deluxe."

The man gave me change, took a key from a rack and tossed it onto the counter. He jerked his thumb at a sign on the wall behind him and quoted it without looking: "No refunds." Then he said, "third floor," and nodded at the stairs on my left.

Two flights up, I emerged from the stairwell into a corridor covered with wire mesh. Had I made a mistake? Bent low under the weight of my duffle, I checked the big red number in the stairwell. Yes, I was on the third floor. Now, as my eyes adjusted to the yellow light, I made out doors. Two rows of cubicles faced each other across the corridor. Finally it hit me. I was going deluxe in a flophouse.

I staggered down the hall to my cubicle and swung through the door. Found a cot, a hard-backed chair and just enough floor space for my duffle. Flimsy sheets of wall-board separated the cubicle from its neighbors. They ended, like the walls of a public-toilet stall, six inches above the floor. The wire mesh ran over the top and through it I could see the beams of the roof. I lowered my duffle onto the floor with a grunt and the guy in the next cubicle told me to keep the noise down.

The cot looked clean enough, but I threw back the covers to check. Nothing. I stripped down to my T-shirt and undershorts and crawled between the sheets. On the wall above my bed was a yellow 40-watt lightbulb. When I tried to turn it off the string broke, so I reached up and unscrewed the bulb, burning my fingers.

I lay in the darkness listening to drunks snore and moan in their sleep. At the far end of the corridor somebody retched. Somebody else couldn't stop coughing. Still, I congratulated myself: this beat lugging a monster duffle around the streets of Chicago. I closed my eyes to sleep, then found myself scratching. Realized I was itchy all over. Bedbugs?

I twisted on the light and threw back the covers. Nothing. I turned off the light and tried to relax but the itching resumed. Quick now, on with the light, back with the covers. Still nothing. Maybe the bedbugs were too small to see? I looked up. Maybe they fell down through the chicken wire mesh. No, that was crazy. The guy in the next cubicle muttered something about my fucking light.

"Just a minute, just a minute."

I'd paid money for this cubicle. I wasn't going back outside to stagger the streets. I pulled on my jeans and tucked them into my socks. Then my sweaty workshirt. Again I lay down, this time on top of the sheets, though under the blankets. I turned off the light and immediately started itching again. My legs, my arms, even my face.

But no way I was going back outside. Instead I dozed fitfully, tossing and turning and scratching until six in the morning, when finally I rolled out of bed, pulled on the rest of my clothes and stumbled into the streets of Chicago. Map in hand, kitbag on shoulder, I made for the Greyhound bus depot. There, after removing my shaving kit, face-cloth and towel, I deposited my duffle in a locker. Things were looking up.

Then, in the washroom mirror, another surprise: red blotches covered my face and neck. My God! Had I caught some disease? Worried now, I made for the downtown YMCA, strolled in nonchalant and went straight to the elevators. I got off at the ninth floor, found a communal washroom and spent twenty minutes in the shower. After drying myself and dressing, I checked the blotches again. Looked like they were disappearing. Could it be?

At a nearby cafeteria, I downed toast and coffee. This time, when I checked in the washroom, the blotches were gone. Who cared what it meant? Feeling good again, though tired from lack of sleep, I roamed the now-crowded streets looking for Carl Sandburg's city, the unforgettable hog butcher of the world, but found only glass canyons and windy waterfront. Enough! I retrieved my kitbag and caught a bus to the outskirts of town.

Now fate or chance or whatever dealt me a card that sent me indirectly to jail, so justifying my later use of this term "accident." Its form? A parked police car. If that police car had not been parked opposite the ramp onto the main highway north, probably I'd have reached Winnipeg within two days. The car was there, however, directly opposite a sign blaring NO HITCHHIKING, and with a wide-awake policeman in it, when just before noon I stepped off the city bus.

What could I do? I walked past the ramp, nonchalant, my duffle wildly suspicious, and kept walking while avidly the policeman watched. And so got shunted onto a secondary road. Nine hours later, I'd covered less than one hundred miles. And in Madison, Wisconsin, exhausted, I splurged on a room at the YMCA.

The next two days brought more short rides and three-hour waits. I spent one night in a train shelter in St. Cloud, another in a field outside Grand Forks, North Dakota. Late the following morning, near a town called Drayton, a car with a flashing light pulled over beside me. A potbellied man in a brown uniform jumped out with a gun in his hand. He yelled at me to put my hands on the roof, then kicked my feet apart, patted me up and down and told me to get into the car.

He was wearing a badge. I said, "What's this all about, sheriff?"

"Don't make me tell you again."

The sheriff drove me back down the highway to a town called Grafton, where he pulled into a restaurant and left me sitting in the car behind bullet-proof glass. The back doors had no inside handles. After about twenty minutes, another car, North Dakota State Police, pulled into the parking lot with its siren blaring.

Two state troopers got out — one grey-haired, almost fatherly, the other young, crewcut, looked like a marine. They talked with the sheriff, then transferred me and my kitbag to their car. Drove me back the way I'd come.

At the police station in Grand Forks, everything happened so fast I couldn't think. A uniformed woman took my finger prints. Then the crewcut trooper led me down a hall and shoved me into a jail cell, iron bars floor to ceiling. Shut the door and locked it. I asked what was going on, but he just glared and walked away down the hall.

Except for me the jail was empty. My knees felt wobbly. I sat on my bunk — the only furniture in the cell — with my head in my hands. Until now I'd remained unshaken, secure in my innocence. I'd done nothing wrong. Nothing but hitchhike and that wasn't a jailing offence, was it? Now I remembered stories of innocent people spending years in jail. I could see myself phoning home: "Hi, mom. Got a map handy?"

Two hours later, I was still elaborating this dismal fantasy when the older trooper returned and unlocked the cell. "You got a guardian angel or what?"

The previous night, someone tall, dark and bearded had robbed a convenience store. I had no beard but maybe I'd shaved. Anyway, they'd caught the thief at a laundromat in a nearby town. At the front desk I collected my belongings. Then, as I swung my duffle bag onto my back, the crewcut trooper grinned at me: "Too bad the guy confessed. You'd have had a place to spend the night."

The older trooper drove me to the border and watched while I re-entered Canada. Twenty minutes later, still more shaken than I realized, I got a ride with a retired high-school teacher. He kept insisting that I was an ex-student of his from St. Boniface, a certain Jack St. Clair. Finally, as he dropped me off in the heart of Winnipeg, I admitted this and he drove away happy.

I sat on a bench at Portage and Main and put North Dakota behind me. Four o'clock. But today was Thursday and here I was in Winnipeg, right on schedule. I had eleven dollars in my jeans and Duggins was sending me twenty more. The telegraph office was just around the corner. Nothing there yet so I whipped off a telegram: "ARRIVED WINNIPEG STOP STILL ON ROAD STOP SEND TWENTY FAST STOP."

At the YMCA the desk clerk wanted $5 for a room, but turned out he had a small one for $3.50. I took the cheaper room, showered and found a restaurant. My mouth watered at the thought of a T-bone steak with baked potatoes and mushrooms, but I settled for a hot chicken sandwich with fries. No sense being frivolous.

Next morning, early, I hit the telegraph office. No money yet, but not to worry. Duggins had solemnly promised. I'd planned to stay another night at the YMCA, get rested, but now I had to check out. No way I could lug my monster duffle around all day. I carted it to the Greyhound bus depot, crammed it into a stand-up locker and deposited a quarter.

Starting to worry, though I denied it to myself, I called Canada Manpower. Explained that a bizarre series of accidents and misadventures had stranded me in Winnipeg short of funds. An unpredictable sequence of mishaps, setbacks and reversals. The woman on the other end of the line listened politely but had no temporary job listings. She said there would be no pay cheque anyway until next Friday, because here that was how it worked.

Back outside, I turned up cast-away copies of both *The Free Press* and *The Winnipeg Tribune*, but neither advertised temporary jobs. I rambled the streets and repeatedly checked the telegraph office. At noon I decided that when I got my money I'd return to the YMCA and stay one more night, even if I had to pay the higher rate. It was three before I let myself believe that Duggins might not come through after all, and began seriously to regret my extravagance of the night before.

At five I sat on a park bench and counted my money. Two dollars and change. Since breakfast — bacon and eggs, toast and coffee — I'd eaten only a bowl of clam chowder. Now I craved another hot chicken sandwich — my mouth watered — but settled for a hot dog. The temperature was dropping and I made for the bus depot.

From my duffle I retrieved an extra sweater. Then I stuffed the oversized kitbag back into the locker, took out a quarter and stopped: Why not save the money? Who could steal a bag this size? The bus depot closed at eleven, I'd already checked. Overnight, my bag would be safe. I waited until nobody was around, then closed the locker and walked away.

Back at the telegraph office, the clerk had taken to shaking his head as I stepped through the door. Come nine o'clock, when the office closed, I'd received no money. I could hardly believe it. Now it was dark. I checked the bus depot one last time, made certain my duffle was safe, then headed for Union Station.

The place was empty, ominously quiet, but I remembered my grade-six geography: Winnipeg was an important railway centre. Surely the train station would stay open all night, like Central Station in Montreal? I sat down on an out-of-the-way bench and picked up an abandoned *Free Press*. I was reading the letters to the editor when a man in a red cap arrived. "Sorry, sir. Station's closing."

"But Winnipeg's an important railway centre!"

Across the street, in yet another greasy spoon, I drank black coffee and brooded. The restaurant closed at one o'clock. I tried and failed to pick up the waitress and spent the rest of the night walking dark streets and ducking into hotel lobbies to get warm.

Morning became sixty-seven cents in my pocket.

At nine, when it opened, I checked the telegraph office. Still nothing. I tried phoning Duggins in Toronto, reversing the charges, but an operator said the number was no longer in service. No longer in service?

Over a ten-cent coffee I weighed options. I could proceed to Vancouver as planned, maybe get lucky. Or I could turn back, make for Toronto, where I still had a place to stay. That way, if the worst happened, I could continue to Montreal and crash at my old apartment with Baxter.

At the bus depot my kitbag was gone.

Methodically, refusing to panic, I checked every full-sized locker. Then, still calm, I went around the corner to the baggage counter.

"We've got the bag, all right," a grinning baggage handler said. "It'll cost you fifty cents."

I tried reason — "look, the locker cost only a quarter" — but his grin just widened. I paid and staggered out of the depot with my duffle on my back and seven cents in my jeans.

Three days it took me to reach Toronto. Three days and two nights of cold and tired and hungry, of flapping my arms by the side of the highway and singing *Wabash Cannonball* to keep a trucker awake and riding bone-jarred and freezing in the back of a farmer's half-ton pick-up. Three days and two nights it took me, but finally I reached north Toronto, and bummed a subway token and rode the train south. I transferred onto a streetcar and early evening found me lugging my duffle down Jameson Avenue.

At the apartment, nobody was home.

I sat in the hall to wait forever, but along came one of the guys who lived next door. He acknowledged my greeting without warmth. I explained that I'd forgotten my key and, grudgingly, he let me go through his apartment onto the balcony. I climbed the railing and entered my former abode through the sliding back door, which hadn't locked properly since the free-for-all.

A couple of battered suitcases sat in a corner of the living room. Otherwise the place hadn't changed: still no furniture, lots of dirty clothes. I dragged my monster duffle out of the hall, then went to the fridge. There, on the unwashed kitchen counter, lay the telegram I'd sent Duggins. "ARRIVED WINNIPEG STOP STILL ON ROAD STOP SEND TWENTY FAST STOP."

Next to the telegram lay a fat brown envelope addressed to me care of General Delivery, Vancouver. Inside I found an unemployment insurance cheque for fifty-four dollars. I'd been accepted! Also a letter from Baxter, who'd forwarded the cheque from Montreal. And a note from Duggins.

This last I read twice, then a third time. Dixon had been fired from his stock-control job. And Duggins had realized that moving furniture wasn't for him. The two of them were planning to sneak out of the apartment without paying the rent. "We've decided to drive to Vancouver in the TR-3, leaving mid-week. It's good that you're already there. Can you imagine the three of us crossing the country in bucket seats? Sorry I couldn't send money to Winnipeg, but Dixon and I need every cent we've got for gas...."

The fridge was almost bare. I made myself two peanut-butter sandwiches, then sat down on the floor, leaned against a wall and began to eat. So Duggins didn't like moving furniture. He'd talked Dixon into driving to Vancouver. AND THEY NEEDED MY MONEY FOR GAS, DID THEY?

The sandwiches finished, I sat breathing deeply. Finally I stood up, went to the closet and yes, there it was: Duggins' houndstooth jacket. I checked the secret pocket and couldn't believe my eyes. Fifty-seven dollars! I pocketed the four tens Duggins owed me and replaced the rest. Now we were even.

I hoisted my kitbag onto my back and strode to the door. My hand on the handle, I stopped. I thought of the Chicago flophouse, of the North Dakota jail cell, of Winnipeg streets at three in the morning—and put down my duffle. Why stay even?

I returned to the closet, retrieved the remaining seventeen dollars and pocketed them. Quickly now, I took the brown envelope Duggins had intended to send me, maybe, in Vancouver. Across the back of it, before stuffing it into the secret pocket of his houndstooth jacket and clearing out, chuckling, I scrawled: "Going west, talker? Do it or back down."

5

Nobody forgets a First Time, even if it's otherwise unremarkable. Remember riding a bicycle? Falling in love? If you're a Child of the Sixties, you'll remember the first time you drank alcohol, the first time you smoked grass. A First Time is with you forever.

So it is even after you've given up the ghost. And for me, 1970 was a First Time: young Frankie McCracken on Mount Jubilation. Those initial rushes? Try making sense of tumbling images in a kaleidoscope.

Here was Frankie in Chicago, nineteen years old, lugging a giant duffle bag through late-night empty streets. Here he was at age twelve, sprinting down a school corridor, racing to report a theft. Now here he was in New York City, nineteen again, trying to pacify an angry ex-footballer with a peanut butter sandwich.

Frankie brought me back to Jubilation with a fair-enough question: "How'd you know my name, anyway?"

He'd waited until bedtime to ask. We were in the cabin. I was rooting in my rucksack for a flashlight, getting ready to take my sleeping bag outside, and Frankie was using the flickering light of the kerosene lamp to make finger shadows on the wall.

That afternoon, before quitting the tower, I'd said something about sleeping under the stars, how sublime it would be at this elevation.

"You've got a sleeping bag?" Frankie said. "You're welcome to spend the night."

Later he'd given me the grand tour — showed me the weather instruments, the wood-chopping block, the path to the stream where he fetched water. Then the tool shed and the outhouse, tilted crazily into the mountain, and finally the one-room cabin in the trees.

The cabin, like the out-buildings, was regulation maroon. Around it someone had built a fence of trimmed white logs — probably the same madman who'd lined the nearby paths with painted stones. Inside the cabin: a gas burner, a wood stove, a sagging bunk and a built-in table with a moveable bench. Also a doorless cupboard, a wide shelf arrayed with canned goods and instead of a sink — no running water — an old dishpan. Two-by-four girts ran horizontally between studs and served as shelves, mostly for books.

We'd tucked into dinner, baked beans and carrots and rice, and washed it down with apple cider. Then, as I made coffee, I noticed that Frankie was sinking into a depression — he was remembering Camille — so I started reminiscing about my sixty-three days on Desolation Peak: "For a while I thought I'd found the perfect arrangement. Two months of each year I'd be an exemplary Buddhist, a Mahayana fire lookout chopping wood, writing haiku and praying for all living creatures. The rest of the time I'd live cheaply in Mexico."

I took a beat, evoked no response and so plunged on:

"The loneliness wore me down. And Hozomeen! Mount Hozomeen looming in my window."

Frankie snorted and shook his head: "You've got this Kerouac rap down pat, haven't you?"

I grinned at him.

As we did the dishes I felt Frankie sink again and said, "You're lucky to have a separate fire tower. Some other place to go. On Desolation the lookout was all one building — just a cabin with windows."

"This has advantages," he agreed, "but what about lightning storms? To mark strikes, I have to go outside and climb into that sucker. All you had to do was roll out of bed."

"Fair enough, but how's it go?" I swung into a take-off on *Stormy Weather*: "Way up high, there is lightning in the sky, stormy weather."

Maybe you had to be there, but Frankie laughed and we began comparing notes on Old Blue Eyes. I told him how on Desolation I'd stand at the edge of the cliff and shout Sinatra standards into the wind: *I'll Never Smile Again, They Say It's Wonderful, All or Nothing At All.*

Between songs, I said it was unusual, someone his age — "what? twenty-three?" — relishing Sinatra. Turned out Frankie owed the man his Christian name: "My father's a Sinatra nut. Caught his act in Montreal."

"Back in the forties? I saw him then myself, at Carnegie Hall — me and two thousand screaming females. Sinatra wore a white suit, sang *Mighty Like a Rose.*

Frankie made eyes at the ceiling, because how could someone my age have caught Old Blue Eyes in his prime? But he said: "Nobody could sing like the early Sinatra. That magic voice. And clarity?"

"His enunciation was exquisite. And what about his phrasing? The way he'd sing a song, not according to its melodic structure, but the fall of the words."

"Learned that from Bing, my father said."

So it went.

The dishes done, Frankie picked up his guitar. Somewhere along the line he'd mastered not only bar chords but diminished sevenths and augmented fifths and soon we were crooning Sinatra hits: *Imagination, Without A Song, Everything Happens To Me.* Finally we did such a rousing rendition of *Stardust* that we dissolved into laughter and Frankie set aside his guitar knowing we'd never get higher.

By now it was ten o'clock, bed-time, and I stood and stretched. I untied my sleeping bag and rooted for the flashlight and that's when Frankie, idly making finger shadows by lantern-light, asked casually, "How'd you know my name, anyway?"

I said, "Frankie, I know everything about you."

"Stop putting me on. Who are you?"

"I told you. I'm Jack Kerouac."

"Okay, Kerouac, who's Dean Moriarty?"

"The hero of *On The Road.* In real life, my best old buddy, Neal Cassady."

"Japhy Ryder?"

"Gary Snyder. Come on, Frankie, you can do better than that."

"Which Kerouac novel was about life on the fire lookout? Or, no. That's too easy. Which one focused on Kerouac's French-Canadian boyhood in Maine?"

"Nice try, Frankie. I didn't grow up in Maine, but in Lowell, Massachussetts. Stinktown on the Merrimack, my father called it. *Dr. Sax? Visions of Gerard? Maggie Cassidy?* I treated my boyhood in all of them. *The Town and The City*, too, except there I buried the French-Canadian side. A fragment called "Memory Babe". Even *Vanity of Duluoz*. And I wrote about my days on Desolation in three different books."

"All right, so you know Kerouac's work. Proves nothing."

"I've got nothing to prove." I located my flashlight and waved it triumphantly. "Knew it was here somewhere."

I stood up to go.

"One more glass?" Without waiting for an answer, Frankie poured us each another tumbler of cider. "Okay, let's pretend you're Kerouac," he said and shifted smoothly into *joual*, that slangy Québécois French only natives and their descendents understand: "*Qu'est-ce tu fais icitte?*"

That's when I realized whose rhythms I was borrowing. I hadn't known because I'd taken the French in my mind for granted. Why not? All my life I'd dreamed and heard prophecies in that language. "*Tu ne laches pas, toi!*" I said. "You don't let go! You invited me."

Frankie laughed but persisted in French: "What do you take me for? An idiot? I never invited you."

"*Mais oui, tu l'as fais!*" I rattled on in *joual* for the sheer joy of it: "Sure, you did! Remember last January, the day you climbed Tunnel Mountain? Discovered the cabin on top, all boarded up for the winter? You were peeking in the windows when you realized it was a fire lookout. The kind of place Old Kerouac had written about in *Desolation Angels*."

Now I had his attention.

"Back in town you ran into a fellow dish-washer from the Banff Springs Hotel. He told you some government types were coming to town next day, that they'd be interviewing for summer jobs in the park — and fire lookout was one of them. Later, at home in your two-room cabin, you shook your hands in the air and did a dance: 'Kerouac! Kerouac! Be with me now!' *C'était bien un invitation, non?'*

Frankie reverted to English: "Where'd you learn all this?"

I followed him into his native tongue. "I don't fully understand it myself. Somehow we're linked outside of Time. I get flashes."

"What are you doing here?"

"Frankie, you need help."

"Help? With what?"

"How's *Funeral Song* coming?" His stalled novel.

"That's nothing. You saw the manuscript on the table in the tower."

"That so? And what about Camille?"

"That's it!" Frankie slapped his forehead. "You've been talking to Camille! She's the only one who knew about 'Kerouac! Kerouac! Be with me now.'" He laughed and shook his head. "For a moment there you had me going. How is Camille, anyway?"

"She's faring better than you — though I've never met her, not in the flesh."

"Why don't we cut the crap?"

Secretly, I relished his resistance, but I said, "Frankie, lighten up." I emptied my glass, put on my jacket and picked up my sleeping bag and flashlight. "Come see the stars."

Frankie knocked back the last of his cider.

We went out the door, stepped off the porch and strolled to the middle of the white-fenced yard. The night air was cool, the sky alive with stars.

"That's Cygnus, directly above us," I said. "The Northern Cross. God, what a night. There's Hercules. And Draco, the serpent. Look! A shooting star."

"Really a meteorite. Should I make a wish?"

The star rocketed through Cygnus and disappeared. "Remember when you were twelve years old, Frankie? And your least favorite chore was bringing the rent money to Madame Francoeur?"

For a few seconds, Frankie was silent. Then he said, "Yeah?"

"Somebody robbed you. That night you stood in your back yard in Ste. Thérèse, looking up at the star-spangled night. You swore on a shooting star that you'd repay your mother — every last cent."

Frankie stood silent for a long time, staring up at the sky. Finally he said, "I never told anybody that. Not even Camille."

I put on my best W. C. Fields' voice: "Right you are, my boy."

Back in my own voice, I said, "Sleep tight."

Then spun on my heel and walked out the gate.

6

Flash forward to 1983 and I'm not the world-famous novelist I'd expected to be in my thirties. Instead I'm a small-town journalist, editor-in-chief of *The Rocky Mountain Miracle*. What can I say? We create the weekly *Miracle* out of a three-room office in downtown Banff, heart of the Canadian Rockies. We're a high-tech operation and, as editor-in-chief, I keep a computer-with-modem here at home, in the back room of this humble rented house.

From where I sit at this moment, almost ten years later still, I can look out and see the top of Tunnel Mountain: rounded, atypical, undramatic, white with snow. The lookout tower that once marked its top — the tower I discovered with Camille early in 1970 — is long gone. So, too, the tower on Mount Jubilation, where as a fire lookout, alone, I worked the following summer.

I know the Jubilation tower was gone by 1983 because Gerald Nicosia published *Memory Babe* that year, his critical biography of Jack Kerouac, and I lugged the tome up Mount Jubilation to read it. I knew helicopters had replaced the lookout system, that they swept the national park as necessary. Still, I expected to find the wooden tower standing, and certainly the one-room cabin. But no. I stayed on Jubilation anyway, for three days and two nights, slept out under the stars. When I came down I celebrated Nicosia's biography in *The Miracle*.

Today, I find annoying the reportorial choppiness of this review. But mainly I'm struck by my failure to question easy explanations of Kerouac's too-early death. The piece opens with six paragraphs of context, then focuses on the biography's polemical strain: "Nicosia is out to prove that Kerouac is a major American writer, and the extent of his success will astonish many...."

BUT HERE, AT THE RISK OF CAUSING CONFUSION, I BOLD-
LY INTERRUPT. FRANKIE THE NARRATOR THREATENS
TO QUOTE HIMSELF AT LENGTH. SO WHAT, YOU SAY?
LET HIM RAMBLE? NO, THANKS. I CAN SEE WHERE HE'D
TAKE US. ALSO, HOW SLOWLY. BETTER, I THINK, TO
SHOUT, "TRUST ME!" THEN OUTRAGE THE CONVEN-
TIONS AND PREPARE TO STAND TRIAL. HEAVY-
HANDED? CALLING SOFTLY, I ENTER THE TEXT:
— Frankie! Frankie, can you hear me?
— Pardon? Is that you, Jack?
— Is Jack who you want me to be?
— You'll have to speak up.
— PLEASE ABANDON THIS TEDIOUS REVIEW. IT'S IN-
TRUSIVE, UNWORTHY.
— But what better way to dramatize my intellectual evolution?
Concrete newspaper articles. Documentary evidence. I'm show-
ing rather than telling.
— YOU'RE INDULGING YOURSELF.
— Same to you.
— YOU FORGET, FRANKIE, THAT WITH A SINGLE PITHY
PHRASE I CAN WALK YOU OUT THE DOOR, TROT YOU
DOWN THE STREET AND GET YOU HIT BY A TRUCK.
— That's three empty clauses.
— DESPITE HIMSELF, FRANKIE THE NARRATOR LEAPT
OUT OF HIS CHAIR, CART-WHEELED ACROSS THE ROOM
AND JERKED OPEN THE BACK DOOR.
— Okay! Okay! We'll do it your way.
— HAVING COME TO HIS SENSES, FRANKIE SHUT THE
DOOR, RESUMED HIS SEAT AND SPECIFIED HIS OBJEC-
TIVE:
— I want to establish Nicosia's biography as the source, for
starters, of my erstwhile belief that celebrity-hood destroyed
Kerouac.
— THE SOLE SOURCE?
— No, the biography caught the Beat-American Zeitgeist.
— ARGUE FIRST THAT NICOSIA OVERSTATES HIS CASE.
GET THE READER ON YOUR SIDE.

— To suggest, as Nicosia does, that the six novels Kerouac wrote between 1951 and 1953 represent "an explosion of creativity unmatched in American literature since Melville" is pushing it.
— CITE FAULKNER.
— Consider William Faulkner, late twenties, early thirties. Furthermore, to claim that *San Francisco Blues*, a collection of 79 poems, "is one of the most important poetic works in the second half of the 20th century" is, well, patently ridiculous.
— VERY NICE.
— On the other hand, I have to admit that Nicosia makes a compelling case for the notion that *Dr. Sax*, with its mix of fantasy and realism, is the first postmodern novel in America.
— THOUGH HE DOESN'T DWELL SUFFICIENTLY ON THE TEXT WITHIN THE TEXT, DOES HE? THAT SPECTACULAR EXAMPLE OF PARODISTIC SELF-REFLEXIVITY, WHEN DR. SAX, HIS COUNTENANCE PURPLISH, SWEEPS INTO THE SALON AND HOWLS GREETINGS?
— You're worse than I am. Nicosia draws attention, as well, to Kerouac's Joycean ear for harmony and sound, for idiom, and to "the breathless race of dependent clauses that is the hallmark" of his prose. And the essence of his unique contribution.
— ENOUGH! TO THE LIFE.
— What about suggesting that, if Nicosia's critical expositions get in the way of his story, they are nonetheless welcome, even necessary, because critics have treated Kerouac with shameful superciliousness?
— KEROUAC LIVED AN IMPETUOUS LIFE.
— Nor, for two reasons, was it happy. First, Kerouac lacked the ability to handle his own genius.
— THIS YOU HOLD TO BE TRUE?
— No, it's what I took from Nicosia.
— KEEP THAT STRAIGHT. ELABORATE THIS PATRONIZING ASSERTION.
— Kerouac's gifts included a phenomenal ear for language, a photographic memory and an astronomical IQ. But he grew up in a French-Canadian ghetto. This didn't prepare him for celebrity — and vilification — as King of the Beats. His prodigal

talent picked him up and wrung him out like a sponge. Finally, having turned him into a caricature of himself — a pot-bellied redneck with delusions of grandeur — it tossed him away.

— REASON TWO ALLEGED FOR UNHAPPINESS?

— Kerouac was a college football star, a merchant seaman, a railroad brakeman, a forest fire lookout — but first, last and always, he was a mama's boy. As a result, he had sexual problems. One woman described him as "a minuteman" and others made this allegation sound kind. Kerouac suffered from chronic impotence and agonizing ambivalence. He participated in homosexual orgies and then endured days of guilt and anguish.

— THE ORGIES, THE RAMBLINGS, THE BROKEN DREAMS: NICOSIA BRINGS THEM ALL BACK HOME TO MEMERE?

— So, too, the relationships Kerouac couldn't sustain, and that couldn't, ultimately, sustain him — with Allen Ginsberg, William Burroughs, Neal Cassady, John Clellon Holmes, Gary Snyder. Nicosia writes that Kerouac "left two wives, a daughter, numerous lovers and friends, and several careers as though they were just way stations on the road to his final dissolution." When he died, in 1969 at the age of 47, Jack Kerouac was living with his mother.

— THE SUGGESTION IS THAT KEROUAC COMMITTED SUICIDE-BY-DRINK BECAUSE HE FAILED MORALLY?

— Correct. He never escaped his mother. Never grew up.

— THIS TENET IS CENTRAL TO THE BEAT-AMERICAN INTERPRETATION OF KEROUAC?

— Yes, to an interpretation I now regard as false.

— TAKE US TO NEW YORK.

7

There's no city like the first city, and for Jack Kerouac that was New York. Seventeen, eighteen, nineteen years old, Kerouac fell in love with the Big Apple — with Times Square and Greenwich Village, with Harlem, the Bowery and the Brooklyn Bridge, with the uptown jazz clubs, the waterfront bars, the never-ending bus ride through the red-brick sprawl of the Bronx.

For Kerouac, New York City was French films at the Apollo Theatre and wolfing down hot dogs at Times Square while digging hustlers, junkies and petty thieves flogging stolen watches; it was leather-jacketed pimps and red-haired hookers and solitary walks à la Walt Whitman and Thomas Wolfe and riding the Staten Island Ferry with a childhood friend, drunk as the sun came up, to shout Byron's poetry at the Statue of Liberty.

Kerouac's New York was romantic enough for me, and early in the summer of 1966, having recovered from my Do-It-Or-Back-Down fiasco, and eager to renew my Kerouwacky quest for experience, I rode a train south out of Montreal. I carried sixty dollars and a small travelling bag and never dreamed that experience might take shape as frustration and disappointment or a desperate chase through night-time dangerous streets.

A few days before I'd tried to hitchhike across the American border but suspicious guards had checked my wallet and turned me back. This time I lied to a customs officer who strolled through the train and, full of self-congratulation, got out at Plattsburgh, New York. There, on a park bench, I spent the night.

Next morning I hit the highway. Rides were short but numerous and the sun was setting when a trucker dropped me at a subway stop on the northern outskirts of New York. I rode the subway south, one eye on the overhead map, rattled happily

41

through the soot-smelling dark. Finally, at Forty-Second Street, I trotted up out of the subway station to Times Square.

It was grubbier than I'd imagined, despite the bright lights and neon signs, but I bought two hotdogs and stood wolfing them down. A few hookers strolled past. A man with no legs paddled by on a platform. A red convertible pulled up, three men in it, and one hollered, "Hey, slim! You looking for a place to spend the night?"

I started walking. I bought a city map at a kiosk, rented a room at the YMCA on 34th Street and slept like a dead man. Next morning, travelling bag in hand, I tumbled into the streets: New York City! In daylight I couldn't get over the scale of the place. I'd seen hundred-storey skyscrapers but not like this, not in this concentration. Even Chicago hadn't prepared me.

In Greenwich Village, the only quarter I'd consider, I quickly discovered hotel prices. Worried, though not panicked, I entered a grubby-looking place I'd at first dismissed: the Greenwich Hotel. The lobby was full of rheumy-eyed men and ominous signs — "No Women Allowed" and "Check Out Time 7 a.m." — but I'd survived worse. The desk clerk said the cheapest rooms rented for $11 a week. I said, "We're talking rooms, right? Walls that extend from ceiling to floor?"

The clerk stared at me, but I insisted on seeing for myself and rode an unsafe elevator to the sixth floor. I passed a communal bathroom, old men in their undershirts, but already I could see that the Greenwich was at least one step up from your average flophouse. The room was cupboard-size with a cot in it, but boasted floor-to-ceiling walls and even a sink. A tiny window looked out onto an air shaft. Here day was night but who cared? I didn't intend to stay inside.

During the next few days I wore holes in my sneakers, bought cheap sandals and kept going: Grand Central Station, Madison Square Garden, Radio City Music Hall, the Port Authority Bus Terminal, Columbia University, Broadway, Fifth Avenue, the Brooklyn Bridge, the Algonquin Hotel. I spent an hour at the top of the Empire State Building. I considered taking the ferry to Staten Island, decided against it when I learned what it cost.

One night I caught Shakespeare in the Park, *A Midsummer Night's Dream*, fantastic. But most evenings I spent in The Village shuffling from one cafe to another, half-expecting to round a corner and bump into Bob Dylan or Allen Ginsberg or even Old Kerouac himself — who, though I didn't know it, was drunkenly roaring around Hyannis, Massachussetts.

A freakishly early heat wave hit New York. The temperature reached 102 degrees Farenheit, then 103, 104. Humidity you wouldn't believe. Night two, as I lay sweating in my glorified cupboard, I thought of Lawrence Ferlinghetti's *Coney Island of the Mind* — not the poems but the title image. And dug out my subway map.

The next three days I spent at Coney Island. I strolled the boardwalk, lay in the sand, took the odd dip — the water not yet polluted beyond use — and lived on pizza and ice cream. Finally the heat wave broke and I resumed rambling around Manhattan, though now I was running out of money.

I'd listened in a bar to the agonizing of a would-be draft dodger and fled a males-only party into which I'd been hailed from a third-floor window. But that was it for excitement until my last night in New York. I was sitting at the fountain in Washington Square when a pretty girl caught my eye — a black girl in a summer dress strolling around the fountain arm-in-arm with two white guys.

When she passed a second time, I nodded and smiled and to my surprise she dragged the two men over and said, "Man, you're sending out good vibes. You high or what?"

"High? Oh, you mean on grass! Don't I wish!"

"Come walk with us." The girl held out her hand and I took it. She asked my name, introduced the two men, one of them older, tough-looking, and said, "My friends call me Jeunesse."

"Jeunesse! I love it!"

She prattled on, then, as if we were alone. Hadn't she seen me at the fountain last night? I said probably she had. That I was from Montreal, had been in New York two weeks — stretching it — and spent most evenings here in The Village.

Suddenly the younger man said he had to split, had to work tomorrow. As we waved goodbye, Jeunesse said, "Come on, Sylvester. Don't be an old grump. Let's get this man high."

Sylvester didn't warm to the idea, but Jeunesse kept pushing and finally we caught a subway train bound for Central Park. As we rode I told my story — a young Kerouac seeks experience in New York — and learned that Jeunesse had arrived from upstate only three days before.

She'd met Sylvester and his friend last night. They'd smoked grass together and today Jeunesse had moved a suitcase into Sylvester's apartment. She planned to stay a couple of days, just until she received some money she was expecting.

Sylvester's apartment was on the fourth floor of a red-brick building on 119th Street. It was a spotless one-bedroom with a gurgling bowl of goldfish and a wall full of books on eastern religions. Sylvester, who had to be pushing thirty, worked as a hospital orderly at a place called Mount Sinai. He was studying yoga, and lately he'd been experimenting with psychokinesis: "You know: moving things with your mind."

The three of us sat on the floor and shared a joint. Jeunesse showed me how to suck in the smoke and hold my breath and laughed when I had a coughing fit. She was sitting next to me, cross-legged, our knees almost touching. Big brown eyes, full lips. The word, I thought, was gorgeous.

When we finished the joint — gave me a buzz, nothing memorable — Jeunesse urged Sylvester to demonstrate mind over matter. He produced a tiny windmill he'd rigged up using paper, popsicle sticks and elastic bands. "The grass we've smoked will increase our mental power," he said. "If we work together, we should be able to make the windmill spin without touching it."

Nothing happened the first time, so Sylvester passed around a second joint and told us to focus, to get onto nature's wavelength. This time I saw the windmill move.

"Amazing," I said. But my attention was on my left knee, where Jeunesse had laid her hand. Without warning, she jumped to her feet: "Let's go up on the roof and look at the lights."

"It's getting late," Sylvester said. "I work tomorrow."

But Jeunesse insisted. She led us up five flights of stairs and through a small door onto the gravel-covered roof. She showed me her favorite vantage point and we stood at the rail oohing and aahing, looking out at the lights. Then she remembered the binoculars — they'd used them last night — and asked Sylvester to fetch them. He said no way, but Jeunesse pouted and he capitulated.

Alone with Jeunesse, I put my hands on her shoulders. She leaned back against me. I turned her around, she came into my arms. We kissed and I ran my hands lightly over her breasts. She moaned. When we came up for air, I said I wanted to spend the night with her. She said, "Hmmmm, okay. I'll come back to your place."

"Jesus, I just realized that's impossible! I'm staying at a men's hostel."

"Can't you sneak me in?"

"There's an all-night desk clerk. What if —"

Sylvester, puffing hard, reappeared with the binoculars. We took turns looking through them, seeing nothing, then headed back downstairs. I asked Sylvester if I, too, could stay overnight — save myself a subway ride.

"No way, man," he said. "No visitors allowed after eleven. Already, by letting Jeunesse stay, I'm taking a chance."

Jeunesse walked me downstairs. At the side of the building, we stood necking. I explained that The Greenwich had a no-refunds policy on by-the-week rentals, so I couldn't switch. And that I had less than five dollars in my jeans. Maybe we could cross the street and duck into Central Park?

Jeunesse said let's wait. Tonight she'd sleep on Sylvester's couch. Tomorrow, her father would send money. She and I would rent an apartment together.

"Fabulous," I said. "I'll get a friend in Montreal to forward my unemployment cheques!"

We agreed that, tomorrow afternoon, I'd pick her up from Sylvester's. Into the night, I went whistling.

Next morning, after breakfast, I checked out of the Greenwich Hotel. I rambled the streets congratulating myself that I was carrying only a small bag, and also on clicking with Jeunesse, and eventually made my way uptown. I arrived at Sylvester's at two o'clock, as arranged. Jeunesse answered the door, put a finger to her lips and gestured with her thumb.

Sylvester called, "Who is it?"

I whispered, "What's he doing here?"

"He called in sick." She made a face, then led me into the living room. "Look who's here!"

Sylvester was sitting on the floor surrounded by stereo components. He grunted but didn't get up. I sat down on the couch. Jeunesse looked sharper than ever, but when she went into the kitchen to make coffee, I didn't dare follow.

I tried small talk. Sylvester responded with grunts. Jeunesse returned and said, "He's just an old grump, aren't you, Sylvester?"

Jeunesse and I agreed that the weather had improved mightily since the heat wave. I asked whether she'd heard from her father and she said no, she hadn't. Then Sylvester said, "I'm getting hungry. Did you take those chicken wings out of the freezer?"

Since breakfast, I'd eaten nothing but a slice of pizza. Emboldened by hunger, I said, "You're having chicken wings?"

"Sorry we can't ask you to stay," Sylvester said. "But we don't have enough to go three ways."

"No, no. I understand." There was a long silence. Finally, I got up. "Guess I'll be on my way."

Jeunesse said, "I'll walk you to the door."

Sylvester, who hadn't moved from the floor, got up and came with us. At the door, I said: "Sylvester, do you mind if I have a private word with Jeunesse."

Sylvester glared but Jeunesse said, "Please, Sylvester."

The man turned and stomped into the living room. Jeunesse stepped into the hall and pulled the door shut behind her.

I said, "What's happening here?"

"Nothing. That's why Sylvester's so grumpy."

"What about you and me? You still want to get an apartment?"

"Yes, yes. But I didn't get my money. He'll send it tomorrow."

"And tonight?"

"Oh, I'm all right here."

"You sure?" I tried to take her in my arms and kiss her, but she pushed me away. "Not now. Tomorrow. Come by tomorrow morning. He'll be at work."

"What time does he leave?"

"I don't know. Come after nine. That'll be safe."

"You sure you'll be all right?"

"Don't worry." She kissed me on the cheek. "I can handle Sylvester."

"Tomorrow morning, then." I started down the hall, swinging my bag, then turned. "Hey, wait. Why don't you keep this for me? Save me carting it around."

Jeunesse took my bag, kissed me again, this time on the lips, and disappeared into the apartment.

Back on the sidewalk, I counted my money. Three dollars and change. I decided against another slice of pizza, opted instead for a loaf of bread and a small jar of peanut butter — more protein. Then, having nothing better to do, I walked down Broadway to Washington Square, swinging my plastic-wrapped loaf. I visited bookstores, filched a plastic knife from a hotdog stand and sat at the fountain eating peanut-butter sandwiches.

As evening fell I figured why wait? I might as well hike back uptown tonight. Fifth Avenue, West 42nd, Times Square, Broadway, Central Park West — to me they were still magical. By the time I got within hailing distance of Sylvester's, street lights were blazing and I was exhausted. I knew better than to venture deep into Central Park, and found a bench in a well-lit area adjacent to the street.

By now, ten o'clock, nobody was a pedestrian. I lay down on the bench and closed my eyes. Cars streamed steadily past on

Central Park West and I dozed off thinking about tomorrow morning — how I'd head up to Sylvester's apartment and crawl into bed with Jeunesse. Afterwards, I'd sleep. Come afternoon, she'd receive her money. We'd rent a room....

A hand touched my thigh. Startled, I opened my eyes. A giant black man stood grinning down at me. "Didn't mean to scare you." I sat up. The man wore a T-shirt that showed off his pectorals, his biceps. He stood about six-foot-five, weighed maybe two-sixty — looked like a football player. He said, "People call me Angel." And sat down beside me on the bench. Not another soul in sight. "What's your name?"

"Jack." I don't know why I lied, maybe just a reflex, but I stuck to it. "My name's Jack. I'm visiting from Montreal."

"Tell me, Jack. What you looking for, out here in Central Park all by yourself?" Angel grinned again, showing off a gold tooth.

"Nothing. Nothing at all. Just trying to get some shut-eye."

"You like sex, Jack?"

"Women, you mean? Sure, I like women." I reached under the bench, no sudden movements, and retrieved my bread and peanut butter. "Want a sandwich?"

"How you like sex with men?"

"Angel, I don't." I'd stuffed my plastic knife down the side of the loaf and couldn't get it out. I opened the peanut butter and, using my finger, spread some of it onto a slice of bread.

Angel said, "Let's you and me crawl into them bushes over there."

"Nothing personal, Angel. But I don't swing that way." I took a bite of my open-faced peanut-butter sandwich, glanced at my watch. Three o'clock. Few cars on the street. "You sure you don't want a sandwich?"

"You playing games with me, Jack!" Angel grabbed me by my left arm. "Let's shake it!"

He began dragging me toward the bushes.

"Hey! Let go!" I kicked and fought but Angel was a power-house. Finally I managed to swing around and shove my slice of bread and peanut butter into Angel's face. The big man roared and loosened his grip. I jerked free, stumbled onto the sidewalk and exploded into a sprint. Back in high school I'd run the hundred-yard-dash and I figured I was gone. But Angel didn't give up. Then I realized that, for a guy his size, he was amazingly fast. Also in fantastic shape. And I was wearing sandals.

Three cars went past. "Police!" I yelled. "Police! Police!" Nobody even slowed down.

I gritted my teeth and for three blocks ran all out. I had a stitch in my side when finally I glanced over my shoulder and saw that Angel had given up. He stood on the sidewalk shaking his fist and wiping peanut butter off his face.

The rest of the night I spent circling Columbia University, Kerouac's alma mater. I regretted the loss of my bread and peanut butter, but wouldn't go back for it. Kept myself going by thinking of Jeunesse. I walked until nine o'clock in the morning, then made for Sylvester's. I knocked on the door, no answer. I knocked again and Sylvester appeared — wearing only a towel.

"Sylvester? Uh, hi. How's it going?"

"You again?"

"Jeunesse around?"

"She doesn't want to see you."

"Well, I want to see her."

"She's finished with you, dig?" Sylvester reached down behind the door, tossed my travelling bag at my feet, then closed the door in my face.

I knocked again, harder than before. Sylvester opened the door. "Didn't you hear me, bright boy?"

"I want to see Jeunesse."

"She doesn't want to see you."

"I want her to tell me that herself."

"She asked me to deliver the message."

"Jeunesse!" I called. "Jeunesse, are you —"

"Hey, asshole!" Jeunesse shouted from inside the apartment. "Can't you take a hint?"

Sylvester grinned and slammed the door in my face.

I raised my fist to knock again — but to what end?

Back on the street, I unzipped my travelling bag and checked inside. Everything was there: shaving gear, dirty socks,

Kerouac's *The Subterraneans*. I zipped up the bag and counted my money: one dollar and eighty-five cents.

If I left right away, I could make it to Montreal before I starved. But first I found a telephone booth and looked up Mount Sinai Medical Center. I asked for the personnel department, the senior person in charge, and told the woman who came on the line to check out an orderly named Sylvester who'd booked off work for the past two days. He wasn't sick, I said, he was home doing drugs.

The woman wanted to know more but I hung up.

8

On Desolation Peak in 1956, by the light of an old kerosene lantern, I read a book called *The God That Failed*. It consisted of confessions of ex-communists who had repented when they discovered the totalitarian beastliness of the system they'd worshipped. All about spies and dictators, plots and assassination attempts, people fighting for the sake of fighting, purges and failed revolutions and murders at midnight. Depressing.

Yet I remember my fascination, and the marvellous strangeness of reading that in February 1922, one month before I was born, such-and-such was happening in Moscow and something else in the streets of Vienna. How could there have been a Vienna, I wondered, or even a concept of Vienna, before I was born?

It's because the One Mental Nature rolls on, of course, regardless of arrivals and departures, indifferent to those who fare in this Nature and are fared in by it. Step back far enough and individuals dwindle to Nothingness. Me, I don't like to remain at that distance. With Neal Cassady I spent hours laying out Timelines and looking for connections, for echoes and reflections, signs and synchronicities.

And I remember lying in bed with my real-life "Mardou Fox," my quintessential Subterranean, the two of us realizing that in 1944, when I was twenty-two and she was thirteen, we were both living in New York City, and oh, God, let's see, at Easter you were downtown, rambling around Times Square? So was I! We must have passed each other in the street.

You can learn a lot by comparing chronologies. And when, outside of Time, I began laying the life of Frankie McCracken alongside my own, I discovered all the requisite parallels. The Celtic and French-Canadian heritage, tinged with Iroquois. The tragic father, the indomitable mother. The ubiquitous Catholicism. Later, the travels. The descent into the maelstrom.

On Mount Jubilation, that first night under the stars, it all came flooding back. I remembered that in Frankie I'd recognized the distinctive traits of an eternal companion — the hapless Sancho Panza of my soul. In emulating me, Frankie had sought a difficult passage, one in which he could develop humility, perseverance and love. The Kerouac family motto, by comparison, is *Aimer, Travailler, Souffrir*. To love, work and suffer. See the fit?

But as Frankie stared into the maelstrom of Time, preparing to plunge, he heard a thousand voices buzzing with the Ancient Counsel: "No, no, don't do it! Don't be born! Darkness will engulf you!"

Plunging into the flesh meant risking drowning. Frankie might forget himself and so waste a life. In the Darkness, he realized, thematic parallels might not blaze brightly enough. He remembered that I take joy in comparing chronologies and seized upon the idea of planting markers — signs and omens and portents — that, should he find himself in trouble, would certainly catch my eye.

Date of conception would be the first signpost, and Frankie decided to signal my father, who died of cancer in May of 1946. That meant being born in February of 1947, or maybe early March. He'd never be able to hang on until my own birthday, March 22, but he wanted a double signpost at birth and settled on one that would identify him with my blood-brother, Neal Cassady.

I'd met Neal in December of 1946, when he'd arrived in New York from Denver, and I was still getting to know him early the following year. Having discerned this and more, Frankie decided to enter the world prematurely, on Feb. 8, 1947 — the day Neal Cassady turned twenty-one.

Still he didn't feel safe.

While analyzing the options available to his parents-in-waiting, Frankie discovered the village of Ste. Thérèse Sur-le-lac. And thought immediately of Ste. Thérèse de Lisieux, the Little Flower of Jesus — as he knew I would. Because never, not even at the height of my Buddhist phase, did I ever stop praying to Ste. Thérèse.

Ste. Thérèse Sur-le-lac lies twenty miles west of Montreal on the north shore of the Lake of Two Mountains, the Lac des Deux Montagnes. Today it's a suburb, a bedroom community, but in those days — the late forties and on through the fifties — a two-lane highway, Chemin St. Esprit, ran through the centre of town.

Ste. Thérèse boasted a general store (Marché Champroux), a hotel (La Fin Du Monde) and a gas station (Esso). Further west, up the highway towards St. Narcisse, Ste. Anne de la Providence and St. Rédempteur, there was a French elementary school and a Roman Catholic church. Farm fields lined the highway, and beyond them lay nothing but woods.

Streets in Ste. Thérèse were hard-packed dirt roads, most of them running south from Chemin St. Esprit to the lake: Avenue des Anges, Avenue des Archanges, Avenue des Oracles. But two such roads, Avenue des Fantômes and Avenue des Cherubins, ran north from the highway to the train tracks. Houses in those days were rickety, clapboard affairs on stilts — uninsulated summer camps raised high off the ground because of spring flooding. People who lived year-round in the town winterized these places, put foundations under them.

For nine months of the year, Ste. Thérèse Sur-le-lac was home to three hundred souls — among them a few *Anglais*. But in June, July and August, because of the lake and the sandy beach, the town was a poor-man's resort, its population exploding into the thousands. Montrealers would commute daily by train, coming and going from a tiny open-front station north of the highway. The rest of the year, the train came only as far as the nearby town of Coeur d'Aimée, and from there commuters took taxis.

To Frankie McCracken, contemplating his plunge, Ste. Thérèse looked painfully isolated. Still, it was more like working-class Lowell, Massachussetts, like Centralville and Pawtucket-ville, where I'd grown up, than a tough Montreal *quartier* would be. And the French Catholic ambience was perfect. Frankie needed that reinforcement because his parents-to-be spoke English together, while mine had spoken French. Also because his mother would insist on raising him Protestant.

What finally decided him, though, was the town's name. Ste. Thérèse Sur-le-lac would serve as a final signpost, and so keep him safe in the dark. From outside of Time, Frankie nudged Destiny.

His parents-to-be, Maurice McCracken and Margaret (Maggie) Granger, had married in Halifax in 1944 — a civil ceremony with one of Maurice's Air Force buddies acting as best man. When the war ended, the young couple had moved to Montreal and rented a room in a downtown flat. For weeks Maggie complained about noise and crowdedness and urged her young husband to take her out of Montreal, to show her the surrounding country-side.

Finally Maurice, an amateur film-maker, roughed out a script that called, though he didn't know why, for desert scenes and mirages and also a lake. Where to shoot them? As a boy, Maurice had attended a family picnic in the north-shore town of St. Eustache. Vaguely, he remembered a lake.

Maurice convinced his movie-making partner — Henry owned the camera — of the need to scout locations. And one Sunday morning in May of 1946, he and Maggie piled into Henry's old car and drove north out of Montreal.

They crossed the Cartierville Bridge, then followed the twisting, two-lane highway as it meandered along Rivière-des-Prairies through St. Martin, Ste. Dorothée and Laval Ouest. Finally they arrived in St. Eustache, where Maurice asked a gas station attendant for directions. The man told them to keep driving west, to follow the highway, Chemin St. Esprit, to Ste. Thérèse Sur-le-lac. Turn left at the hotel, La Fin Du Monde, and at the bottom of the street they'd find the best beach in the world.

They followed the man's directions, and as they drove slowly down Avenue des Archanges, looking out at the boarded-up houses, Maggie noticed signs saying, "*A Louer.*" That meant "For Rent." At the beach, where a light breeze was blowing in off the lake, Maggie remembered Nova Scotia: This is more like it, she thought. Only the seagulls are missing. And the smell of the salt sea air.

On the way back to the car, Henry having walked on ahead, Maggie said to Maurice, "This town wouldn't be a bad place to raise children."

"This is the sticks, Maggie. We'd die out here."

"Maurice, I'm dying in the city."

That night, Frankie plunged. And when he surfaced in darkness on the eighth day of February, 1947 — eight and a half months after the death of my father, and on the day my blood-brother, Neal Cassady, turned twenty-one — Frankie McCracken did so in a drafty, three-room house in Ste. Thérèse Sur-le-lac. Under the protection of the Little Flower of Jesus.

9

Twenty years after visiting New York City, still obsessed with the so-called King of the Beats, I drove from Banff to Calgary and back — spent three hours on the road — to view a documentary film entitled *Kerouac*. In reviewing it for *The Rocky Mountain Miracle*, I noted early that in 1959, two years after he published *On The Road*, and while he was still the toast of New York, Kerouac appeared on Steve Allen's syndicated television program: "Director John Antonelli opens and closes this too-brief (71-minute) film biography with clips from that telecast — a wise move."

— FRANKIE, I'M DISAPPOINTED.
— You're not Jack Kerouac.
— YOU'VE GOT A JOB TO DO.
— Who are you?
— THINK OF ME AS A KIND OF HOLY GHOST.
— Get real, will you? I'll settle for where.
— WHERE AM I? WITHIN AND WITHOUT. HOW DID THE PHILOSOPHER PUT IT? I AM NOT WHERE I THINK, AND I THINK WHERE I AM NOT.
— Sophistry and bafflegab! Postmodern Jabberwocky!
— AS NARRATOR, FRANKIE, YOU'VE GOT A JOB TO DO. I'M HERE TO SEE YOU DO IT.
— Then quit interrupting the narrative.
— YOU'RE THE ONE WHO'S INTERRUPTING. THESE NEWSPAPER CLIPPINGS? THIS DOCUMENTARY AP-PROACH? YOUR EGO IS SHOWING. YOU'RE TRYING TO DEMONSTRATE WHAT A HOT-SHOT JOURNALIST YOU ARE. EITHER THAT OR YOU'RE BONE LAZY.

— Foundationless allegations. In my 1986 review of the Antonelli documentary, any fair-minded reader will discern a first flicker of awareness, an impending realization that, in the Beat-American Interpretation of Kerouac, something is rotten.

— YOU ATTRIBUTE THE WRITER'S DEATH TO HIS HAVING BECOME A SOCIAL PHENOMENON. THAT'S BEAT.

— Admittedly. And wrong, wrong, wrong.

—AND AGAIN YOU CASTIGATE POOR MEMERE.

— Also wrong. But note my suggestion that America wanted Kerouac to be the romantic, hard-driving outsider. To be that and nothing more.

— YOU BEGIN TO INTRIGUE ME.

— In opening with clips from the Steve Allen show, Antonelli establishes his documentary method and also creates a context. Kerouac was a writer, yes — but also a social phenomenon. Eventually, this awkward duality, this conflict, destroyed him.

— THIS IS YOUR POSITION?

— No, no. Antonelli's. But admire his method. In closing with footage from that same Steve Allen show, clips of Kerouac reading from *On The Road* and *Visions of Cody*, the film-maker leaves us with an image of the writer at the peak of his powers. This is clearly preferable to bowing to chronological time and ending with an equally potent image of Kerouac just nine years later, drunk and incoherent on William F. Buckley's *Firing Line*.

— LET'S GET THIS STRAIGHT. INTO THIS NARRATIVE, YOU'RE SEEKING TO INTRODUCE A DOCUMENT ABOUT A DOCUMENT THAT MIXES AND MATCHES DOCUMENTS?

— Well, I do say the documentary footage of the real Kerouac is the most compelling stuff in the film. Though Antonelli also dramatizes incidents and events. Fortunately, actor Jack Coulter looks enough like Kerouac that the documentary survives.

—BUT WHAT'S THIS ABOUT HOW, IN A LUCKY REVERSAL OF STEREOTYPES, COULTER'S NOT AS HANDSOME AS EARLY-DAYS KEROUAC? FRANKIE, WHO CARES?

— The review also enters a chronology into the narrative. After the opening, we find ourselves in Lowell, where Kerouac grew up Catholic and French-Canadian. We follow him to New York City on a football scholarship, watch him drop out of Columbia University, see him ship out as a merchant seaman. We go on the road with him, see him down and out in Mexico and San Francisco.

— ALL OF WHICH WILL EMERGE, FRANKIE. AND LOOK: HERE YOU SAY THE FILM MINIMIZES KEROUAC'S BIZARRE RELATIONSHIP WITH HIS MOTHER.

— True. But then I say it's probably because the image that emerges from an exploration of that relationship — the image of Kerouac as a mama's boy — doesn't jibe with that of the romantic, hard-driving outsider. And that reckless, hard-driving outsider is what all of America wishes Kerouac had been — that and nothing else. That's an anti-Beat flash.

— IMPOSSIBLY CONVOLUTED, FRANKIE. MARGINAL AND BOTTOM-LINE BORING. GO DIRECTLY TO BOSTON. DO NOT PASS GO. DO NOT COLLECT TWO HUNDRED DOLLARS.

10

If male chauvinism means reducing women to sex objects, then Jack Kerouac stands guilty. Why rehearse specifics? In mitigation I note that he was a man of his times. And that, of worse crimes, he was innocent. I think of Old Jesus, of his famous invitation to cast the first stone and fall silent remembering my own salad-days response to a vision of airline stewardesses.

Early summer, 1966. New York City. See me muttering to myself as I arrived at the George Washington Bridge, fuming still over Jeunesse and Sylvester and my late-night chase around Central Park, so distracted that I spent several moments standing beside a ramp that spiraled onto the bridge before realizing this was no good. A driver couldn't stop here without getting rear-ended. Besides, where was I going? Hartford? Providence?

I swung up the ramp, rounded a bend and there, in an even-worse spot, stood another hitchhiker. Blond, early twenties, he sported a button-down shirt and a red-and-white cardigan and right away I pegged him: Joe College. On his left foot he had a white cast that reached almost to his knee. He was holding a cardboard sign that said "Boston."

I stopped to chat, as you did in those days, ended up revealing my plan: "I'm going to cross the bridge and try my luck on the other side."

The blond guy put his sign under his arm. "Hell, I should do that very thing." Broad southern accent. "I've been here over an hour. Mind if I walk with you?"

I pointed at his cast: "You think you can make it?"

"Nothing to it." The blond guy swung up to me grinning, held out his hand. "Bubba's my handle. Bubba Dunkley, Georgia."

"Frankie McCracken, Montreal."

We shook hands and started across the bridge, cars whizzing past and a wind blowing hard enough that we had to yell. "What'd you do to your foot?"

"Chipped a bone playing tennis. Ain't nothing, really."

Besides the fancy shirt, Bubba was wearing a pricey wristwatch and well-pressed trousers, the left leg cut open neatly, at the seam, to allow for the cast. He wasn't carrying any kind of bag and I said, "First time on the road?"

"How'd you guess? It sure as hell ain't by choice."

Swinging along in his cast, plonking it down and then dragging it, *thonk, tshht,* Bubba told me he'd just completed third-year economics at the University of Texas. When school let out, he'd flown north for a holiday. New York was more expensive than he'd expected, and a couple of days ago he'd had to phone home and get his father to wire two hundred dollars. Then last night, he'd met a woman in a bar. He didn't want to go into details, but this morning when he woke, both the woman and his money were gone: "Can you beat that?"

Bubba wasn't worried because he had friends in Boston: three airline stewardesses. They were expecting him. They would feed him steak and wine, chauffeur him around town, show him a great old time. He'd visited before. In fact, he'd stashed a complete wardrobe at their apartment. "What about you?"

I'd had a good time in New York, I said, but now I was down to my last couple of dollars and had to get home.

"Well, at least you're not flat broke," Bubba said, looking me up and down. "You know, we're about the same size. You'd look all right in one of my suits. Why don't you come to Boston? We'll have ourselves a time."

By now we'd reached the end of the bridge. Ahead lay Highway 87 and Montreal; the road to Boston, Highway 95, ran through an underpass below. Three stewardesses waiting for Bubba? Too good to be true. I said I had friends waiting in Montreal.

Bubba tried to change my mind, but finally, disappointed, he climbed over the guard rail, waved goodbye and disappeared down a grassy slope.

Three stewardesses waiting in Boston? Ha! I crossed a median, dropped my travelling bag at my feet and stuck out my thumb. My heart wasn't in it. If Bubba had been telling the truth, I'd thrown away the chance of a life-time. If I let him go now, I'd never know. And that, I realized, grabbing my bag, I couldn't bear. "Bubba!" I raced back across the highway and scrambled down the slope. "Bubba, wait! I've changed my mind!"

At my insistence, Bubba stationed himself in front of me, his casted foot propped on my bag. Almost immediately a Buick Roadmaster pulled over. We piled into the front seat, me first to do the talking. The driver was a swarthy, muscular man in his mid-forties, looked like a furniture mover. He was going all the way to Boston and had picked us up so we could chip in for gas. "That's how it works, right?"

"I've got two dollars," I said, "but we were hoping to get something to eat."

The driver, who'd grunted that his name was Bruno, looked around me. Bubba said he'd been robbed, but he'd take Bruno's address and send him fifty dollars.

For a while Bruno drove in angry silence and I thought he was going to kick us out. Bubba was boasting about how his father owned several companies — oil and gas refiners, mostly, but also a chocolate-making outfit — and one day they'd all be his. If we gave him our addresses, he'd send us boxes of liqueur-filled chocolates like we'd never tasted.

Bruno slashed his arm through the air: "Cut the bullshit!"

Bubba flushed. To me, he whispered, "Damn it, I'm telling the truth!"

For half an hour we drove in silence. Then Bruno pulled into a service centre. He filled his Roadmaster with gas before parking in front of the restaurant. "Fifteen minutes," he said. "You guys are on your own."

Bruno took a booth and polished off a clubhouse with fries. At the counter, Bubba and I shared a cheeseburger. Bruno finished eating while Bubba was in the washroom and outside, at the car, I had to tell him: "Hey! Wait for Bubba!"

Back on the highway I watched the speedometer. We were doing seventy-five, eighty miles an hour and I was thinking, well, at least we're really tooling along when a police car came out of nowhere, zoomed up behind us, lights flashing. Through a loudspeaker, the policeman ordered us to pull over onto the side of the highway. As Bruno got out, shaking with fury, Bubba said: "Hey, don't worry. I'll take care of it."

Five minutes later, Bruno swung into the car waving a speeding ticket: "This is what I get for picking up hitchhikers."

"I'll take care of that," Bubba said. "We're in Massachussetts, right? A judge here owes my father. Pull over at the next gas station and I'll make a phone call."

Bruno looked at me and I shrugged. Bubba insisted that he wanted to phone this judge. And next service centre, Bruno pulled in: "I don't know why I'm doing this."

"Come and listen!" Bubba said. "I insist that you both listen!"

Bruno and I stood outside the telephone booth while Bubba placed a collect call to Hyannis. He gave his name and somebody accepted charges. Bubba said, "I want to talk to Judge Hackett personally. No, it's a private matter."

We waited a couple of moments, and then Bubba was extending his father's regards and explaining that he'd run into a problem with a speeding ticket. He read the ticket number to the judge, said, "You're sure this won't be any problem."

Goodbyes completed, Bubba emerged grinning from the phone booth and tore up the ticket with a flourish. "That takes care of that. Shall we go?"

On our way back to the car, I danced a little jig. Bubba had made sure we'd heard the voices at the other end. This guy was for real — and that meant three stewardess were waiting.

Bruno insisted on buying coffees all around.

At four o'clock we rolled into Boston. Bruno was late for an appointment. He was going downtown and where did we want to get out? Bubba said near Harvard but Bruno said that was out of his way. I checked my map and suggested the Greyhound bus depot.

Bruno dropped us there and disappeared into the rush-hour traffic. In the depot, Bubba said, "The girls will pick us up, no problem. Jackie's mine. The other two...."

I handed him my last dime, having saved it for this purpose, and sat on a bench to wait. Bubba reappeared almost immediately, looking confused. "There's no answer."

"Are they expecting you?"

"I've already told you: yes!"

"Maybe they're shopping for groceries or something."

"They should be home. Their plane was due to arrive from Miami three hours ago."

"You mean they're flying in?"

"They should be here already."

"Bubba, relax. Try calling again. Maybe you dialed the wrong number. If there's still no answer, call the airline and see if the plane's delayed."

This time I followed Bubba to the phone booth. Still no answer at the apartment, so Bubba called United Airlines. He mentioned Miama and waited. Then he said, "Grounded! What do you mean, grounded? I'm waiting for people on that plane."

Silence. Then Bubba was yelling: "Tomorrow's not good enough! Do you realize who you're talking to? My name's Dunkley! I'm Bubba Dunkley Junior! My father owns most of Georgia and half of Arkansas! I want to speak to the president of this airline! I don't give a damn about company policy! What's your name? My father's going to hear about this! Do you understand me?"

Bubba slammed down the receiver. He stood a moment looking around, wild-eyed, then made for the front door. I caught him out front, on the sidewalk, told him to relax, take a few deep breaths. "Okay, so the stewardesses don't arrive until tomorrow. It's not the end of the world. You can phone your father now, get him to wire some money and presto! We're back in business."

"We haven't got a dime to make another call."

"No problem," I said.

Out front of the bus depot, while Bubba paced, looking the other way, I tried to bum a dime. Finally a bearded black man stopped to listen. I told him I was from Montreal, that through a bizarre series of accidents — but he waved off the rest of my story, handed me a dollar.

Back inside the depot, Bubba made a collect call to Georgia. Again I stood listening.

"Accept the charges, Cassie," Bubba said. "It's me, Junior. Tell the operator you accept the charges." Suddenly, he was roaring: "Cassie, god-dammit! You accept these charges, you hear, or you'll be out on your ass! You hear me, Cassie? Out on your fat black ass! Listen, operator, she accepts the charges. Operator, she accepts the charges."

From Bubba's end of the conversation that ensued, I deduced that Bubba Dunkley Senior had flown to Houston, some emergency business meeting. His wife was still in San Diego. Cassie was in mid-sentence — I could hear her voice — when Bubba smashed down the receiver. Again he made for the front door.

Again I ran after him. Talked him into returning once more to the counter. We sat on stools, drank coffee and shared a donut. Bubba kept looking around, distracted. To settle him down, I told the story of Jeunesse and Sylvester and how I'd evened the score with a phone call. Bubba just stared at me. "This place stinks," he said. "I've got to get out of here."

Might be wiser, I said, to stay right where we were. Night was falling. Outside looked like rain. At least in the depot we'd be warm and dry. "Tomorrow morning we'll phone the steward-esses and —

"This place stinks!" Bubba jumped up to his feet. "I've got to walk."

"What about your foot?"

"Walking will be good for it. If I sit still all night my foot will stiffen up."

"Bubba, you're not making sense."

"You coming or not?"

The darkness, the cold, the gathering storm — I ran through it all again. Why not just sit in the bus depot and wait, keep phoning the stewardesses to check. But Bubba was adamant. Finally I took our last dime, deposited my bag in a locker and followed him out the door.

"Which way's Harvard?"

I pointed and Bubba stomped into the night, refused to say where we were going or why. "I don't want to talk."

I didn't believe he could maintain the pace, not with one foot in a cast, but after fifteen, twenty minutes, Bubba was still pounding ahead, teeth clenched, eyes fixed in front of him, ramming the base of his cast down onto the sidewalk, then swinging his foot up beside it. *Thonk, tshht, thonk, tshht.*

Tomorrow, I told myself, everything would change. Stewardesses would whisk us away to hot showers, steak dinners and God knew what else.

After about an hour the sidewalk turned into a dirt-and-gravel shoulder but Bubba pounded on. I paused under a street-lamp, checked my map and decided we were still heading for Harvard. I caught Bubba and strode along beside him in silence for another fifteen minutes. Then I said: "Storm's blowing up."

Bubba ignored me. Again I reminded myself that only this bad-tempered lunatic could lead me to the heavenly stewardesses. "Maybe we should head back to the bus depot."

Thonk, tshht. Thonk, tshht.

Sooner or later I'd have to go back for my bag. The faster we walked now, the farther I'd have to travel later. I'd already tried slowing the pace for short stretches, but Bubba had pounded ahead. *Thonk, tshht. Thonk, tshht.* Now I slowed down again, only this time I didn't bother to catch up as soon as he pulled ahead. Twenty yards. Thirty yards. Fifty. I let Bubba get almost out of sight. Wanted to get rid of me, did he? I considered letting it happen, but thought again of the stewardesses, of how tomorrow everything would change. I stumbled into a trot and didn't stop running until I caught up.

Together now, Bubba and I pounded silently into the night. *Thonk, tshht.* Shoulder to shoulder. *Thonk, tshht. Thonk, tshht.* My legs ached and I craved sleep but I went onto automatic pilot and lost track of time. *Thonk, tshht. Thonk, tshht.*

Rain on my face. I came out of my trance. We'd long since passed the walled grounds of Harvard University, where we might have sheltered under trees. Now, as we pounded into the wet night, I could see only the dark shapes and lit windows of apartment buildings. What was I doing here? As I pulled my jacket over my head I thought of the Ghost of the Susquehanna, bound for "Canaday." Remembered that somewhere, on yet another rainy night, Kerouac had followed this ghostly, white-haired old hobo seven miles in a downpour, sweating, ex-hausted, the old man urging him to walk faster, the two of them making desperately for a bridge to "Canaday" — a bridge that didn't exist.

"Bubba, this is crazy!" I pointed across the street at a three-sided bus shelter. "Let's get out of the rain."

"I've got to keep walking," Bubba said. "Don't want my foot to seize up."

"You bloody-minded fool!"

I trotted across the street into the shelter. As I dried my face on my sweater, the rain really began to pound. Cars pulled over because drivers couldn't see. I smiled grimly and stretched out on one of the benches. I was dropping off to sleep, my arms crossed on my chest, when Bubba erupted into the shelter. He mumbled something about not wanting to catch his death and lay down on the bench along the opposite wall.

Children woke me. They chattered as they passed on their way to school. The sun was shining. I rubbed my face and sat up. Bubba was already sitting. He looked grey but said he wanted to resume walking.

"You're making for the apartment," I said. "Figure you'll sit outside until the stewardesses arrive. But what if they don't turn up until tomorrow?"

"Got any better ideas?"

"I'm going back to the bus depot. Wash my face. Maybe pawn my watch and get something to eat."

Bubba said he wasn't going back to the depot. Anyway, he was certain the stewardesses would arrive this morning. "Wait for me at the depot. We'll pick you up."

I said, "Give me the girls' phone number."

"Can't do that. It's unlisted. But we'll pick you up at the bus depot. Two o'clock. You have my word."

"See you at two," I said. I waved goodbye to Bubba, then stepped off the sidewalk and stuck out my thumb. I got a ride with a Harvard student, business administration, who said I was in luck, he was heading downtown. I told him I was starving but he didn't take the hint. Suddenly, I couldn't believe how quickly, here was the bus depot. Last night we'd walked forever.

Two nearby pawnships refused my watch, said it was worthless. I went into the depot, retrieved my bag and brushed my teeth in the men's room. That made me feel better. Out front, through sheer doggedness, I bummed a dollar and a half. I sat down at the counter and spent most of it on bacon and eggs. This cleared my head.

It was eleven o'clock and maybe the stewardesses were already in Boston. They'd feed me steak and wine. Chauffeur me around town. God knew what else. All I had to do was wait until two.

Then I thought: Who are you kidding? Bubba has no intention of returning for you — not if the stewardesses arrive. He wants you here in case they don't, so you can save his ass. By now I was sitting on a bench. The depot was quieter than last night, far less crowded. And as I looked around, suddenly the missing piece clicked into place, and I understood why Bubba had refused to stay here last night, why instead he'd plunged into the streets: Most of the people around me were black. Bubba was a racist.

I sat a moment, digesting this.

Then I called United Airlines. The flight from Miami was on its way. I said I wanted to leave a message for one of the stewardesses, a woman named Jackie. "No, I don't know her last name," I said, "but I'm a friend of a friend. Please write this down. Tell her to ask Bubba how he lost his money in New York.

Tell her a friend thinks Bubba caught something. Got that? Bubba Dunkley caught something terrible in New York."

When the woman asked my name, I said, "Jack Kerouac." I spelled this for her, then rode a city bus north to the outskirts. Climbed onto a highway and stuck out my thumb.

11

D id I mention taking joy in comparing chronologies? That first night on Jubilation, as I lay looking up at the stars, I realized that in April of 1956, while I was living in a shack in Berkeley, California, and writing *The Scripture of the Golden Eternity*, in which I explored the Buddhist idea that, know it or not, all things are One and related, a farmer in Ste. Thérèse Sur-le-lac, Quebec, decided to raise money by selling three tiny houses, one of which he rented to the parents of Frankie McCracken.

In early May, when I launched into writing *Old Angel Midnight*, that wild experiment in which I berated myself for ever having dreamed I could get rich by madly scribbling, Frankie's father visited friends and relations, raised a down payment of $300 — and discovered it wasn't enough. The McCrackens would have to move.

Later that month, while I rambled San Francisco drinking Muscatel, Frankie's parents hunted houses in Ste. Thérèse. On Avenue des Archanges, halfway between the highway and the lake, his mother found a summer camp selling for two thousand dollars. The annual spring flood threatened the place, but Madame Francoeur, the owner, said forget the down payment, just pay me forty dollars a month.

And in June of that year, 1956, while I hitchhiked north to Desolation Peak, still hoping at age thirty-four to have a vision that would change my life, nine-year-old Frankie McCracken helped his parents pile their belongings into a half-ton truck, three separate loads, then rode his bicycle across the highway and down Avenue des Archanges to the place he'd call home for the next eight years.

The property, fifty feet wide and one hundred deep, boasted six or eight trees, three fully grown: two poplars out front, one on each side of the yard, and a weeping willow at the foot of the sandy driveway. The back yard was a swamp of waist-high grasses and bullrushes. In July of 1956, while on Desolation Peak I wrestled Buddha and shouted Sinatra into the wind, Frankie and his father attacked the grass with a scythe, covered their handiwork with three truckloads of sand.

The house lacked a foundation. It sat, not on the usual stilts, but on horizontal beams, once telephone poles. The roof leaked, the clapboard walls needed paint and the double windows didn't fit. "At least it's ours," Frankie's mother said. "Or will be soon. We can fix it up."

The house included a kitchen and an adjoining front room, three tiny bedrooms with curtains for doors and two porches, obviously after-thoughts. The front porch was windows from the waist up, several different sizes, and winter would mean sealing it off. The back porch ran along the side of the house from the middle, where the kitchen door opened onto the steps. It was dark and enclosed and at the far end, behind a door with a latch, was the toilet — a seat with a hole in it.

By September of 1956, when I left Desolation, Frankie's father had partitioned the kitchen and, with the help of his oldest son — "Pliers? Dad, they're right beside you!" — installed a septic tank and an indoor flush toilet.

Fourteen years later, on Mount Jubilation, I stayed with the house as Frankie's father enlarged the front room by taking out part of a wall and boarding up some front-porch windows. He helped a local contractor raise the residence and put a cement-block foundation under it. To the bathroom he added a sink. And he replaced the hand pump in the kitchen — it required endless priming — with an electric pump that worked automatically.

In the beginning, the kitchen sink was the only sink and often backed up. Bad news. Next to the sink stood an ice-box. In summer, once or twice a week, depending on the weather, a man came around selling blocks of ice out of the back of a truck. In winter, Frankie had to fetch ice-blocks from the man's house a mile up the highway, trundle west under the train bridge and on past the French school, the BP Station and the Roman Catholic church.

That's where Frankie went to get stove oil, as well, when the drum in the back yard ran empty, hauling a two-gallon bottle on either a wagon or a toboggan, depending on season. The oil stove was opposite the back door. Black stove pipes ran up the wall behind the stove and then across the kitchen, suspended by wires. They joined the pipes from the front room and disappeared into the ceiling above the back door. "Looks like Hell," his father admitted, "but we have to heat the place somehow."

Above the ice-box, to the right of the kitchen-sink window, open shelves displayed cereal boxes, bags of flour and sugar, cans of soup and beans — everything Frankie's mother needed, or at least all she had, to feed a family of five and then six. There were more shelves in a waist-high counter which separated the kitchen from the front room, though the same worn linoleum, red-and-green checks, ran from one end of the house to the other.

Besides the wood stove, the front room boasted a worn couch, a ratty arm chair and a rocker. A black-and-white television set picked up two channels, one French, one English. Beyond it was the front porch, where, in an old buffet and on makeshift shelves, Frankie's father stored books and records.

Of the three bedrooms, Frankie's sisters shared the only one big enough for two beds. It lay to the right as through the back door, really at the side, you entered the house. His parents, with their double bed, shared the next largest, off the front room. Frankie and his brother had bunkbeds, so they got the smallest bedroom, at the back corner of the house.

Frankie was almost eleven before a classmate who'd visited gave him a North American perspective on his home. The boy shook his head as Frankie joined a circle of laughing friends in the hall, a circle gone suddenly silent: "I don't understand it, Frankie. How can a guy like you come out of a place like that?"

Frankie was twelve, the only seventh grader on the high school basketball team, before the house contributed further. Two mornings a week, he attended practices that began at 8 a.m. — one hour before classes. He would finish his *Gazette* route, and then, instead of returning to bed for an hour, eat breakfast and hitchhike into Coeur d'Aimée. Usually he'd get a ride right away and stand at the front door of the school flapping his arms to keep warm until the janitor arrived.

If he didn't get a ride within the first fifteen minutes, he'd start walking, hitching as he went. This particular morning, Frankie had to walk all the way to school, almost three miles, and so arrived late for practice. He changed as quickly as he could and ran down the hall to the gym, just in time for scrimmage.

Not until first period, scripture, did he remember the rent money. That's what they called it, rent money, though really it was payments on the house. Once a month after school, Frankie had to deliver this rent money, trudging twenty minutes along the highway to Madame Francoeur's house in St. Eustache. He hated this chore. He didn't mind missing the school bus and having to hitchhike home. And Madame Francoeur he liked. She'd invite him inside, offer him milk and cookies.

What Frankie hated was accepting May's rent receipt in October, or last November's in July. And watching Madame Francoeur, honestly confused, flip through her records, saying, "Can that be right?" And having to say, "Yes. Yes, that's right."

So always he'd drive the rent money out of his mind until he had to deliver it. Remembering it suddenly that morning, first period, Frankie realized that in his rush to get to the gym for basketball practice he'd neglected to lock his locker. He decided to check, just in case.

At the front of the room, the teacher was droning on about loaves and fishes. Under his desk, Frankie opened his wallet. He couldn't believe it. The rent money was gone. The classroom began to spin. Frankie stumbled to his feet and made for the door.

His teacher, startled, jumped out of the way: "Frankie?"

"Got to call my mother!"

Out the door, along the corridor and down the stairs he ran, taking the steps two at a time. He didn't stop running until he reached the principal's office, where he banged on the door until it opened.

"Mr. Herder, I've been robbed!"

"Are you trying to break down the door?" The principal, a myopic man who stood six-foot-five, looked down at Frankie through thick glasses, his eyes huge and blue and watery. "Come in, then."

Mr. Herder closed the door and motioned Frankie into a chair, then sat down behind his desk. "Now, Frankie, what's happened."

"I've been robbed. I — "

"You mean something is missing. Don't be too anxious to accuse." He leaned forward and made a steeple with his fingers. "What's missing?"

"Forty dollars."

Mr. Herder's eyebrows went up.

"I had it in my wallet. Now it's gone. I want to talk to my mother."

"What were you doing, carrying that much money?"

"It was rent money. I was supposed to deliver it."

"Where did you lose this rent money?"

"In the locker room." Frankie's voice quavered. "I went to basketball practice and … and I left it in my locker."

"Ahhhhh." Mr. Herder, satisfied, sat back in his chair. "You forgot to lock your locker."

Frankie didn't trust himself to speak. He nodded at the floor.

"How many times do I have to tell you people? Never leave your lockers unlocked. Never, never, never."

"Mr. Herder, could I use your telephone, please?"

"So now you've lost forty dollars. "

"I want to call my mother."

"All right, go ahead." Mr. Herder got up from his desk, stepped to the window and stood looking out, his hands clasped behind his back.

"Mom? It's me, Frankie."

"Frankie? Is something wrong?"

"Mom, I've lost the rent money."

"The rent money?"

"Yes, Mom." His voice broke. "I forgot to lock my locker. When I got back from practice, the money was gone."

"Okay, Frankie. Don't cry."

"Mom, we're already late. And bills just keep coming. What are we going to do?"

"Don't worry, Frankie. I'll think of something."

"I'll pay it back, Mom."

"Don't talk foolishness. And stop crying, now. Where are you calling from?"

"The principal's office. Mom, I'll pay it back."

"Stop crying, Frankie, please. Forget the rent money. It's not the end of the world."

"I'll pay it back, Mom. You'll see. I'll pay it back."

12

By the mid-eighties I was seriously questioning the Beat-American interpretation of Kerouac. But it wasn't until 1987, at the now-famous Quebec City conference, that I discovered a second comprehensive analysis. I wrote about it in *The Rocky Mountain Miracle*: "QUEBEC CITY — Jack Kerouac, the wild-man American writer who died in Florida in 1969, turned up last week in *la belle province*. Kerouac sprang vividly to life in the minds and hearts of roughly 200 people — among them poets, novelists and scholars of international reputation — who gathered in the author's ancestral homeland to celebrate his life and work."

— THAT'S ENOUGH, FRANKIE.

— "Participants came from all over the United States of America: from California and Ohio, from Wisconsin and Massachusetts and New York. They came, too, from across Canada: from Ontario and New Brunswick and Alberta. But most of them came from the province of Quebec, where French-Canadians recently awakened in numbers to shout: *'Ciboire!* Kerouac's one of us!'"

— FRANKIE!

— Surely even you see the need for Quebec City?

— YES, BUT NOT FOR REPORTAGE.

— This article turned up in newspapers and magazines all over the world.

— TO QUOTE IT HERE, HOWEVER, WOULD BE SHAME-LESSLY SELF-INDULGENT.

— Objection! I'm offering documentary evidence of a key development.

— DOCUMENTARY EVIDENCE IS NOT PRIVILEGED HERE, FRANKIE. IT'S JUST MORE WORDS ON A PAGE. OBJECTION OVER-RULED.

— That so? Listen: "This was no academic conference, with professors delivering esoteric papers and scoring debating points. Nor was it a literary festival, with big-name authors reading from their works on a dais, socializing among themselves and granting the occasional interview. Rather it was a bilingual, four-day *rencontre* that some called a sacramental experience, others an old-style happening and still others a rip-roaring wake."

— SUCH RECALCITRANCE, FRANKIE. YOU LEAVE ME NO CHOICE: FRANKIE THE NARRATOR FELT HIMSELF SEIZED BY THE BACK OF THE NECK, AS IF BY A GIANT HAND. THIS ALL-POWERFUL HAND FROG-MARCHED HIM ACROSS THE ROOM AND THRUST HIM UN-CEREMONIOUSLY OUT THE DOOR. THE OLD FAMILIAR SURROUNDINGS, INCLUDING THE GROUND ON WHICH HE NORMALLY WALKED, HAD CEASED TO EXIST. FRANKIE FOUND HIMSELF TUMBLING THROUGH A CLOUDLESS BLUE SKY. FAR BELOW, THOUGH RAPIDLY DRAWING NEARER, LAY A RANGE OF SNOW-CAPPED MOUNTAINS. FRANKIE RECOGNIZED MOUNT JUBILA-TION. BUT WHAT WAS THAT? A DIRT ROAD? A DIRT ROAD MEANDERING THROUGH MOUNTAIN PEAKS? FRANKIE REALIZED WITH GROWING HORROR THAT HE WAS HEADING STRAIGHT FOR THE MIDDLE OF THIS IMPOSSIBLE DIRT ROAD, THAT WITHIN SECONDS HE WOULD LAND WITH A SPLAT.

— "You!" he hollered. "You've made your point!"

— FRANKIE THE NARRATOR CLOSED HIS EYES. WHEN HE OPENED THEM AGAIN — WHAT? NO SPLAT? — HE FOUND HIMSELF SEATED SAFELY IN FRONT OF HIS COMPUTER. SULKILY, HE SAID:

— I might have been hurt.

— HURT, YES. CRUCIFIED, RESURRECTED. TRANSFORMED INTO A GIANT DUNG BEETLE. YOU CAN BE REPLACED, FRANKIE. INSTEAD, PRESTO! YOU'RE FULLY RECOVERED. NOW TELL ME ABOUT THE *RENCONTRE*.

— The gathering happened in the back rooms and bars, the winding streets and small hotels of *Vieux Québec*. There were panel discussions at the international youth hostel, lunch-time debates at a downtown pub and late-night shows at an aptly named bar, *Le Grand Dérangement*. Videos, film premieres, book launchings, slide shows, book-and-photo exhibits, posters, cassette tapes, T-shirts — for four days Kerouac was king of Quebec City.

— SPECIFIC RESPONSES?

— Biographer Ann Charters said the gathering represented "a true rebirth, a renaissance." Allen Ginsberg declared: "I haven't seen anything like this since the 1960s."

— HISTORICAL SIGNIFICANCE?

— The occasion had as many meanings as participants. I described it as a confluence of two rivers of thought, one essentially American, the other French-Canadian. Each of them roiling with tensions and contradictions, all of which Kerouac himself manifested, many of which were personified at the gathering.

— TWO DISCOURSES, THEN. ELABORATE.

— Most serious discussion has treated Kerouac in an American context, depicting him as a Beat Generation writer who rebelled against the consumerism and conformity of the 1950s. Here the sub-themes have been well-articulated: spontaneous prose, Buddhism, autobiographical fiction, colloquial language, identification with the underdog.

— CUT TO THE GENIAL BUSINESSMAN.

— Lawrence Ferlinghetti wondered aloud if the gathering wasn't wildly exaggerating Kerouac's *Québécois*-ness. Which fits my emerging theory.

— AND CAROLYN CASSADY?

— She came from England and stole the show: "An elegant, well-spoken woman, Cassady is the ex-wife of Neal Cassady, real-life model for Kerouac's most famous hero, Dean Moriarty. In describing her long, complex love affair with Kerouac, Cassady evoked an indisputable truth: Old Jack was a great spirit, a great heart."

— FRANKIE, DON'T TEMPT ME.

— The second roiling river of interpretation flows directly out of the decades-old Quebec-independence debate and focuses on the author's French-Canadian heritage. Franco-Americans from Lowell have insisted for years that the Beat-American Interpretation of Kerouac is inadequate. But no heavyweight intellectual has arisen among them to state the case convincingly or explore its implications.

— THAT CHANGED IN QUEBEC CITY?

— French-Canadian poets, novelists and scholars exploded into the debate, challenging Kerouac buffs from around the world to investigate questions about *Le Grand Jack* that, as Ferlinghetti noted, "nobody in America has ever asked." Does Kerouac symbolize what happens to French-speaking Quebecers who leave their province? Was he unable to return to Quebec because the province wasn't mature enough to welcome him?

— THE CRUCIAL DOCUMENT IN THIS AWAKENING?

— A videotape from 1967, when Kerouac gave a television interview in Montreal. The program was *Le Sel de la Semaine*. And the truth was there, in gesture and expression, and despite his uniquely accented French, for all to see: Kerouac was a French-Canadian — *un de nous autres*.

— THIS VERDICT WAS UNANIMOUS?

— You kidding? Novelist Victor-Levy Beaulieu reiterated the intransigent Quebec-nationalist position he staked out in his book *Jack Kerouac: essai-poulet*. He insisted that Kerouac, though a great artist, has nothing to do with Quebec.

— GIVE ME A VARIATION.

— A poet named Francoeur depicted Kerouac as a minor writer experimenting in a major language, and stated flatly that Quebec has no place for him as a Beat writer.

— ON THE OTHER HAND?

— One cultural geographer drew parallels between Kerouac and the martyr Louis Riel, arguing that the writer could not return to Quebec during his lifetime because the province wasn't mature enough to accept him. Another elaborated, claiming that until now French-speaking Quebecers have not been secure enough to perceive themselves as Franco-Americans, and thus to accept

Kerouac — a universal genius who wrote a unique blend of literature and lived truth: "vecriture."

—WHAT'S THIS ABOUT A QUEBEC PLAYWRIGHT?

— The Quebec City gathering recalled an experiment by Michel Tremblay. He took actors who'd appeared in two of his plays, put them on stage and told them to interact, remaining in character. The experiment ended in disaster. One set of actors drove the other from the stage.

—YOU ANTICIPATED SOMETHING SIMILAR?

— Part way through the *rencontre*, as Beaulieu castigated Ginsberg and tempers flared, I couldn't help wondering whether a similar debacle was about to unfold within the personified worlds of Kerouac.

—SCRATCH THE ANALOGY.

— Wait! That no disaster ensued was a tribute to the spirit of Kerouac, don't you see? It proves Jack Kerouac is still *On The Road*.

—WE READ YOU, JUBILATION. COME IN.

13

That first morning on Jubilation I awoke to the sounds of Frankie in the tower, windows open, trying to raise the park warden on his two-way radio. "Jubilation Lookout calling Saskatchewan River Crossing. Jubilation Lookout calling the Crossing."

For a moment I didn't know who, what, where, when or why I was, never mind how. I was a stranger to myself, lost, haunted and alone, and then I remembered waking to that same feeling in a fleabag hotel by the railroad tracks, my first time seriously on the road. And smiled sadly to think that now, in 1970, I'd become the ghost I imagined then — a ghost lost in the echo chamber of somebody else's life.

"Jubilation Lookout calling Saskatchewan River Crossing. Come in, please."

"Crossing here. Good morning, Jubilation."

From the tower, Frankie relayed his weather report: current temperature, minimum last night, maximum yesterday. Relative humidity twenty-seven per cent, wind west south west at six miles per hour, visibility excellent, barometer steady.

While Frankie made small talk with the warden, I crawled out of my sleeping bag — the air tingled, pine-scented — and walked to the edge of the mountain. I stood looking out over the green valley and up at snow-capped mountain peaks etched white against the sky.

Frankie signed off and clambered down the ladder with a thick brown envelope under one arm. As his feet touched the ground, I called: "Race you to the cabin!"

Then grabbed my bag and beat him to the gate.

This he didn't like: "Get you next time."

The cabin smelled of buckwheat pancakes. "Had to use condensed milk," Frankie said as he shovelled them onto plates. "But look." He held up a can. "Real maple syrup. My mother sent it from Quebec."

We ate the pancakes smothered in syrup and washed them down with coffee, black and bad. Frankie asked about my plan for the day and I said, "Guess I'll hit the trail."

"You're kidding! You just got here!"

"Come September third, I turn into a pumpkin."

"Today's only the first!" Earlier, in the tower, he'd entered weather readings in his dated log-book. "I've been alone on this mountain for three months. Why don't you stay?"

I held out my arm: "Twist it."

Frankie slapped it away. "Glad that's settled," he said, "because last night in bed I got thinking." From a shelf he retrieved the thick brown envelope he'd carried out of the tower. "I don't know how you knew about the rent money. Guess I told Camille and forgot myself." He stared intently but my face gave nothing away and he continued: "Anyway, you mentioned my novel and I thought you might want to glance at it."

As I took the manuscript, a flash-flood hit me. Here was Frankie as a boy in Ste. Thérèse, lying awake and praying that tonight his father wouldn't come home. Here he was pedaling up Avenue des Archanges in autumn sunshine, anxious and fearful about entering La Fin du Monde. And what was I to make of Frankie in rainy-night San Francisco, nineteen years old, stripped to jeans and T-shirt and wading alone into the storm-tossed Pacific Ocean?

I knew I'd seen it all before, that this was a Great Remembering. Yet still I felt myself swept off my feet and floundering, going under, fighting for breath as white waves of remembrance crashed over my head. One day Frankie would write his life and mine. But the tenor of his tale — whether for Magic or against — was open to argument. Could I rouse him?

I searched these visions, these new images, but found no hint of how to proceed. Then, as if on cue, a spectacular double-whammy washed over me, a white flash involving Camille that opened in Banff and sent me reeling across the cabin, left me shaking my head, holding my eyes.

Frankie said, "You okay?"

"You're blocked and don't know why," I said, waving off his concern. "You figure anybody who knows Kerouac's work as well as I do might be able to help."

"Listen, if you're not feeling well — "

He reached for the manuscript but I pushed away his hand and sat down. "You've got the language skills," I said. "Terrific ear for language, a fine sense of rhythm. Also, you can be funny."

"You haven't even read the thing!"

"You do have a penchant for telling. You tell us your father loved Sinatra, for example. But you never show him sitting at the kitchen table, still in his overcoat, playing the same old records over and over."

Slowly, without taking his eyes off me, Frankie sat down on the edge of the bed. "Wait a minute!" He smacked his forehead. "I see what's happened. You read the book last night. You climbed into the tower and used your flashlight. The rest is extrapolation."

Frankie laughed, satisfied. "You had me going there. What I'm wondering, since obviously you've read the manuscript, is whether my approach is too autobiographical."

"All serious fiction is autobiographical, Frankie, in that it's a projection of the creative mind behind it." Still at the table, I poured more coffee. "What you're after is a shift from the literal to the allegorical — a symbolic encounter with the deepest self."

As I spoke I realized again that Death had radically changed me. My memories were intact, the facts as before. But my attitudes were new. My language, my rhythms. A symbolic encounter with the deepest self? Once I would have fled howling. Now, curious to see what I'd say next, I plunged on: "Ever wonder, Frankie, why so many novelists write about growing up?"

"No — but you're going to tell me."

"It's because growing up, everything you experience, you experience for the first time. And that makes an indelible impression. Your first home run, your first day of school. Who could forget them? Your first kiss? Your first disaster in love."

"Ah, we're back to my novel."

"No, we're not." I indicated his manuscript. "Here you treat a minor mishap in puppy love. The disaster didn't come until later — with a woman you met at a Montreal art gallery."

"I don't like where you're taking this."

"Disaster in love means being haunted by visions of what might have been. I'm talking shame and self-loathing, Frankie, and aching for a second chance. I'm talking Beat. I'm talking the way you feel right now — now that you've driven away Camille. Now that, for the first time, you stand to lose her forever."

Frankie went white. "Camille is none of your business!"

"All of which goes to show," I said lightly, realizing I'd taken him too far too fast, "that the problem here is not autobiography but vision." I tapped the manuscript. "Change the vision and the details will take care of themselves." I handed Frankie his un-opened manuscript, knocked back the last of my coffee and stood up. "Which way to the outhouse? I've forgotten."

"Turn right out the back gate and follow the path uphill. But wait a minute. What do you mean: change the vision?"

"Ah, youth. What powers of recovery." I assumed the voice of W. C. Fields: "My boy, existential angst just doesn't become you." Back in my own voice: "All this God-is-dead stuff, Frankie. So cold, so isolating. So false. You're back where you were when you said a first goodbye to Montreal."

"But God IS dead." He was getting used to me. "That's what shapes the novel, gives it coherence."

"Frankie, you're more driven by ideas than I was or ever wanted to be. But if you must have some heavyweight thinker in your corner, forget Friedrich Nietzsche. Check out Carl Jung. Archetypes, synchronicity, the collective unconscious. The good doctor's not bad, either, on relations between Self and Ego."

"Camille told me to read Jung. Wanted me to go back to university."

"Maybe she was right."

"Get real. I'm twenty-three years old."

"Frankie, I was twenty-six when I enrolled at the New School of Social Research. And I'd drafted *The Town and The City.*"

"You've got this Kerouac rap down," Frankie said as he adjusted his pillow against the wall, "but your continuity needs work. "One minute you're the quintessential bohemian, the non-conformist par excellence. The next you're urging me to join the fraternity crowd."

"I never acquired survival skills, Frankie. Couldn't earn a decent living until too late."

"You think I care that" — he snapped his fingers — "about earning a living? Don't you get it? I'm an artist."

"My sentiments, exactly, when I was your age. And even later. Having published a novel, I travelled to California expecting the *San Francisco Chronicle* to cry, 'Genius!' And make me a sports columnist. Found out the world doesn't work that way."

"You want me to sell out."

"Frankie, as a summer job, fire lookout beats most." I stood up and stretched. "But if you do go back to school, don't neglect literary karate. Develop some polemical skills. Make the Truman Capotes think twice before pulling their knives."

"This is getting weird. The real Kerouac wouldn't spout higher education but spontaneous prose."

"Ah, my spontaneity rap." I chuckled, remembering. "That was a reaction to the death I found around me."

"The conventions of psychological realism?"

"More the celebrating of the superficial. The idea that literature is a value-free word-game and never mind the spiritual, never mind the heart."

"Kerouac said writers shouldn't revise."

"I revised like a fiend and didn't admit it. But in knocking revision, I didn't go far enough. I didn't push the idea out the other side. I'm telling you, Frankie, that RE-vision is all. Change your vision and the rest will follow — which brings us full circle."

"So can we quit this charade? You don't sound even remotely like Kerouac."

"Frankie, I've got to run. But which Kerouac don't I sound like? Kerouac at twenty-eight? At forty-five? Your problem is vision."

"There's nothing wrong with my vision!"

"*Au contraire, mon ami.*" I bolted out the door and hollered over my shoulder as I ran: "You don't believe in miracles!"

14

There's no city like the first city, and for young Frankie McCracken, for me at seventeen, eighteen and nineteen years old, that city was Montreal. I said goodbye to The Town, to Ste. Thérèse Sur-le-lac, in the fall of 1964, having graduated from high school in nearby Coeur d'Aimée, and spent the next two years falling in love with what Kerouac might have called the cityCityCITY of Montreal. Three times I left Montreal and went on the road — dry runs, though I didn't realize it, for my San Francisco Vision Quest — but never for more than weeks at a stretch and quickly returning to stock-pile more memories. Or so it seems now, the nostalgia of middle-age in full flood.

So for young Frankie, for myself at seventeen, eighteen, nineteen years old, Montreal was a three-D kaleidoscope of images and associations, a whirl of red-brick apartment buildings and odd-smelling rooming houses, of fast food in cheap restaurants, movies in theatres both uptown and down, English and French, and live music in folk clubs and *boites à chanson* and down-and-dirty bars like the Black Bottom and the Esquire Showbar, this last going strong until three in the morning, so you'd turn up after midnight if you found yourself alone and the crew-cut bouncer would wave you past the line-up for tables and you'd perch on a stool at the bar, knock back Labatt's and lose yourself in the frenetic magic of rhythm and blues.

For me at seventeen, eighteen and nineteen years old, or so it seems now, Montreal was a city of seasons. Autumn was evening courses at Sir George Williams University, sitting in an over-heated cavern with four hundred other students, mostly fellow office workers, listening to lectures on constellations and black holes or Chaucer and the "Knight's Tale". Autumn was cool, crisp air and playing touch football with a gang from the office, startling them into new admiration with Kerouwacky razzle-dazzle, with crazy-man broken-field running.

Winter in Montreal was partying with a bunch of college guys who'd chipped in to rent a house for all-night blow-outs with the lights low and everybody drunk and dancing, shouting along with the Rolling Stones, and losing myself in in the beer and smoke and *Satisfaction*. Winter was paralyzing cold and blizzards, people abandoning their cars in snowbanks and me striding to work, so cold I could see my breath, wearing rubbers instead of boots, earmuffs instead of a hat and a well-cut blue overcoat instead of my old favorite duffle because lately I'd become a young Turk in pin-stripes with a go-getter image to proclaim.

In spring the big, bulky coats came off and Montreal was pretty girls in summer dresses and trying to focus on *The Subterraneans* while sitting on a cement bench at Place Ville Marie, a light spray from the fountain drifting over me, the square a profusion of secretaries and receptionists, eyes closed in the sunshine, leaning back, skirts riding high. Spring meant climbing the "mountain" in the middle of town, Mont-Royal, so named by an explorer who'd obviously never seen the Alps or the Canadian Rockies, walking the tree-lined road that spirals up it, horse-drawn caleches spinning past, and climbing steep wooden stairs to the Lookout, where I'd eat ice cream, lean against the balustrade and look out at the office towers and bridges of my cityCityCITY.

Montreal in summer was steam-room hot, ninety degrees in the shade and stupifying humidity. Summer was evenings riding around town on the Bus To Nowhere, two regular bus tickets and you could neck for hours in the life-giving air conditioning, but mostly it was mornings pounding away at a typewriter and afternoons shuffling the downtown streets in khaki shorts and sandals, the heat smacking up off the sidewalks, until finally I could stand it no longer and I'd catch a train to Ste. Thérèse.

So finally summer was my parents' house in the almost-country, where I'd sit in the kitchen trying to explain what I was doing with my life. And here my nostalgia begins to wind down.

"It's time you settled down, young man," my mother would say. "You should get yourself a job, move home here and help out with the bills."

"They're your bills, not mine."

"Maurice, you're his father. You tell him."

"You can't tell these guys anything, Maggie. He'll find out."

This would be the summer of 1966, after my sorties to Chicago and New York. The real battle wasn't joined until early autumn. By then I'd spent three weeks in southern Ontario, priming tobacco. I'd amassed five hundred dollars — a small fortune — and didn't intend to fritter it away. I visited Ste. Thérèse on a weekday, my mother home alone.

"Collecting unemployment insurance," she said. "A hulking brute like you. It's a disgrace."

"Not to worry, Mom. I'm going to Mexico."

"Mexico?" She finished rinsing the lunch dishes and poured dishwater down the sink, careful not to splash any on her housedress. "What are you talking about, Mexico?"

"I'm going to be a writer, Mom. I need experience."

"Frankie, you're nineteen years old. It's time you settled down, got a steady job."

I tilted my chair back on two legs, folded my arms across my chest and groaned dramatically. With the usual results.

"I don't understand it, that's all." She took two dish towels from a rack and tossed one to me. "Why Mexico? You could get experience in Montreal. Or right here in Ste. Thérèse if you put your mind to it."

"What do you want me to do?" I snapped the dish towel in the air. "Go back to delivering *Gazettes*?"

"You had a good job at that personnel agency."

"Mother, I don't want a job." I stood up so I could tower over her. "I'm going to be famous, understand?"

"Oh, Frankie, stop talking nonsense. Your father was going to be a movie star."

"My father didn't have my talent."

"Maybe not, Frankie. But what have you accomplished?"

"What have I accomplished?" Astonished, I appealed to the ceiling. "Eighteen years old, I was interviewing people for jobs. The youngest vocational counsellor in the history of Montreal."

"Why not get another job like that one?"

"What have I accomplished?" Waving my arms, still addressing the ceiling, tea-towel in hand, I paced around the kitchen. "Mother, I've been around. I've visited Chicago and Boston. I've lived in New York City. Greenwich Village? Frankie McCracken was there."

"Oh, for the love of God."

"What have I accomplished? I've read Dostoevsky. I've read Nietzsche. To the Superman all things are possible. I've read Jack Kerouac!"

"For the past six months you've done nothing but gallivant around the countryside. Or else sit on your bum in that filthy room downtown."

"I've been writing, remember? Writing!"

"So what have you published, Frankie?"

"That isn't the point, mother." I stopped pacing, stung, and brought my face close to hers. "Don't you know anything?"

"You're going off half-cocked, that's all I know. When you could be staying home here and helping out with the bills."

"I just lent you twenty-five bucks." I tossed the dish towel on the table. "What do you want, blood?"

Two steps and I was out the door.

"A no-good drunken bum!" Red-faced, shouting, my mother followed me to the top of the stairs. "That's what you're turning into. A good-for-nothing alcoholic, just like your father."

"That's right!" I plunged down the driveway, hurling immortal words over my shoulder: "I'm going to be just like my father, I tell you! Just like him!"

And with that stormed into the world.

15

D id I mention disaster in love?

Consider only Springtime Mary, who in my fiction, melded with the wife of my best friend, the lovely Carolyn, became the improbable Maggie Cassidy. Twenty, twenty-five years after saying goodbye to Springtime Mary, I'd flick on the radio, catch Sinatra mid-song and find myself back in Carnegie Hall, a teenager forever and Mary beside me, listening to Sinatra croon *Mighty Like A Rose*. You want melancholy, Frankie? You want shame and self-loathing? You want Beat?

This outburst was prompted by the rush I'd just taken out of his recent past — that spectacular, double-whammy flash involving Camille, early 1970.

"Frankie, it meant nothing."

"Don't say another word."

"I hadn't seen him in years. We got drunk."

"No more, please! I can't bear it!"

Frankie had just returned from a second furious hike to the top of Tunnel Mountain. He was pacing around the two-room cabin they'd lucked into on arrival in Banff, punching his hand with his fist.

"This is childish, Frankie. You've been carrying on for two days. Why don't we—"

"Childish! You sleep with some bozo—"

"Frankie, it had nothing to do with you and me."

"You sleep with some bozo passing through town. And then have the nerve to tell me I'm childish."

"All right, it was stupid."

"How'd you find each other, anyway? Some scrawl on a toilet door?"

"It was stupid, I apologize, it won't happen again."

"That's it! 'Looking for a good time? Call Camille at the School of Fine Arts.' "

Camille started to cry: "What about Barbara, Frankie? I forgave you, remember?"

Now, on Jubilation, the flash curled and crashed like a wave, swept me back to Montreal and the previous autumn, 1969. The autumn I died and Frankie, finally recovered from San Francisco, began again to live. Every Friday after teaching school Camille would drive into Montreal to spend the weekend with him. Usually they stayed in the city, rambled from the top of Mount Royal to Rue St. Denis, visiting bookstores and art galleries and coffee houses. The Matter of Opinion. *Les Trois Amants*.

When winter came Camille drove Frankie to the Laurentians and taught him to ski, laughing until she cried when by mistake they wandered onto an expert slope and he refused to remove his skis. And paid the price. Later he laughed about it, too.

But their affinity was rooted in parallel passions. Camille's architect father, long dead, had painted watercolors on weekends. Since childhood Camille had doodled on notepads and napkins, but lately she'd grown serious. The house she shared with two other teachers was crammed with her work, everything from delicate pen-and-ink sketches to spectacular acrylics that filled half a wall. In her passion for painting, Frankie rediscovered his writing. But hesitated.

Since returning from San Francisco, he'd determined that a never-ending series of one-night stands wasn't the answer. Yet alone in his room he'd lie awake nights: "My God! This relationship with Camille is getting too hot." He'd phone and suggest they cool it. Then, after moping around all weekend, he'd break down and call her. When he didn't see Camille, he missed her. He'd never resolved to be faithful. My God! Was he drifting into death?

So Frankie was wondering one Friday as he swung home from an office job at which he couldn't last much longer. As he approached McGill University, Frankie recognized a young woman half a block ahead. She was struggling with two bags of groceries. He caught her and offered to help. Six months before, Frankie had run into Barbara at a bar and remembered her from high school — a pretty girl, athletic, but two grades younger. Now she worked as a bank teller and lived alone just one block away. He'd gone home with her that night — turned out she'd always had a crush on him — but hadn't seen her since.

Now, as they passed his street, Aylmer, Barbara said, "Why don't you show me where you live? I could use a coffee."

Frankie hesitated, glanced at his watch — Camille wasn't due for two hours — and led Barbara up the street, telling himself nothing would happen. But no sooner had he put the groceries on the kitchen table than Barbara was in his arms, her tongue halfway down his throat. They tumbled onto the mattress and tore off each other's clothes. As he entered her, Frankie heard footsteps.

Having resided in the rooming house for six months, Frankie had inherited the best quarters — one and a half rooms on the ground floor at the front. Now, glancing up, he saw that he hadn't closed his blind properly, that along one edge it flapped open six inches. Through this crack, unable to breathe, he watched Camille, ninety minutes early, climb the last few stairs. Maybe she wouldn't see him? But she did. Her face registered surprise, then shock, then horror. And then, just before she turned and fled, it split open.

Frankie lost his erection. He felt sick. He asked Barbara to leave and she did — though not before cursing him out.

Camille didn't return. Next day and the day after, she refused to take his calls. Finally, mid-week, Frankie called in sick, caught a bus to the north shore and intercepted Camille after school. Rather than create a scene in the parking lot she let him into her car and drove him back to the house.

Taking up with him had been a mistake, she said. He was sick and disgusting. She never wanted to see him again. Having intended to make a dignified plea, Frankie found himself on his knees. He clung weeping to Camille's legs, said he knew he wasn't worthy, promised that nothing like this would ever happen again.

Camille relented.

They made love.

Afterwards, as he stared into Camille's eyes, Frankie realized that he was more deeply involved than he'd ever dreamed possible. Here was a woman who'd seen his worst self and still found it possible to love him.

Now, in Banff, he said: "Barbara was different. You and I were just starting out."

"That's not true and you know it." Tears ran down Camille's cheeks. "I've said I was sorry!"

"Sorry's not good enough."

"I love you, Frankie. But I can't take any more of this."

"Better brace yourself, then, because you've got a summer of it coming."

"No, Frankie, I haven't. I'm not going onto Jubilation with you."

"Okay with me." Frankie grabbed his jacket. "Go on back to Montreal, Camille! Find your bozo! See if I care!"

Frankie slammed out the door.

Three hours later, when he came home drunk, Camille was gone. She'd left a pen-and-ink sketch she'd done on Mount Royal. It showed Frankie sitting on the balustrade near the top, looking out over the skyline of the city.

16

MORE THAN TWENTY YEARS LATER, WHILE CON-TEMPLATING HIS QUEBEC CITY SIDEBAR, FRANKIE FOUND HIMSELF THINKING HE'D BEEN AFRAID FOR NO REASON:

— Early in the narrative game, you might have dumped me. But we're deep into the story. You can't do anything drastic.

— THINK NOT, FRANKIE?

— There are laws about these things, aesthetic rules that can't be broken. If you killed me off, or turned me into a giant bug, readers would be outraged.

— WHAT YOU DON'T REALIZE IS THAT, KNOWING YOUR REBARBATIVE NATURE, I'VE PREPARED FOR ANY CON-TINGENCY.

— You're bluffing. You can't harm me. Without me, you've got no story.

— YOU'VE HEARD OF OMNISCIENT NARRATION?

— Too late for that now.

— NOT NECESSARILY. THOUGH IN THE EVENT OF YOUR ACCIDENTAL DEATH AND DISMEMBERMENT, I'D TURN THIS TALE OVER TO OUR ALTERNATE NARRATOR.

— Alternate narrator, my eye! Ain't nobody here but us chickens.

— SORRY, FRANKIE. AN ALTERNATE NARRATOR HAS BEEN AT WORK IN THIS TEXT ALMOST SINCE THE BEGIN-NING.

— You're lying. If this alternate exists, produce him.

— THAT WOULD INTRODUCE A DIALECTIC, FRANKIE. I PREFER MY CONTRADICTIONS UNRESOLVED.

— Yeah, yeah.

— ENOUGH! IN QUEBEC CITY YOU DISCOVERED A SECOND MAJOR INTERPRETATION OF KEROUAC. BUT

YOU DIDN'T SEE IT AS INCOMPATIBLE WITH THE BEAT-AMERICAN.

— Right. I described the *rencontre* as a confluence of rivers, remember?

— FRANKIE THE NARRATOR JUMPED TO HIS FEET, STOOD AT ATTENTION AND, KNOWING WHAT WAS GOOD FOR HIM, ANSWERED ALL QUESTIONS TO THE BEST OF HIS ABILITY. ASKED WHETHER, IN A SIDEBAR FOCUSING ON ALLEN GINSBERG, HE REVEALED AN UNCONSCIOUS BIAS, FRANKIE SAID:

— Yes, I did. Despite myself, I dramatized my belief that the Beat-American interpretation would subsume the French-Canadian. That really the latter was a tributary.

— EXPLAIN.

— I suggested that Allen Ginsberg embodied the largeness of heart and spirit which in the end made the gathering what it was.

— WHY NOT? MANY WHO REGARD KEROUAC AS A WACKY AMERICAN SAINT OF SORTS SEE GINSBERG AS HIS PROPHET.

— That's Beat, all right. Most French-Canadians, however, perceive Ginsberg as a dark angel. They say he helped destroy Kerouac.

— IN QUEBEC, THE POET ANSWERED THIS CHARGE?

— OBLIQUELY. I mean, obliquely. He stressed that Kerouac was not only his friend but his teacher, and that he'd come to Quebec City to pay homage. Then launched into an hour-long Zen-Buddhist interpretation of Kerouac that focused on the author's spiritual greatness.

— HE TRIED TO ANSWER THAT RECURRING QUESTION: "WHAT HAPPENED TO KEROUAC? WHY DID HE DRINK HIMSELF TO DEATH?"

— Quebec writer Victor-Levy Beaulieu had suggested it was because Kerouac was a lost Québécois, *un de nous autres*. That "Ti-Jean" suffered because the English-speaking world has never understood French-Canadians.

— GINSBERG RESPONDED WITH PARABLES?

— He offered the Buddhist view, a strain of the Beat-American, that Kerouac despaired because all life is suffering and he never found a teacher to resolve certain contradictions.

— IN ANSWER TO A SUGGESTION THAT KEROUAC WAS A MINOR, EXPERIMENTAL WRITER, GINSBERG ASSERTED THAT THE BEAT KING WAS MAJOR.

— He said Kerouac was always undervalued, misunderstood and ridiculed, and insisted that even today he is not properly appreciated.

— THE KEY MOMENT IN THE CONFERENCE?

— Victor-Levy Beaulieu made a brilliant speech reiterating the interpretation he offered in his 1972 book, *Jack Kerouac: essai-poulet*.

— THAT WAS IT?

— No, that prepared the moment. Beaulieu raised the temperature in the crowded hall by thirty degrees. He ruffled the feathers of those Québécois who consider his nationalist politics dangerous. Of French-Canadians outside Quebec who intend to survive as themselves. Of Anglo-Montrealers who don't believe every trace of their existence should be obliterated. And of Americans who object to being stereotyped.

— BEAULIEU DISMISSED GINSBERG'S WORK?

— With a supercilious shrug. Others leapt to the microphones and the poet's defence, but Ginsberg remained in his seat, leaning on his cane. I approached him immediately afterwards, as people filed towards the exits. Tension still in the air, Ginsberg spoke of Beaulieu's sensitivity and beautiful language and said he was "like Jack."

— HE THEN RUSHED OFF TO FIND BEAULIEU IN THE THRONG?

— So I later determined. Apparently, Ginsberg congratulated him on a fine speech and invited him to dinner. Beaulieu went. Ferlinghetti played interpretor. But for most observers, or so I reported, the symbolic, incidental lesson was still unclear.

— NEXT DAY AT THE PODIUM, GINSBERG DESCRIBED HOW, WHEN ATTACKED, KEROUAC NEVER FOUGHT BACK?

— He talked of the Beat King's incredible empathy, of his "panoramic awareness," and finally of his ability to hold contradictory ideas in his mind.

— YOUR POINT?

— "Yes, Kerouac is yours," Ginsberg was saying to Beaulieu and his followers. "But he is not yours alone. *Le Grand Jack* belongs to the world."

— SUDDENLY RELEASED, HIS KNEES RUBBERY, FRANKIE THE NARRATOR RESUMED HIS SEAT. HIS UNCONSCIOUS BIAS STOOD REVEALED, AND WITH THAT HE WAS WELL-SATISFIED. THE PROCESS THAT HAD INDUCED REVELATION, HOWEVER, PLEASED HIM NOT AT ALL. IN FACT, FRANKIE WAS OUTRAGED. HE RESOLVED NOT TO LET IT SHOW. CUT TO JUBILATION.

17

Fire hazard is at its peak between noon and two o'clock, so Frankie left the tower just long enough to eat some alphabet soup, a peanut-butter sandwich and half a dozen chocolate-chip cookies. He brought his coffee back into the tower. From below I could hear him clacking away at the typewriter, making notes about this lunatic visitor who wouldn't quit pretending he was Jack Kerouac. I chuckled, stretched out on a blanket in the sun and lost myself in the echo chamber of his life.

At three Frankie shook me awake. The sky had clouded over and we were going for water. Frankie had a four-gallon steel carrier, an ancient back-pack contraption. On the front porch, while shrugging it on, he waved away my offer of help. "Empty, it weighs nothing," he said. "Coming back we can maybe take turns."

Out the back gate, we swung left and marched south along the side of the mountain. An overgrown path branched off and wound away into the trees. It led to an older stream, Frankie said, long since dried up. The stream we wanted was half a mile farther. He had to visit every second or third day, but preferred this to the alternative. "End of May, when I arrived, this trail was waist deep in snow. I had two big barrels catching water off the roof, but every morning I'd find a dead mouse floating. I ended up melting snow. Ever drink coffee flavored with pine needles?"

We broke into a clearing sprinkled with tiny alpine flowers, blue and red and purple and yellow and white. Above us, to the right, towered the summit of Jubilation, massive and rocky. Scrub gave way to shale and scree. Then came boulders, sheer cliff and, thousands of feet above, the jagged, snow-capped peak.

To our left, down the mountain, an avalanche or rock slide had cut a swath through the forest. The scrub was waist-high and we enjoyed an unobstructed view of the valley, the Mistaya River rolling away. The clearing was noisy with chirping and buzzing and I slapped at mosquitoes and remembered hiking down off Desolation, what? fourteen years before? A seventy-pound pack on my back, my shoes worn through in the soles. Agonizing.

"Awake and alert," Frankie said as we re-entered the trees, the underbrush thicker here. "Keep an eye out for wood ticks."

I'd been listening to what sounded like a stream: "Say what?"

"No ticks in the Cascades?" Derisive, this, as if he'd finally caught me out, and I grinned at his post-California scepticism. "They're tiny insects, almost invisible, that hang on the leaves of plants," he said. "You walk by, brush the plants and the ticks cling to your clothes. They climb your leg, up your torso, burrow into your hair, crawl into your ear — decidedly unpleasant."

"Shades of the Joycean earwig."

"As in James Joyce?"

"The Master himself. *Finnegan's Wake*? If you —"

Frankie grabbed my arm, put a finger to his lips and pointed through the trees. A fawn stood splay-legged, drinking from a stream. Behind him, almost invisible, loomed a great-antlered elk. The animal gazed at us, alert and protective. We waited in silence. When the fawn had finished drinking, the elk nudged his flank, then turned and disappeared into the trees: three leaps, a flash of white and he was gone. The fawn scrambled after him.

Strangely, the sight moved us both. Frankie fell silent, became aware for the first time of our telepathic rapport. "We can hear each other."

"You finally noticed."

Spooked, disbelieving, Frankie withdrew.

Here, again, an avalanche had cut a swath through the trees. The stream tumbled past, its source a melting glacier far above. Frankie shrugged off his water carrier. He knelt beside the stream and scooped water into his mouth, then splashed his face. When he'd finished, I did the same. The water was freezing cold, invigorating.

Frankie made a mill race — uncapped the metal carrier and wedged it into the stream so water ran bugless and sparkling into its mouth. Then he sat on a rock to wait and I joined him. We chewed straws and sought shapes in the scudding clouds and I almost lost myself in a Haight-Ashbury acid flash.

Frankie kept me on the mountain: "So what's a miracle?"

For this I'd roughed out a plan, but I said: "Come again?"

"You knocked my scepticism, remember? So what's a miracle? Stumbling on those elk?"

"That was magical, not miraculous. A miracle implies divine intervention."

"Give me a for-instance."

"Well, the miracles I know best are my own."

Flatly, no question implied, Frankie said, "Your own miracles."

"The three I worked in my lifetime. But you've read *Dharma Bums.*"

"Loved the novel." He took a beat. "Didn't think it miraculous."

I laughed. "It isn't. But it does report two miracles. Remember how I cured my mother?"

"Can't say I do."

"We were living in North Carolina, my mother and me, with my sister and her family. It was 1956. The spring before Desolation. I was heavy into Buddhism and fancied myself a religious wanderer — a *bhikku* in modern clothes. I was roaming the world to turn the wheel of True Meaning and so gain merit for myself as an Awakener, a future hero in Paradise. I was praying and meditating and felt I was getting stronger, spiritually."

"You're kidding, right?"

"Mémère came down with a bad cold. Her nose was running, her throat hurt. She was sneezing continually and getting worse. On the night of March 12, 1956 — it was my thirty-fourth birthday — I lay on the back porch listening to her cough until finally I could stand it no longer. I sat up in my sleeping bag and meditated, went into a deep trance while concentrating on my mother's cold. Before long I had a vision, saw three images: Heet liniment, a bottle of brandy and white flowers."

"You had a vision of Heet liniment? Tell me you're kidding."

"By now it was midnight. I got out of bed, went into Memere's room and took away this vase of white flowers, bachelor's buttons. My sister had brought them into the house and scattered them everywhere. I went and collected all these white flowers and put them out on the porch. Next morning, when my mother woke, I treated her with Heet and brandy. By night, I'd cured her."

"And that was it."

"Yup."

"That was your miracle."

"My first miracle." I'd moved to a massive boulder that was flat on top, almost perfectly level, and I brushed it clean with my hand. "For a long time I thought it would be my last. I warned myself against becoming obsessed with working miracles. I mean, what a responsibility!"

Frankie snorted, shook his head: "I've heard ridiculous, but this beats all."

"It stands up." I positioned my hands on the rock. "It stands up as my first miracle."

I swung into a headstand and Frankie laughed despite himself: "Now what?"

I began methodically lowering and raising my feet. "Not to worry," I said. "There's nothing sublime about this." I did twenty-five leg raises, added five for good luck, then quit and sat up straight. "Come to think of it, I used to do that even when I was drinking heavily. That's pretty miraculous, *n'est-ce pas?*"

Frankie grunted. The water carrier had overflowed and he removed it from the stream. As he screwed on the top he said, "All right, I'll play straight man. In *Dharma Bums* there's a second miracle?"

"It was a prophecy."

"A prophecy's not a miracle. Not the way you've defined it."

"Don't be a pedant, Frankie. It counts, I tell you."

"Okay, hit me. But this better be good."

"The rucksack revolution. I predicted it in *Dharma Bums* in the fifties, prophesied that millions of young people would take to the roads with packs on their backs, having refused to worship the great god Consumption."

"Wasn't that Japhy Ryder's prophecy?"

"Gary Snyder gets an assist. I was the one who put it in print."

"Tell me you're kidding."

I grinned and picked up the water carrier. Now it weighed at least sixty pounds and Frankie helped me into the harness. Then put his hand on my shoulder. "You're talking Jabberwocky —"

"Make that Kerouwacky."

"— but I can't stand an unfinished story. The third miracle?"

"That came later. I was living with Mémère in Northport, Long Island. I had a painter friend, a Polish guy I called Stashou, and in New York City, commuting distance away, a girlfriend named Dody who was also a painter."

"Wait! Don't tell me! You started painting."

"You got it. I was having visions and most of my work had a religious theme. I especially liked painting pietas — the Virgin Mary mourning over the dead body of Jesus?"

The water carrier weighed six tons and my shirt was getting wet from condensation. I decided to keep it short. "Finally, I had a vision of this cardinal, Giovanni Montini. I saw him wearing papal robes and painted him that way. Four years later — are you ready for this? — Montini became Pope Paul the Sixth."

"That painting was it?"

"Technically, it's nothing special — almost like a cartoon. But I gave the Pope these big blue eyes. They follow you around."

"You call that a miracle? Even if that painting did exist, it would prove nothing."

"Miracles never prove, Frankie. They signify and suggest. But let's move out."

I swung onto the trail, but not twenty strides out I felt freezing water running down the backs of my legs. Condensation? "What the —"

"Oh, I forgot to tell you," Frankie said, deadpan. "You fill that old carrier, it leaks like one of your stories."

18

In Los Angeles, Camille had spent a day visiting a friend from college while I'd taken the children to Disneyland. Yet again. Today, in San Francisco, was turn-about. Camille and company went to the zoo. I rode a bus up Market Street, swung off into sunshine at the corner of Haight and Ashbury, notebook and pencil in hand, and started to walk.

The Magic was gone — or so I quickly decided. The Psychedelic Shop had become a pizza parlour and The I/Thou Coffee House a shoe store called The Taming of the Shoe. Tracy's Donuts, an early-days hang-out, was now an empty storefront. Here and there, colorful posters recalled the sixties. "Token psychedelia," I scribbled. "Haight still funky but Magic is gone."

Two blocks south, a Digger-run crash pad, The Free Frame of Reference, was now a laundromat called The Wash Club. And the Donut Shoppe around the corner? Where one night in 1967 I'd watched Allen Ginsberg pump quarters into a juke box, thinking, where's Kerouac? Any minute now, he'll walk in the door. The Donut Shoppe was now Stanyon Printing Services.

Back on Haight Street, the Straight Theatre had long since been demolished — but that I'd read about. I stood a moment remembering a drizzly afternoon when I'd wandered into the theatre, attracted by the sounds of rock 'n' roll, some band rehearsing, to discover Janis Joplin at work. That's when it started to come back, with that memory of Janis howling *Summertime*, the Haight-Ashbury working Magic after all.

Again it was 1966, Thanksgiving Day, and I'd just arrived in California. Nineteen years old, a yea-saying rucksack warrior in jeans and a turtle-neck sweater, I'd hitchhiked and ridden freights across the continent and stumbled into what looked like a social revolution. A few days before, while driving me to San

Francisco in a Volkswagen van, a sociology professor from Berkeley had raised his eyebrows: "The Haight-Ashbury? You've never heard of the Haight?"

He rhapsodized for twenty, twenty-five miles, describing the Haight as the most interesting social experiment America had ever spawned. "But you've heard of Timothy Leary and LSD?"

I'd read the famous *Playboy* interview, found it fascinating and said so, and when the professor dropped me off in downtown San Francisco, he not only directed me to the Haight-Ashbury but reached into his shirt pocket and extracted a ball of tinfoil. "This is all I've got with me. Just half a tab, but it's pure LSD — primo acid." He handed me the ball. "Wait for the right moment."

Now it was Thanksgiving Day, free turkey dinner in the Haight, and I stood in the middle of a dirt-floor garage, the original Free Frame of Reference, grinning and nodding, unable to believe my stumbling good luck, a turkey leg in one hand, a cup of wine in the other, the half-tab of acid safe in my wallet.

The feast was courtesy of a group called The Diggers, self-styled Merry Men who regarded the Haight as a kind of Sherwood Forest. Beautiful people were everywhere. A guy wearing a W.C. Fields mask and an old top hat hovered over a turntable playing *Visions of Johanna*, the same verse, over and over again, Bob Dylan observing repeatedly that little boy lost, he takes himself so seriously. Nobody minded. A girl wearing a see-through American flag and nothing else climbed onto a table and made like the Statue of Liberty. Nobody minded that, either — certainly not me.

I stood nodding, guzzling red wine, stuffing my face with turkey. People were jostling me, climbing back and forth over a Mad-Hatter type stretched out on the floor, his arms crossed on his chest. Reaching for another cup of wine I took an elbow in the ribs. Turned to see an older guy, mid-thirties, chubby, with a light-bulb nose, pale blue eyes and thin brown hair that hung lifeless over his ears.

He said sorry, I said no problem. Had I just arrived? Yes, I said, and suddenly I was talking, telling this guy that I'd hitchhiked and ridden freights from Montreal, that I was chasing experience, gathering material for a novel.

"Experience you want?" He held out his hand. "My name's Oscar."

We both laughed. Turned out Oscar, too, was a writer, more specifically a poet, and that got me babbling particulars: "I call my latest story "A Piece of Wandering Orgasm". It's like my hero's…"

"Sorry, a what?"

"A Piece of Wandering Orgasm. My hero's so alive he's experiencing orgasm all the time. You know, just walking around. It's an advance of sorts on Kerouac."

Oscar nodded as he received this nonsense, rocked back and forth on the balls of his feet, his hands in the pockets of his baggy green trousers, his paunch out over his belt. He reminded me of a toy I'd had as a child, a roly-poly man I'd push over onto his back, but who always rolled to his feet again. Wanted to know if I'd published anything. "Oh, a couple of stories. I've got others making the rounds. What about you?"

"Short poems here and there," he said. "The usual literary mags. Just finished a long one, though, a sixteen-pager. It'll be in an anthology that a friend of mine's publishing."

That got my attention. "An anthology?"

We talked until Oscar said come on back to the house and read my poetry: "I share the place with some beautiful people."

"Hey, why not?"

A light rain was falling but Oscar's house was just around the corner, a two-storey Victorian that over-looked the panhandle of Golden Gate Park. "The Fell Street House, we call it," Oscar said, opening the double front doors and ushering me inside.

Oscar shared the ground floor with a married couple, their disturbed son and a painter named Ruth, none of whom was home. Angry paintings adorned the walls, mostly of whores draped in American flags and surrounded by cars and airplanes and TV sets. "Ruth works part-time as a topless dancer in North

Beach," Oscar said, as if that explained the pictures. My face must have said something because he added: "She's a lesbian."

Oscar sat me down in an overstuffed armchair in the living room. He handed me a hard-cover binder containing fifty or sixty poems, all neatly typed, double-spaced, and left me alone. The poem for the anthology, the sixteen-pager, was all about Oscar's early life but with African mythology mixed in: God laughed once, *cha*, twice, *cha cha*, seven times in all, *cha cha cha cha cha cha cha*, created the world that way. All about the magic of New Orleans, how his mother conceived him in the back seat of a car and he never knew his father. Full of esoteric references and allusions and ending with a vision of Africa, a night-time initiation rite and thirteen-year-old boys dancing around a bonfire.

Fantastic. But I admired even more a series of poems about terrible angels who couldn't tell whether they moved among the living or the dead. This confusion had to do, somehow, with Eros and Agape, with Realizing Duality and the Seventeen Scale.

"Ah'gapay," Oscar said when I asked him to explain. "Pronounce it ah' gapay. Eros and Agape, lust and compassion — they're two sides of the same Duality. The challenge is to realize this Duality by reconciling the opposites in experience."

"Run that by me again?"

Turned out Realizing Duality was the secret of the Seventeen Scale, a way of measuring writers. Only the greatest writers and poets, Oscar said, the ones who had Realized Duality, could hope to become Seventeens. They were the True Artists. Most writers were Sixes or Sevens, Eights or Nines. And it wasn't just a matter of craft.

A Nine could be as skilled a craftsman as a Seventeen, as fine a wordsmith, but because he hadn't died and been born again, and so reconciled the Opposites, he could write nothing that would last — nothing that would echo forever in the minds of men. Ten was the turning point. A superb craftsman could become a Nine, but he couldn't get into those double digits, couldn't become an angel, unless he Realized Duality. And to do that he had to die and be born again.

"I don't understand."

"Duality isn't something you understand, Frankie. It's something you realize. You've got to die and be born again."

Impossible to imagine bafflegab more suited to a would-be writer, and a few days later, bent on Realizing Duality, I sat in that same armchair waiting for my half-tab of acid to work magic. I'd given up on a rational approach, having cross-examined Oscar in The Blue Unicorn, the Donut Shoppe, the I and Thou — the sundry cafes and coffee houses of the Haight. Oscar said Rainer Maria Rilke was the Greatest Poet Who Ever Lived. He was especially big on *The Duino Elegies*, which had Transformed Poetry. He himself was probably the Greatest Poet Alive Today, if only because he treated the Duality of Love. "I am a bridge," he said. "A bridge you must cross."

I understood, of course, that Oscar was gay. But I told myself, so what? That was part of his fascination. As a teenager, Oscar had peddled his ass in upscale Miami. Then he lost his looks and considered becoming a priest. Finally, he'd opted for poetry. And followed his muse wherever she led: New Orleans, San Francisco, New York City — round and round and round. Somewhere he married and tried to go straight. Somewhere else he divorced. For years he worked as a counsellor for disturbed children.

"Half a tab," he said, disappointed, when I showed him the acid I'd received as a gift. "Not enough for both of us."

"Guess I'll have to do it alone."

"Your first trip?" Oscar shrugged. "No guide? It's your life, baby."

I thought a moment, then said, "Maybe you'll be my guide."

"No way. Sharing a trip is one thing. Guiding's another."

"Oscar, you'd be perfect."

He shook his head: "Acid's like a pair of glasses. You can see more clearly. And you, Frankie — you'd see the evil in me but not the good."

"I'd see both."

"How could you, Frankie? You haven't Realized Duality."

"But that's what I want to do. Don't you see, Oscar? You're the perfect guide."

Now, at The Fell Street House, I lounged in the arm chair while Oscar sat reading on the inside stairs that led to the second floor. Nothing was happening. I was growing impatient, irritable, and was ready to pronounce the experiment a failure when the cross piece in the window opposite rushed at me, then rushed back into place again. It was like seeing it through the zoom lens of a movie camera: "The acid! It's working!"

Settling deeper into the overstuffed chair, I inadvertantly brushed one hand along its arm. My hand tingled pleasurably. I rubbed it along the arm. Felt even better the second time, all pins and needles. Both hands down my thighs. This was fantastic. The acid had sensitized my whole body. I ran my hands up and down my legs, then noticed the mattress on the floor against the far wall. On the mattress lay an old pink bedspread with thousands of tiny ridges. Rougher texture.

"Where are you going?"

I crossed the room and slid, face down, onto the mattress. "Oooooooooo." The feeling was unbelievable. My hands, my legs, my chest, my stomach — my whole body was pins and needles. "Ooooooooo." I began writhing against the bedspread, squirming. Oscar was standing over me, looking down, but I couldn't stop. "Oooooooooooo." Back and forth on the bedspread. "Oooooooooo." Nothing but the bedspread. "Oooooooooo. Oooooooooo. Oooooooooo."

"Frankie." I heard a voice. "Frankie." A hollow voice was calling my name. "Frankie, isn't there something you have to do?"

Something I had to do? Yes, there was — but I couldn't remember what it was. Didn't care. I didn't want to stop writhing on the bedspread. "Oooooooooo."

"Frankie." The voice persisted. "Isn't there something you have to do for Oscar?"

"Oscar?" The name sounded familiar but I couldn't place it. "Oscar?"

"Yes, Oscar. Don't be selfish, Frankie."

I looked up from the mattress and saw a man standing over me. That was Oscar. The man's name was Oscar — but I knew nothing else about him.

"Frankie, you've been rolling around on that mattress for three hours."

I tried to stop writhing, couldn't. "Oooooooooo, it feels good. It feels just so good."

"Look, Frankie." Oscar held a clock in front of my face. "Three hours."

"Three hours." The words meant nothing. Somewhere, Time existed. But that was in a world I'd left behind. Again I let go. "Ooooooooooooooo."

"Frankie! I've been watching this long enough."

"Ooooooo, but it feels good."

"Where's your Agape, Frankie? Your compassion? Stop thinking of yourself. Think of Oscar."

"Oscar?"

"Yes, think of poor Oscar, sitting and watching this. Don't be selfish, Frankie. Think! Isn't there something you have to do? Here, look at this."

Oscar was sitting on the mattress, showing me a piece of paper. There was a poem on it. I tried to read the poem but the typed words kept changing shape, bending and twisting. It was like trying to read in a fun-house mirror. "Footsteps on the stairs." I heard footsteps. "Not for me." The footsteps went past the door. "A bed, a chair ... this tiny room ... an unknown city." The poem blurred.

"What's the matter, Frankie?"

"Nothing. It's just —" My voice cracked. "It's just so lonely."

"Hey, now." Oscar patted my head. "Oscar's here."

I buried my face against Oscar's chest.

A hand was unbuttoning my shirt. It was just a hand. It didn't belong to anybody. One button. Two buttons. Three. The hand was under my shirt, running lightly over my chest. This was wrong.

"Frankie." The voice again. "Frankie, will you wait here while Oscar goes to the bathroom?"

The hand belonged to Oscar. It was Oscar's hand.

"Will you wait, Frankie?"

"Uh hunh." If I didn't say yes, it didn't count.

"You won't move now? Promise?"

"Uh hunh." I watched Oscar go down the hall and into the kitchen. Then I dragged myself from the mattress and stumbled across the room into the armchair. I hung sideways over the arm, noticed specks of white paint on the grey floorboards. I'd seen them before but now they arranged themselves into a pattern. Suddenly, the pattern changed, became more intricate. Then it changed again. Amazing. The specks didn't move but the pattern changed anyway.

And what was that — a foot? A foot and a leg? They were just sitting there by themselves. I couldn't figure it out. No, wait! That was my foot! And that was my leg! That foot and that leg were part of my body! I sat up straight and looked down at my body. My body wasn't me. It was something I used. A vehicle. The real me was thinking thoughts. That body wasn't me at all. It was just a vehicle that —

"Frankie! You promised not to move."

A strange man was standing over me. Oscar! The man was Oscar. But he was smaller than before. Far away, somehow. In the distance, he sat down on the mattress. "Come here, Frankie." He patted the mattress. "Don't you want to realize Duality?"

"Duality?"

"You promised, remember? Are you going to break your promise?"

"I didn't promise."

"Yes, you did, Frankie. But it looks like I was right about you. You've got no compassion." Oscar stood up. "That's your problem, Frankie. You're selfish."

"I've got compassion, Oscar."

"No you haven't. Eros, baby! You understand nothing but lust. You'll never be anything but a Nine."

"A Nine!" This was terrible. I couldn't remember what a Nine was, but I knew I didn't want to be one. "No, Oscar. Seventeen! I'll be a Seventeen."

"No way, baby." He shook his head sadly. This had been a test. Oscar was a judge of some kind, an agent for a higher order. Now the matter was out of his hands: "Nine."

"Seventeen." The room was hot. Stifling. I had to get outdoors.

"Sorry, Frankie. Eight."

"SEVENTEEN, OSCAR!" I spotted a hallway, pulled myself out of the chair. "SEVENTEEN!"

Again Oscar shook his head: "Seven."

Yelling, I made for the hallway: "SEVENTEEN, OSCAR! SEVENTEEN! SEVENTEEN!"

19

If human consciousness is a neural metropolis, then a psychedelic trip is an earthquake. It reduces buildings to rubble, knocks out communications, plunges the city into wounded silence. And if that city is a San Francisco of the Psyche? If it straddles a major fault-line?

On Mount Jubilation, the rush of Frankie's first trip brought me not only his Haight-Ashbury but my Newton Center, Massachussetts, where with Allen Ginsberg, in January of 1961, I visited Timothy Leary. The guru-to-be was still a psychology professor at Harvard and hunting a cure for alcoholism.

Leary told me psychedelic drugs could work miracles, change the world, that they made religious experience universally accessible. I popped his mushrooms and relived a nervous breakdown I'd had in the navy, ended up in the psychiatric ward — horrible days when I thought I could see inside people's heads.

That first trip shook me to my foundations. But it didn't raze me. And later that year, when Leary produced more mushrooms in Ginsberg's New York City apartment, I chewed a dozen or so. Leary took me walking through the snowy streets of the Lower East Side and we tossed a loaf of bread like a football. Then I started hallucinating: buildings toppling, people turning into cackling demons. The usual horror show. Only this time everything happened on several planes. Every sentence Leary uttered had five or six meanings.

Next day, I awoke to myself — but I wasn't the same. It was the morning after an earthquake. In some sectors destruction was minimal. But nerve centres and filters had been knocked out. I was disoriented. If objects could change essence without changing shape, a simple chair becoming a golden throne, then how did I know what I thought I knew? Reality was provisional. Our modes of perception were conditioned responses. Anything was possible.

Despite my highly differentiated consciousness, then, and my thirty-nine years of age, psychedelic drugs had reduced me to pre-adolescence. And here's the worst of it: the effect stayed with me. Months after that second trip, during a thirty-day drinking binge that brought me, red-faced and ranting, to an old favorite bar in Lowell, I met a ne'er-do-well steeplejack named Paul Bourgeois, an ex-thief who'd spent twelve years in jail. After listening to me rave drunkenly that my ancestors included not only French Canadians but North American Indians, Bourgeois concocted an insane story that spoke directly to the drug-traumatized twelve-year-old in me.

Bourgeois was Moon Cloud Chief of the Four Nations of the Iroquois. He'd just returned from Prince of Wales Island near the North Pole, where 3,000 of our people, half-French, half-Iroquois, were starving to death. Trouble was, nuclear submarines were cruising beneath the polar ice cap, polluting the water and contaminating the fish. The Moon Cloud Chief was on his way to Washington to complain. What's more, we were cousins, he and I, because two of the four tribes in the North were named Kirouac and L'Evesque —Memere's maiden name.

Yes, I believed this — even sober. I wrote letters to friends telling them that soon I'd be heading North to join my Iroquois brothers. And I clung to this fantasy for six months. Eventually, I brought Bourgeois home to Florida where, under pressure from Mémère, he confessed and made me listen.

Nobody understood it — how a cheap con artist seeking beer money could snooker a celebrated author. But that was because nobody understood the destructive power of psychedelic drugs. Nobody understood that, months after my second trip, my psychic defences were still down.

Next thing I knew, Leary was hounding me to publish an upbeat letter I'd written after my first trip, when I was still innocent. I told him to forget it — that psychedelic drugs stupify hand and brain for weeks on end. That tyrants and mad doctors would one day use them for brainwashing.

In 1967, six years after that second trip, while Ginsberg was travelling America urging every man, woman and child over fourteen to drop acid and welcome the ensuing nervous break-down, I was telling friends I'd never fully recovered. And I was mature when I popped — almost forty.

While Ginsberg and Leary chanted paens to psychedelic drugs, I denounced LSD as a communist plot to destroy the country — the only way I could hope to get through. Metaphorical truth-telling. These were the oh-so-hip sixties, you see, and I was derided as a boor and a has-been: Cracker Jack Kerouac, once King of the Beats, had become a know-nothing redneck, a broken-down drunk. Only half of which was true.

20

That San Francisco morning in 1990, standing in the sunshine staring up at the Fell Street House, scene of my first acid trip, I realized that Kerouac was thirty-nine years old when he blew the psychedelic fuses. Fully mature — and not a nobody. A metropolis in a world of cities. Bedevilled by alcoholic slums, it's true, yet functioning, even celebrated. And still it had taken him months to recover.

Me, I hit acid at nineteen. Despite my wise-guy street-smarts, my adolescent bravado, I wasn't a city, much less a metropolis, but a hamlet with pretensions. A small town built on a San Andreas fault. That first acid trip razed me, reduced me to rubble. Yet some final part of me remained standing, some irreducible pillar. And, with all else in ruins, that part took control. The emergency system? The Self?

Whatever the metaphor, I scribbled in my notebook, Oscar and his betrayal, his assault on my self-image, were merely details. Acid itself was the catalyst — or was it a portal? This I knew: a rucksack warrior plunged into the Psychedelic Experience. A little boy lost stumbled out.

Certainly I was still able to function — to smoke grass and buy cheeseburgers in restaurants. But after that first trip I "understood" that some mysterious force had brought me to San Francisco for a purpose. Taking acid had removed my blinders. Now I could discern hidden meanings. These meanings had always existed but I'd never been able to see them.

How clearly the confusion came back.

The world was full of omens and portents. Everything happened on several planes. During the acid trip Oscar had made a pass at me. But that was on the surface. On a deeper level, he'd been acting for some mysterious force. He'd been testing me —

but for what? I'd fled the house screaming, "Seventeen! Seventeen!" But maybe, somehow, I'd passed?

I continued to visit the Fell Street House. Always Oscar welcomed me, though between us I felt a new distance. What did that mean? I needed another sign, another signal. And arrived one afternoon to find the house buzzing. I'd just missed meeting Jessica and Mitchell, the upstairs tenants. The city had shut off their electricity and they'd come down the inside stairs, struggling through the makeshift barrier, to ask if they could run an extension cord.

Oscar had said yes, of course, and the visitors had stayed to chat. Jessica sat on the steps and read palms. Tarot cards, tea leaves — apparently, she did it all. Under a pseudonym, she wrote an astrology column for the *San Francisco Oracle*. Oscar said she was clairvoyant and that Mitchell was beautiful: "An archangel! A beautiful archangel!"

I couldn't believe I'd missed them. Then Oscar said Jessica had invited him upstairs to read poetry. And he didn't want to go alone.

That evening, after a dinner of brown rice and cabbage, Oscar and I went out and around to the side of the house and climbed the rickety stairs. More polite than beating our way through the inside barrier. Jessica opened the door. She was older than I'd expected, at least forty, and wore a floor-length blue dress and a black lace shawl. She led us into the dining room, dark except for three flickering candles. The air smelled of grass.

At the table sat a good-looking guy rolling joints. Neat and precise, wavy black hair, four or five years older than me: Mitchell the archangel. He shook hands solemnly. We all sat down and Jessica closed a hardcover tome that had been lying open at her end of the table. Oscar said, "You've been reading by candlelight?"

Checking a reference, Jessica said. And as Mitchell rolled joints, she explained that the book was a hard-to-find Bible translated directly from Sanskrit, and incorporating much that orthodox Christianity considered apocryphal.

Mitchell sent a joint around the table.

116

Oscar had brought his red binder and we passed joints as he read poems by the light of the flickering candles, using his hollow reading voice and finishing with the long work about God laughing seven times, *cha cha cha cha cha cha cha*, creating the world that way. We all clapped and then Jessica started talking about reincarnation. "In the early eighteenth century,," she said, "in my last life, I was an Indian princess."

I said, "How do you know?"

"I remember."

"You remember a past life?"

"Oh, yes. Not everything but bits and pieces. I remember travelling through mountains in winter. Yes." Jessica touched her fingers to the sides of her head. "Yes, that was the worst of the terrible winters." She was staring straight ahead, seeing nothing. "I almost died in the shadow of the tallest mountain in the world."

Mitchell handed me the joint. I toked and passed it to Oscar without looking away from Jessica. Black eyes, black hair flecked with grey. Forty-five? Fifty? She looked ageless, other-worldly.

After a moment, still staring into the candles, Jessica resumed talking in a younger voice, a strange rhythm. "It was late afternoon when we reached the ridge that faced the tallest mountain in the world. Grey Beaver said we'd camp there overnight and picked up his bow. He didn't have to tell me where he was going. We'd seen elk droppings on the trail and hadn't eaten meat for weeks. I tethered the ponies, built a fire and wrapped myself in buffalo hides. The baby was kicking inside me. I closed my eyes. When I opened them, it was night — and Grey Beaver hadn't returned. The wind was rising. I checked the ponies, then stoked the fire and curled up beside it."

Oscar offered Jessica the joint but she ignored him. She was entranced. I sat directly opposite, watching the candles dance in her eyes. There was a mental bond between us. My head was buzzing with it. Jessica remembered being alive in the seventeen hundreds. This was mind-boggling. Or wait. Maybe she was putting us on?

Again Jessica started talking, the room silent except for her strange, young-woman voice. "When I woke it was morning. A cold wind was blowing snow into drifts and the ponies were gone. As I ate the last of the pemmican, I heard Grey Beaver calling me — not his voice, but his spirit. Telling me to hurry. I plunged down the trail, snow swirling around my knees, calling, 'Grey Beaver! Grey Beaver!' I felt him moving further away. I tried to run but the snow got deeper and I kept falling and getting up, falling and getting up. Finally I couldn't get up any more. I lay there, exhausted, the baby kicking inside me."

Again Jessica paused, only this time, as I stared, I saw her face change. The lines around her eyes disappeared and so did her wrinkles. Her hair fell suddenly to her shoulders, thick and black and shining. For three seconds, four, the woman across the table from me was a beautiful Indian princess.

Then Jessica returned.

"Your face!" I said. "I just saw your face change! You really were an Indian princess!"

"What did I look like?"

"You were… beautiful."

Jessica asked me to describe in detail what I'd seen. When I'd finished she smiled and said, "You see very clearly, Frankie. But why so surprised? You saw the face I wore during my last incarnation."

"That's just it. I've never believed in reincarnation. Though it fits, I guess, with something I discovered on acid."

"What was that?"

"That the body's a vehicle."

"The body dies but the self lives on, moving from one body to another."

"But that changes everything."

"It's astonishing," Oscar said, standing up. "But it's also time for us to be off." He raised his eyebrows at me. "Frankie?"

I couldn't believe he would leave now, in mid-discussion. Then I realized, my head buzzing, that this was all part of the Test. If I wished I could leave now and forget the mysterious force. If I stayed, Jessica would show me my next step. But everything took place on a number of levels. I had to play the surface game, too. "If it's okay with you, Osar, I'll stay a while."

Oscar looked at me strangely but Jessica led him to the door. I shared another joint with Mitchell while they said goodnight. When Jessica returned she resumed her story, described how she'd ended up giving birth in the snow. I said, "What about Duality? How does that tie in?"

"Duality?"

"You know, Realizing Duality, reconciling the opposites. How does that fit with reincarnation?"

Jessica laughed and nodded towards Mitchell: "Maybe you should ask him. He's the wise one here."

"I'm not sure there is a connection," Mitchell said: "Duality is an illusion. It's all One."

"I don't understand."

Jessica laughed and said to Mitchell: "Wouldn't Charmian just love him?"

"With Charmian, who can tell?"

To me, Jessica said: "If you're ever down in Carmel, you must look her up. Charmian Foster." She smiled a special smile. She had nothing further to reveal. If I wished to go forward, I had to see this Charmian Foster. "How do I get to Carmel?"

Mitchell said: "It's down the coast a hundred miles, maybe a bit more."

"Okay, I leave tomorrow morning."

"I didn't mean for you to make a special trip," Jessica said. "Just that if you happened to be down that way you could —"

"No, no." At each step, I had a choice. "I'm going anyway. I've got to go."

"As you wish," Jessica said at last. "But if you do see Charmian, don't tell her who sent you. Tell her… let's see… tell her you don't know whether I'm male or female."

Mitchell looked at the ceiling. He felt she was revealing too much. But Jessica touched my arm. "Tell Charmian you're not sure whether the person who sent you is a man or a woman."

21

"This question about why Kerouac drank himself to death," Camille said. "These guys propose only two alternative answers. Either he did it because he was French-Canadian or else because All Life Is Suffering and he was too sensitive to endure." She shook her head. "What if he drank himself to death because he was an alcoholic?"

October, 1987. Camille had made all the right noises about my Quebec City extravaganza. But lately she'd been studying alcoholism, and talking about it too much, and I said, "That's too easy."

"You think so? Look, you've got a dialectic here. The thesis is Kerouac as Beat King. The antithesis is Kerouac as French-Canadian."

"And the synthesis? Don't tell me! Kerouac as alcoholic."

"Alcoholism was the root cause, yes. The disease came first and determined the rest."

"Kerouac drank because he despaired," I said. "The question is: Why did he despair?"

"No, Frankie. You've got it backwards. Kerouac despaired because he was suffering from alcoholism. Depression is a symptom of the disease."

We agreed to disagree, though secretly I began to wonder. Maybe I'd missed something? I remembered talking in Quebec City with an American critic named Rebecca Rosen, a big blonde woman with a sensitive face and shoulders like a linebacker.

Rosen had recently published *The Impromptu Stylistics of Jack Kerouac*. I considered it brilliant and told her so, though I also confessed I couldn't buy her thesis: that "spontaneous bop prosody" was Kerouac's chief contribution to literature.

Rosen had built her argument around a canon of five "core novels." Of these five, only *On The Road* and parts of *Visions of Cody* exhibited Kerouac at his best. Missing, for example, were *Dr. Sax*, *The Subterraneans*, *The Dharma Bums* and *Big Sur*. Not only that, but Rosen, driven by the logic of her argument, had concluded that Kerouac's finest achievement was *Desolation Angels*. Which to me was complete nonsense.

At this Rosen laughed ruefully. She'd written *Impromptu Stylistics* as a doctoral thesis. But originally she'd proposed to explore, not style and the Divine Comedy of the Buddha, but the effects of mind-altering substances on Kerouac's work. Benzedrine and *On The Road*, marijuana and *Desolation Angels*, alcohol and *Satori In Paris*.

Yes, I liked it. But Rosen's thesis advisor didn't — or didn't believe he could sell it to his colleagues. He told her to think again, maybe choose another author. Certainly come back with a different proposal.

When she'd recovered — I imagined furious tears and savage pillow punching — Rosen remembered something Allen Ginsberg had said about the grand, non-linear design, the stylistic unity of *The Legend of Duluoz*. And decided to explore "spontaneous bop prosody."

Now, prompted by Camille, I wondered if originally Rebecca Rosen hadn't been on track. Academia had derailed her. The resulting book, because it was both brilliant and misconceived, demonstrated the folly of the conventional Beat approach. Taking that tack meant dismissing Kerouac's finest work and celebrating a method — spontaneous prose — the author himself practiced only fitfully.

And the theory built up to support it? This idea of tapping into the Self so deeply that you tap into the One Mind that unites us all? It's the main reflection of Buddhist thinking in Kerouac. And here something clicked. Spontaneous prose is the crucial link between Kerouac and the Buddhism of Allen Ginsberg. To profess "spontaneous bop prosody" doesn't serve Kerouac. It serves "The Beat Generation" at Kerouac's expense.

22

In Pacific Grove, California, heading north up the coast in the summer of 1990, we stayed at an elegant bed-and-breakfast, the big splurge of the trip, a gabled Victorian mansion that was all linen sheets, home-made muffins, vintage carousel horses and ocean view. We lounged by the water at Lover's Point, pedaled a four-person surrey along the ocean-front and drove our rented car seventeen miles around Pebble Beach Drive.

From Pacific Grove we visited nearby Carmel. I hunted signposts but the gingerbread town I remembered from the sixties had become a boutique haven for the rich and wrongly famous. Only the geography remained as before — the two-lane highway winding down hill into town, the spectacular sand beach stretching away forever, the Pacific Ocean rolling in white-capped and incessant.

On the beach, while the children built castles, I scribbled notes about my first visit. Remembered arriving one afternoon in December of 1966, having survived a ninety-mile ride with an out-of-work rock band bound for Big Sur. I lugged my rucksack down hill into town, found a phone booth and flipped open the directory. When a woman answered, I said, "Charmian Foster? This may sound strange, but I've been sent to Carmel to see you."

"Not so strange. Who sent you?"

"The one who sent me said, 'Tell her you're not sure whether I'm a man or a woman.'"

Charmian said, "I see." Then: "A few of us are meeting tonight. Perhaps you'd like to join us?"

That afternoon I spent walking the beach, telling myself this was insane. Signs, omens, mysterious forces — meaningless hallucinations. What was I doing here? Then I'd remember my acid trip — how I'd seen for myself that reality was more complex than I'd dreamed. And what about Jessica's face? The idea of reincarnation had a literature behind it.

At seven o'clock, when I rang the bell of a cosy bungalow I failed to locate in 1990, a dazzling woman in her mid-thirties opened the door: big blue eyes, white-blonde hair to her shoulders, a shimmering floor-length gown, dark blue with silver stars. "Charmian Foster?"

Having shaken my hand, smiling warmly, wide-eyed, Charmian led me into a sunken living room where three men and a young woman sat cross-legged on the floor. Made introductions. I registered Kenneth as a lanky man with an Indian feather behind one ear. Wendy was about my own age, chubby and freckled. Patrick and Bradley were clean-cut guys in their mid-twenties. As I joined the circle with Charmian I spotted a red cross hanging over the fire place: "Are you Rosicrucians?"

"Very observant, Frankie. The answer is yes and no. But tell me: How is Jessica?"

So Charmian knew. I said Jessica was fine and described how, the previous night, I'd seen her face change: "She was once an Indian princess. Beautiful."

Charmian, nodding, looked around the circle, then back at me: "What else?"

"It sounds insane," I said, "but I feel as if some mysterious force is guiding me."

"You're a seeker," Charmian said. Then briskly clapped her hands. "Let's begin."

She led me to a couch on a raised platform and told me to lie down.

"Can't I stay in the circle?"

"You can do that later. Right now we're going to release your astral body."

"My what?"

"Your spiritual body. Your higher self." She laughed, patted me on the arm. "Don't look so concerned. It needs to get out and breathe."

Vaguely, then, I remembered Kerouac mentioning his astral body. Somewhere in *Desolation Angels*? I wished I'd read the book more closely. Something about relaxing and entering a trance?

Following Charmian's instructions, I stretched out on the couch, my arms at my sides, and closed my eyes. Charmian rejoined the circle on the floor. Methodically, Kenneth had been dimming lamps and lighting candles. The darkened room fell silent and those in the circle — I peaked out the corner of one eye — bowed their heads as if in prayer. Again I thought of Kerouac and willed myself to let go, to enjoy the flickering light, but a piercing scream jolted me up onto one elbow: "What the — ?"

"Frankie, you've got to relax." Charmian stood up, laughing, and came over to me. "That's just the signal to begin."

She put me back down, returned to the circle and began again: "EEEEEEEE! EEEDLE EEEDLE EEEDLE EEEDLE EEEDLE EEEDLE EEEEEEEEE!"

Charmian screeched and warbled until she ran out of breath, then began sing-songing in a high-pitched voice, not making any sense: "Shaylasoooooo, incubaaaaaaay, maninaaaaa, por-toseeeeeaaaa."

One of the men added a simple bass background: "Unga, toro, singa, medi, unga, toro, singa, medi" — sounded like Kenneth. Then came another female voice, Wendy, winding up and down against the cadence: "Haytanaya yoowayoowaooo, ganabayeeayee, aaeeaaeeaah."

Finally I could distinguish five voices, each of them chanting something different, Charmian's voice tight-roping high above the others. A man's voice stopped — the unga-toro bass. Out of the corner of my eye I saw Kenneth rise and stride into the kitchen. I could hear him bing-banging around, opening and closing doors. Running water? Smashing ice-cubes?

He returned to the living room carrying a pail full of water and smashed ice. This he sat on the floor in the middle of the circle. Then he rolled up a pantleg, pulled off a sock and plunged his bare foot into the pail. He winced and I almost laughed out loud. Kenneth clenched both fists, stretched one arm towards the ceiling and extended the other in my direction. His eyes closed, he began rolling his head in time to the music.

The chanting grew louder, more intense. It reached a crescendo and then slowly tapered off as, one by one, voices withdrew. Finally Charmian chanted alone: "Shaylasoooooooo, incubaaaaaaay, maninaaaaa, portoseeeeaaaa." She carried on for a few seconds, then warbled and screeched yet again: "EEEDLE EEEDLE EEEDLE EEEDLE EEEDLE EEEDLE EEEEEEEEE!"

Sudden silence. Kenneth went rigid, one arm pointing at me, the other at the ceiling.

"No, don't get up." Charmian approached the couch. "We've released your astral body."

"How do you know?"

"I can see it, floating here above you. It's having a lovely time."

"My astral body? What's it look like?"

"Like your physical body, only lots of different colors. Look: can't you see it too, faintly?"

"No. No, I can't." I squinted but saw nothing. "Maybe it's too dark."

"Not at all. I can see it quite clearly. But how do you feel?"

"Pretty good."

"Don't you feel — lighter?"

I considered this. "Maybe a little lighter."

"What are you thinking?"

Charmian was standing close to the couch, her leg almost touching my arm. She really was quite stunning. Should I lie? If she could see my astral body, probably she could read my mind. "I'm thinking that I wouldn't mind being your lover."

One of the men snorted. Charmian glanced over her shoulder and the noise stopped. "That's not unnatural. What about your astral body? Are you worried about it floating away?"

"Should I be?"

"No, no." Charmian laughed. "It's attached by a sort of umbilical cord."

"Will you be able to get it back in?"

"Oh, yes. But we'll give it a few moments. Obviously it needs some fresh air. Now, shhhhh."

Charmian returned to her place on the floor.

After a brief silence, again she screamed. Again she led a five-voice chant, ended it with a shriek. Kenneth, who had remained rigid throughout, except for this head, suddenly went limp. Groggily, he shook his head. He stepped free of the pail, dried his foot on a towel and carried his paraphernalia back into the kitchen.

Charmian said my astral body was back inside my physical one. She invited me to rejoin the circle on the floor, said: "Now's the time for questions."

"What was Kenneth doing?"

Charmian explained that he'd been acting as lightning rod. Releasing an astral body for the first time required energy. "Afterwards, you can learn to release it yourself, and even to project it from place to place."

"But what's the connection between astral bodies and changing faces? And how does reincarnation fit?"

"It's the astral body that moves from one incarnation to the next."

"So when I saw Jessica as an Indian princess, I was seeing one of the faces of her astral body?"

Wide-eyed, Charmian nodded.

"What about you? Can you see faces?"

"Yes, of course."

"Can you see any of mine?"

"Frankie, I can see all of them. Some of your past lives were very noble indeed."

"So who was I?"

"It's best to explore past lives yourself. Kenneth was once one of Napoleon's soldiers. Wendy was lady to a knight of King Arthur's. Patrick, here, knows a great deal about several of his past lives. All of us lived in Egypt — back in the days of the pharoahs.

"Did I live then, too?"

"Yes, you did. That's often the way it works. Cyclical reincarnation. The same people turning up in different times, different places. Jesus and his disciples. Arthur and his knights."

"You mention Jesus. Was I around then?"

"You were."

I didn't want to ask the question that popped into my mind, but I could see no way around it: "Was I… was I Jesus?"

"No," Charmian said, unruffled. "No — Jesus was a bit different. But you were close to him."

"Was I one of his disciples?"

"Yes, you were."

"Which one?"

"Well, I don't usually tell people about their past lives. I prefer to let them find out for themselves." She looked around the circle. "But in this case, I'll make an exception." She smiled at me. "You were James."

"But weren't there two James?" Wendy asked. "James the Brother of John and another one?"

Charmian beamed at her. "Very good, Wendy."

"Two James? Which one was I?"

"Which one do you think you were?"

"Which one was nearer to Jesus?"

Charmian looked at Wendy and nodded.

"James the Brother of John," she said. "You know: Peter and James and John."

"Was I the Near James?"

Charmian smiled. "That you'll have to find out for yourself."

23

By the time we got back to the lookout I was soaked to the skin. Frankie had offered to take the carrier at the clearing, having laughed until the tears ran down his cheeks, pointing and saying, "Mister.... Mister Omniscience!" But by then I was laughing myself and saw no sense in both of us getting wet.

The crack in the seam of the carrier was near the top, and in the cabin we emptied the remaining water into containers that didn't leak: a kettle, a dishpan, two pots and a bucket hidden beneath the makeshift sink.

Frankie went out to the tower and, as I changed my clothes, I gave myself over to rushes — heard the long, lonely wail of a train from Montreal and pondered the significance of having a tragic father. Lost in this reverie, I was hanging my wet jeans and T-shirt on a front-yard clothes-line when Frankie appeared beside me: "Barometer's falling." He pointed north to where the sky was grey with scudding clouds. "We're in for a storm."

We spent the next couple of hours battening hatches. Frankie carried coal from the tool shed while I swept the cabin. Together we split wood and stacked it on the front porch where it wouldn't get wet. Twice Frankie climbed into the tower to look around. But fire hazard was low and he didn't stay long.

I volunteered to cook supper and whomped up a meal modelled on one I'd shared in Bixby Canyon just ten years before: potatoes wrapped in foil and baked in the wood-stove, along with hunks of roasted spam and cheese and a can of applesauce, all of it washed down, a departure here, with non-alcoholic cider.

Thunder rumbled as we ate and Frankie suggested that tonight I might want to sleep in the cabin. I told him I'd prefer to stay in the tower. "Less claustrophobic."

"Suit yourself." He looked relieved.

After supper, as we did the dishes — Frankie washed and I dried — I noticed a clutch of interrelated books on a shelf above the sink: *Drugs and the Mind, The Doors of Perception, The Varieties of Psychedelic Experience*. When I'd finished drying, I pulled out this last and sat down at the table.

While Frankie put away dishes, I flipped through *Varieties*, an academic tour-de-force by R.E.L. Masters and Jean Houston. Then opted for W. C. Fields: "Ah, yes, the psychedelic experience."

"No doubt you're an authority."

Back to myself. "I survived magic mushrooms, Frankie. But you're right. This psychedelic business has extraordinary dimension." I kept flipping. "Masters and Houston set up a four-tiered model of the unconscious. On the symbolic level, an acid-tripper encounters, let's see here...."

Finally I found the passage I wanted and coasted into it: "The acid-tripper encounters images that are 'predominantly historical, legendary, mythical, ritualistic and archetypal.'"

"That book blew me away."

"The subject may experience, blah, blah, blah... Ah, here it is. 'He may act out myths and legends and pass through initiations and ritual observances often seemingly structured precisely in terms of his own most urgent needs.'"

"Yeah, that's the stuff."

I kept reading aloud: "'Where the symbolic dramas unfold, the individual finds facets of his own existence revealed in the person of Prometheus or Parsifal, Lucifer or Oedipus...' and so forth." I snapped the book shut and shoved it back onto the shelf. "The Self fights back."

"You've lost me."

"Symbolic dramas, archetypal images. Under attack, bent on survival, the Self fights back." Ignoring his confusion, I stood up and stretched: "Let's go play horseshoes. Before the storm hits."

He bounced off the bed. "Didn't know you played."

"Don't expect much. I haven't pitched horseshoes since 1961, when I was gathering myself in Florida to write *Big Sur*."

"Yeah, yeah."

We put on jackets — the evening was cool — and brought the jug of cider.

The horseshoe pit was just south of the tower.

For three months Frankie had been playing nightly, steadily improving, and the first two games he killed me. Then, with a winning score set at twenty-one, he spotted me ten points. We played two games that way and still he won. Every end he tossed at least one ringer and sometimes two. Finally he suggested we go sit on the stump and finish the cider.

"One more game," I said. "Loser makes breakfast tomorrow. And forget the handicap."

"You serious?"

"I'm feeling lucky."

After two turns Frankie was ahead eleven to seven. Then he threw two consecutive ringers, which gave him enough to win. I had one more toss. I turned my back to the peg, flipped the horseshoe casually over my head and heard it settle perfectly atop his two ringers. We were playing last ringer scores all — another concession for my sake — so fifteen points were mine. I'd won.

"What luck!" Frankie cried. "Okay, I'll make breakfast. But let's play one more game."

This time, after three ends, Frankie tossed a lovely ringer, apparently a game-winner, and grinned: "That's that."

Magically, though without flare, I topped it.

With his final shoe, Frankie threw yet another ringer. Chuckling, he wiped his hands in the air: "Who's the better man?"

I closed my eyes tight and spun around three times. Then, my arm extended, hook-shot style, and still with my eyes closed, I flipped the horseshoe skyward. I opened my eyes and watched the wind carry it sideways, this heavy metal horseshoe, and drop it with a gentle thunk around the peg, a perfect ringer. The game was mine.

"What a fluke!" Frankie clasped his head with both hands and staggered around in melodramatic circles. "Talk about a fluke shot!"

I had to laugh. "Magic is alive."

"One more game!"

"Sorry." I rubbed my shoulder. "Pulled my arm with that last toss."

I picked up the jug and our two glasses and led the way to Frankie's favorite tree-stump. Looking north from that gnarled stump, you could see half the valley. Frankie sat down beside me, still shaking his head. "Can't get over that fluke shot. Absolutely incredible."

"I used to play a little pool," I said, "and every so often I'd make what a buddy called a Jesus-Christ shot." Having refilled our glasses, I proposed a toast: "To Jesus-Christ shots!"

We drank and then I gestured with my glass at the clouds, now heavy and dark: "You were right about the storm."

Frankie sipped cider. "What did you mean earlier, when you said miracles signify and suggest, but prove nothing?"

We were still on track. "Miracles provide circumstantial evidence."

"Of what?"

"This and that. Looming sainthood, for example."

Frankie rolled his eyes but I had him: "You yourself once dreamed of sainthood."

"Long ago and far away."

"San Francisco? What, three years back? Maybe I should remind you, Frankie, that I'm a not-so-secret general of the Jesuit and other armies. My novels crackle with proselytizing."

"You mean Kerouac's stuff? Get serious."

"Right from the start. My second published story brought forth an angel."

"Maybe the early work. Before he matured."

"*The Dharma Bums* came later."

"An adventure story, mainly. The religion's irrelevant."

"*Au contraire, mon ami. Visions of Gerard, Dr. Sax, Big Sur,* even *Satori in Paris* — sainthood is always the subtext."

"What are you selling? Kerouac was an impulsive madman, a non-stop sinner."

"My impetuosity was a kind of faith — a reliance on the dharma, on the idea that the universe is self-regulating."

"Kerouac was a drunk."

"Frankie, you're forgetting duality — the dynamic interaction of opposites."

"I don't believe this."

"In my case, addiction to alcohol and the quest for sainthood."

But all this was hitting Frankie too early and he shook his head, disgusted. I refilled our glasses with cider. We drank in silence, staring out at the mountains, the lowering sky. On my face I felt the first droplets of rain.

Frankie said, "So how'd you get onto this sainthood kick?"

"Runs in the family. When my brother, Gerard, was dying of rheumatic fever, age nine, local nuns gathered around his bed to record his last words. I was four and expected him to reappear after he died, huge and powerful and renewed, greater and more Gerard-like than ever. And sure enough, shortly after he died, I was lying in bed when suddenly there he was, standing over my crib, wide-eyed and wild-haired. My big brother, Gerard." I took a sip of cider. "That was all he could manage."

"So this weird fixation of yours springs from a dream you had at age four?"

"Oh, I had many dreams. My mother kept a crucifix in her bedroom and sometimes in the dark I'd see Jesus glowing like a light. Once God spoke to me through that crucifix. He promised to save me, but first I had to suffer and die in pain, frightened and despairing, tormented by doubt and ambiguity."

"You expect me to take this seriously?"

"What do you know about Ste. Thérèse de Lisieux?"

"Only that my home-town owes her its name."

"Thérèse was a Carmelite nun who wrote a spiritual autobiography called *The Story of A Soul*. In it she described how one afternoon, while walking through a thunderstorm, she received a vision. She stumbled and fell into a puddle. After quivering there for a few minutes, she woke to find herself wet and filthy, stood up and shook her fist at the sky: 'Lord, if this is how you treat your friends, no wonder you have so few!'"

Frankie laughed. "Sounds like my kind of saint."

"Thérèse died in 1897 of tuberculosis and was canonized when I was three. My mother kept a statue of her. When I was six or seven I saw it turn, bathed in red light, and look directly at me."

"Another childhood dream."

"Cut to Mexico City, 1950. I was five years older than you are now. I'd just seen my first bullfight and found it revolting. Brutal and bloody and senseless. To forget I smoked grass and focused on my writing. That's when I found the secret of *On The Road*. Had a vision of myself as this Great Walking Saint."

"Drug-induced hallucinations." Frankie waved his hand dismissively. "Best put them behind you."

"North Carolina, 1955. No drugs. I was smelling flowers in the back yard. I stood up, took a deep breath — and woke on my back in the grass. I'd been unconscious, a neighbor said later, for about sixty seconds. That's when I had my vision of the Golden Eternity. Realized that Time is an illusion. That eternity is not just a long time, an eon, but has nothing to do with Time. That dead or alive, we all exist forever in the Golden Eternity."

"Mystical mumbo-jumbo!" Frankie said, snorting. "Kerouac drank and took drugs. He screwed anything that moved. He was a committed hell-raiser, an unrepentant sinner — and you're trying to pass him off as a saint?"

"A saint can serve God as a sinner."

"Ha! Try that one on a priest."

"I'm not here to defend conventional religion, Frankie, but certain men of the cloth might surprise you." Again I refilled our glasses. "One night in Northport, must have been the mid-sixties, a friend arranged for a nymphomaniac to visit me at my house. I didn't want to ruin her pleasure by coming too quickly, so before she arrived I went into the bathroom and took care of business. Later, my friend told a priest. The priest said, 'That's charity! That's real Christian charity!' And demanded to meet me."

"Christian charity!" Frankie almost fell off the stump. "Going into the bathroom to masturbate?"

This time he couldn't stop laughing.

133

24

In Pacific Grove, 1990, I found no trace of the man I remembered as Munsie the Barber. Nor could I find the old house in which I'd rented a room. I did locate the Pacific Grove Public Library, where I'd spent hours each day, unable to borrow books because I wasn't a member, and unable to become a member because I wasn't a resident.

The library was closed for renovations so I couldn't explore the stacks — a major disappointment. I'd hoped to discover some vaguely familiar title — a tome on the prophecies of Nostradumus, perhaps, or a certain impenetrable opus by "Phylo" that celebrated both astral projection and multiple planes of existence.

From across the street I snapped a photo of the building: strikingly long and low, white with a red-tile roof. Spanish arches run the length of the library, and behind them an open-air hallway. Now, as I study my 1990 photograph, I remember being struck, more than two decades before, with the distinctiveness of those arches. For the rest, the photo is silent. No matter. Already it has brought back December, 1966.

In Carmel, having found Charmian Foster, I crashed for two nights at a communal house shared by three of her disciples. The future looked bright until the second evening, when Patrick overheard Wendy inviting me to her room to give her a back rub. Until now, he'd been the only back-rubber. He was also, as it happened, the main payer of rent. Next morning, though I'd declined Wendy's invitation, Patrick told me to clear out. He'd had a dream. I was spiritually disruptive.

I telephoned Charmian Foster, but Kenneth told me she was out of town for a few days. I couldn't believe I'd finished with her — the idea that I'd once been a disciple of Jesus gave me no sense

134

of closure — and felt I had to stay in Carmel. Where room rents were out of sight. A sympathetic waitress told me places were cheaper in nearby Pacific Grove. I spent a night on the beach, shivering in my thin sleeping bag, before realizing her suggestion had been a sign.

I hitchhiked down the highway and, with most of my remaining money, rented a room for a week. From Pacific Grove I reached Charmian Foster, but Patrick had got to her and she wished me many noble lives: "Remember, Frankie: You were one of the disciples — one of two James."

Great. But where did that leave me? Deep in the stacks at the Pacific Grove Public Library. In *Desolation Angels* I found Kerouac's reference to astral bodies. But it shed no light and I plunged into Rosicrucianism, read three or four confusing tomes. Then I discovered Phylo and Nostradamus and explored astral travel and planes of existence and fifteenth-century prophecies of doom. Trouble was, I could find no way to relate any of this to my own experience, to integrate it with what I'd learned since my first acid trip.

Since moving to Pacific Grove, come to think of it, I'd seen precious few signs. Had the mysterious force deserted me? I was out walking one morning, wrestling with this, when some clown in a passing car yelled: "Hey, hippy! Get a haircut!"

I hated the term "hippy." Refused to identify with it. Besides, my hair barely covered my ears. Only, what if that yell was an omen? Maybe the signs were there but, because of the mix-up with Charmian Foster, I hadn't been seeing them? On the other hand, what about money? I'd paid my rent until the end of the week, but for food I was down to four dollars.

Still, a possible sign was a possible sign. It couldn't be ignored. Maybe, for some reason beyond the physical, or on another plane of existence, I did need to get a haircut. I glanced down the street — sneaked a peak, really: no barber poles. Very well: I owed the mysterious force this much. If I passed a barber shop before I reached the end of the block, I'd accept the yell as a sign. Otherwise, no.

I figured I was home free. But ten strides more and there, painted on a window, I discovered a red-and-white barber pole. I couldn't believe it. I peered into the shop. A trim, sandy-haired barber was dusting off an only-customer. A sign listed his prices. I couldn't afford a haircut, not even if I was meant to have one.

Still, a sign was a sign. Having taken two deep breaths, I entered the barber shop as the other customer, an older man with a goatee, paid the barber and left. I waited until I sat in the chair, a bib under my chin, the barber clipping away: "You aren't interested in reincarnation, by any chance? In planes of existence or astral bodies?"

The barber stopped clipping, stepped back and stared, open-mouthed: "Who are you?"

"That's what I'm trying to find out."

While the barber cut my hair, I explained that sometimes I felt a mysterious force was guiding me: "An omen drove me into this shop."

The barber listened in rapt silence, then stepped around from behind me and extended his hand: "My name is Munsie. I'm a spiritualist."

Munsie went and sifted through a pile of magazines and handed me half a dozen: "Take a look at these."

Instead of *Playboy, Time* or *Newsweek*, Munsie stocked *The Winding Path*, the covers of which advertised interviews with beings who lived "on the other side of the veil" and advice on how to stay on the right, true path. I flipped through several of these, fighting to keep an open mind, while Munsie finished my hair. When the barber was done he swept aside his cloth and bowed: "The haircut's on me."

"Thanks, Munsie. To tell the truth, I'm a little low on funds."

"Listen, a few friends are coming over to my place tonight. An informal gathering. I'd like you to join us."

Munsie and his wife lived above the barber shop in a neat, two-bedroom flat. When I arrived, precisely on time, I found half a dozen people there, most of them twice my age and prosperous-looking — no blue jeans. They sat in the living room eating cookies and drinking tea and discussing a friend's passion for curing women by laying on hands. A middle-aged woman in a sequined dress motioned me into the kitchen and whispered, "Are you The One?"

"Which one?"

"The One we're awaiting?"

"I don't know."

Back in the living room, a red-faced man named Gerald said: "Can you see auras, Frankie?"

"Auras? No, I can't."

"Don't be ashamed to admit it," Gerald said, his voice booming. "We've all seen auras. Myrtle, you've seen them, haven't you? Sure you have. Come on, Frankie. Look at Myrtle. Can't you see her aura? Red and blue and just a touch of yellow? I'm sure you can see it. Don't be ashamed to say so. You can see Myrtle's aura, can't you?"

Munsie said: "Gerald gets like this, Frankie. Don't pay any attention."

Later, as the party wound down, Munsie whispered to me that I should remain behind: "I've got something to show you."

When the two of us were alone, his wife having said goodnight and gone off to bed, Munsie rooted in a wooden chest hidden in a back-hall closet.

"Got it!" he said at last, and produced a blue suede jewel box. Munsie sat down on the couch, opened this box and took out a two-inch prism: "With this we can consult the spirits."

The red-and-blue prism was attached to a piece of white thread. Munsie took the end of the thread between the thumb and forefinger of his right hand and jiggled the prism up and down. "A pendulum, see?"

His wife emerged into the living room and picked up a magazine. "Oh, Munsie," she said. "You're not showing him that?"

"I thought you'd gone to bed."

"It's just nervous impulses," the woman said. "Been proven."

She spun on her heel and was gone.

"Pay no attention," Munsie said. "She has little faith." He spun the prism with his finger. "When people die, as you probably know, they don't take new bodies right away. For a while they live on in their astral bodies — pure, disembodied spirits."

I nodded, non-committal: "That fits."

"They know things we don't. And sometimes, if properly addressed, they'll answer questions for us." Munsie jiggled the prism up and down. "They'll spin this pendulum clockwise for yes, counter-clockwise for no." He lowered his voice to a whisper. "Watch."

Munsie dangled the prism over the palm of his left hand. Staring hard, he called: "Spirits! Spirits, can you hear me?"

Nothing happened.

"Spirits! Spirits, please! Will you answer questions for Munsie the Barber? Spin the pendulum clockwise for yes, counter-clockwise for no."

Again nothing.

"Spirits, please! We wait with respect."

The prism began to spin clockwise.

I looked at Munsie's right hand, the one holding the prism. It was perfectly still. Yet the prism spun faster. Munsie asked the spirits half a dozen questions. Had people enjoyed themselves tonight? Would Gerald ever emerge from scepticism? Each time the spirits responded. But I worried that Munsie was moving the thread: "May I try it?"

He handed me the prism. I suspended it over my left palm, careful to keep my hands steady. "Spirits," I called. "Spirits, will you answer questions for Frankie McCracken?"

Munsie said, "For Frankie the Seeker."

Nothing. I handed back the prism — signs or no signs, this business left me cold — but Munsie insisted I try again. This time, at his insistence, I said, "Frankie the Seeker." And to my surprise the prism spun clockwise. Yes, a mysterious force had guided me to California. Yes, that force had wanted me to meet Munsie the Barber.

Munsie clapped his hands: "Ask a tough one."

"Spirits," I called. "Spirits, listen. In one of my past lives, I was a disciple of Jesus — but I don't know which one. Can you tell me? Was I the James of Peter and James and John? The James who was nearer to Jesus?"

Nothing happened.

Munsie cried, "Again!"

"Spirits, yes or no," I called. "Was I James, the brother of John? Was I the Near James?"

The prism spun slowly at first, then gathered momentum and began to revolve.

"I was right!" Munsie cried. "You were James! The Near James!"

25

c/o General Delivery,
San Francisco, California,

Dec. 17, 1966.

Dear Family:

Strange things have been happening to me lately, but I don't know yet what they mean. All I can tell you is that I'm looking for myself. I hope what I find will make you happier with me than you have been.

I love you all very much.

I'm sorry I can't be home for Christmas. Thank you for your kind wishes. You can be sure that I'm thinking of you all. But I have to stay here in California until I find out what it is I've been sent here to learn.

If my last unemployment cheque has come, I would appreciate your sending it along. Also, do you know the precise time of my birth? Mom, this is important. If you don't know to the minute, could you give me an approximation?

I wish there was more I could tell you. I am healthy. I'd like to send you all Christmas presents, but I just haven't got the money. All I can send is this letter and my love.

Joyeux Noel,
Frankie

P.S. Please don't worry about me. Everything will be all right. I have a part-time job at the post office.

26

Nobody learns to be a writer. Not the way you learn to be an accountant or a plumber. You have to be born with a tragic father. So I declared in 1967 during my interview with *The Paris Review*. A wild generalization, but I'd recently written *Vanity of Duluoz*, so I'd been thinking about my own father, Leo Kerouac, and realizing yet again how large he'd loomed in my life.

On Mount Jubilation, at Frankie's unconscious prompting, I remembered how my father would arrive home late for dinner, having gone drinking with his cronies, and Mémère would start in, telling him he was a no-good drunken bum, a *vaurien* who cared nothing for his wife and children, and that she should have listened to her family, she should never have married him.

Leo would respond with something charming, maybe *ferme ta guele, maudite vache*, shut your face, you god-damn cow, *avant que je te fous une baffe*. Before I shut it for you. And the skirmish would begin.

On Jubilation, as I shed my wet clothes, I remembered that when my parents fought like this I'd go stand in the back yard. From there, in the gathering dusk, I'd watch neighbor families in their kitchens eating dinner and imagine they were ghosts eating ghost food, and maybe I was a ghost too. I'd look up at the stars and wonder where the universe ended and think how small my problems were.

If my parents' battle showed no sign of abating, I'd take a long walk, end up sitting on the bank of the Merrimack River, listening to the rush of the water. Sometimes, from upriver, the long, lonely wailing of the train from Montreal would reach me and I'd swear never to become like my father — never to become a drinker.

On Jubilation I discovered that, two decades after I sat on that river bank as a teenager, and not three hundred miles away, in

Ste. Thérèse Sur-le-lac, ten-year-old Frankie McCracken would hear the wailing of a different train from Montreal — and again the long, lonely sound would evoke a tragic father.

Frankie would lie awake in his bed, unable to sleep, waiting to hear the whistle from off in Coeur d'Aimée, one long *wooooooooooo*, one short, and then another long: *wooooooooooo, wooo, woooooooooooooooo.*

This would be any season but summer, because then the train came all the way to Ste. Thérèse and Frankie's mother would take him and Janey and Eddie to meet their father. They'd walk up Avenue des Archanges and along the highway, Chemin St. Esprit, then turn up a dirt road lined with trees and bushes. At the train station — just an open shelter, really — the children would put their ears to the tracks and listen for the rumble that signalled an approaching train.

Far away down the tracks, a light would shine out from against the dark trees. As the train drew near in a long, slow curve, *wooooooooo, woo, woooooooooo*, they'd count the cars — usually six or eight, sometimes ten or twelve. Mothers would yell at children to get off the tracks and into the station. From inside, leaning out, they'd watch the engine thunder past, the engineer waving his big gloved hand, and then the passenger cars clank and shudder to a halt, the whole train steaming and hissing.

Frankie loved to see his father step off the train with the other commuters, his hat on his head, his suit jacket over his arm, his tie askew and his white shirt open at the neck. Down the dirt road they'd go together, a family like all the others.

Only sometimes Frankie's father didn't get off the train. And they would stand, the four of them, looking to see if they'd missed him in the rush — maybe near the engine? — while the train pulled out and everybody else swung laughing down the dirt road.

That meant his father had stayed in town to drink. No telling what time he'd be home. And his mother, biting back tears, would lead the family slowly home.

She'd bought Frankie a third-hand bicycle to use on his *Gazette* route, and now she started sending him alone to meet the train — first the five o'clock, and then, if necessary, the five-thirty.

It was his job to see that his father came home without stopping at the hotel. "Mummy'll be mad," he'd tell his father. "She's been alone all day with the kids and needs a break."

"Yes, yes, I'm just going to stop for a quick one. Need to unwind. Tell your mother I'll be home soon."

That was in summer.

The rest of the year the train from Montreal came only as far as Coeur d'Aimée, and if his father wasn't home before seven-thirty, usually everybody would be in bed when he did arrive. Frankie would lie awake listening for the long lonely howl of the train whistle, which carried on the wind across the corner of the lake: *Woooooooooo, wooo, wooooooooooo*. At the sound, he'd roll over and look at the luminous white hands of his alarm clock.

Twenty minutes, his father took to get home by taxi. Five, ten, fifteen minutes. Twenty and in he'd come, go straight to the front room and dig out his gramophone. Wouldn't stop to remove his hat and coat. He'd crank up the gramophone, sit down at the kitchen table and start playing records, scratchy old 78s, the same ones over and over. "Dream when you're feeling blue. Dream, that's the thing to do. Just let the smoke rings rise in the air. You'll find your share of memories there."

He'd sit at the kitchen table, still in his hat and coat, staring at the floor, listening to Frank Sinatra sing the same songs over and over. "Dream when the day is through. Dream, your dreams might come true. Things never are as bad as they seem. So dream, dream, dream."

But go beyond twenty minutes. Frankie would hear the train whistle and wait. Twenty-five minutes, thirty, thirty-five. Forty minutes and he'd start praying for an exception — that tonight his father wouldn't come home at all. That tomorrow morning in Coeur d'Aimée he'd get off the train all the other commuters got on.

Everybody would see his father and know he'd been out drinking all night, but no shouting match would rip the night open. Either his father would collapse into bed and his mother would call the office, tell them he was sick, or else she'd help him out of his crinkled suit and into clean clothes, then ship him back to

Montreal on the next train. Late for work, smelling of booze. But no shouting match.

That was the exception, because waiting twenty minutes beyond the train whistle usually meant Frankie's father would catch the last train from Montreal, and so arrive home at quarter to two. Or else that he'd got out of the taxi at the hotel, La Fin du Monde, and would stagger home drunk when he ran out of money. Either way, bad news.

Frankie would wake at the creak of the kitchen door. His father would stumble into the house, kick off his boots and throw his coat on the couch. Then, "Maggie, I'm hungry. What have we got to eat?"

"Keep your voice down," his mother would call from bed. "You'll wake the whole house. Your supper's in the oven, where it always is when you get home at this time of night."

His father would open the oven, take out his supper, let the door spring shut. He'd pull a kitchen chair away from the table, make a scraping noise on the hard linoleum floor. After a minute he'd throw down his fork, shout, "Maggie, this is cold."

"What did you expect? Supper was on the table at six o'clock. If you'd get home here after work, like any decent man, you'd find your supper waiting."

"Guy slaves all day with a bunch of philistines, he's got a right to a hot meal when he arrives home. Get out here and make me something to eat."

"Make it yourself. What do you think I am? A bloody servant?"

From there the battle would escalate.

In his bed, Frankie would pull his pillow tight over his head to drown out the noise. Usually, after about half an hour, the shouting would subside. And Frankie would fall asleep.

Then came the night his father lurched muttering into the house. He slammed the door shut and Frankie woke knowing tonight would be bad. He checked his clock. Quarter to twelve, no trains due. His father had stopped off at La Fin du Monde.

Now he was pacing around the kitchen, making a strange smacking sound — pounding his fist into his hand? "Nine years! Nine years I gave them." He bumped into a kitchen chair, knocked

144

it over onto the floor. "Nine years of my life! And this is the thanks I get! Ingrates! Sons of bitches!"

"Maurice, stop slamming around. And shut up that swearing. The kids can hear every word you say. We're all trying to — oh, my God! Look at this mess!" His mother had risen and gone into the kitchen. "You're like a bloody two-year-old. Don't know enough to take off your boots when you come through the door."

His father banged his fist down on the kitchen table and the utensils rattled. "Don't give me any crap, Maggie. I'm not in the mood."

"Take your boots off, then."

His father resumed pacing. "I'll take my boots off when I'm ready." He banged a cupboard door shut — once, twice.

Frankie had never heard him this bad.

"They got me, Maggie. They finally got me."

"Who got you?"

Blam! Blam! His father was pounding the wall behind the oil stove.

"Maurice! For God's sake! You'll break your hand."

Blam! Blam! Blash! Something had given way.

"Are you satisfied? Let me see your hand."

"They got me, Maggie. They finally got me."

"Who got you? What are you talking about?"

"Those bastards at work." His father was crying. Could this be happening?

"Nine years it took them. But they got me."

"What do you mean, they got you?"

"They fired me, Maggie."

"Fired you? Oh, my God! What happened?"

"I borrowed some money out of the accounts receivable. So I could buy lunch."

"So you could buy beer, you mean."

"I was going to hit the bank and put it back this afternoon, as usual. But the auditors came back."

"Weren't they in yesterday?"

"Somebody tipped them off."

"It's because of your drinking. Oh, my God! They were looking for an excuse."

"Nine years of my life, Maggie! Nine years I gave them."

"Oh, my God."

Frankie fell asleep to his father's sobbing.

In the morning, behind the oil stove, he found a hole in the wall. His father had punched his fist through the gyprock. Incredible.

27

They're a hardy breed, these readers of *The Rocky Mountain Miracle*. Also a captive audience. I mean, you want to know what's happening in Banff, Alberta, what are you going to read? That's the attitude I take. Faithful readers know to expect it. They pick up *The Miracle*: "What's that nutcase ranting about this week?" Which is why, despite my history of, shall we say, misdemeanors, the publisher keeps me around.

So, no, I had no qualms about subjecting my readers to more Kerouac, not even after Quebec City. It's just that, for a time, I had nothing to add. Also, certain personal problems intensified. Otherwise irrelevant, they slowed me down.

Anyway, this line I take on spontaneous prose? My contention that the celebration of "spontaneous bop prosody" serves mainly to link Kerouac and the Beats? I didn't explore its implications in *The Miracle* until 1989, when I declared: "It's time to rescue Jack Kerouac from the Beats. This insistence on treating him as a Beat-Generation writer is damaging his reputation. Worse, it's getting in the way of the serious critical appraisal his work deserves."
— YOU CALLED?
— Certainly I knew you'd emerge. Invocation by self-quotation. you've peaked my curiosity. This alternate narrator? Is he more reliable than me?
— HE'S JUST ANOTHER METAPHYSICIAN, FRANKIE. THINKS PROSE, SPONTANEOUS OR OTHERWISE, OFFERS A WINDOW ONTO THE MIND.
— When really it's...
— SOMEWHERE WE LIVE. SOMETHING WE DO.
— If he exists, why can't I see him?

— HE'S ACTIVE IN ANOTHER TYPEFACE. SAME TEXT, DIFFERENT FONT. THINK OF IT AS ANOTHER DIMENSION. A PARALLEL UNIVERSE.

— Now I know you're crazy.

— SUCH SCEPTICISM, FRANKIE. YOU WANT TO SEE YOUR ALTERNATE? BEHOLD: "RAIN SPATTERED THE TOWER WINDOWS AND THUNDER RUMBLED THROUGH THE ROCKIES. I LAY IN DARKNESS, MY JACKET AN UNCOMFORTABLE PILLOW, AND SAVORED IRONIES. FOUR YEARS BEFORE, IN NOVEMBER OF 1966, WHEN FRANKIE HAD ROLLED INTO THE HAIGHT-ASHBURY CHASING HIS LARGER-THAN-LIFE KEROUAC...."

— Agh! Stop!

—... CHASING HIS LARGER-THAN-LIFE KEROUAC, A YEA-SAYING CANUCK WHO ROARED BACK AND FORTH ACROSS THE CONTINENT WITH WILD-EYED BUDDIES, OR ELSE SAT CROSS-LEGGED AND ALONE, SEEKING ENLIGHTENMENT, ON MOUNTAIN-TOPS LIKE THIS ONE...."

— Enough! The horror!

— AND THAT'S THROUGH A GLASS DARKLY.

— The horror! The horror!

— TEMPT ME FURTHER, FRANKIE, AND I'LL MANIFEST YOUR ALTERNATE IN HIS OWN TYPEFACE.

— You'd bring him here?

— BETTER STILL, I'LL GIVE HIM ACCESS TO YOUR FONT.

— You're disgusting.

— I MEAN IT, FRANKIE. NO MORE JOURNALISM. YOU CAN KEEP YOUR TRANSCENDENTAL NONSENSE, YOUR FOOLISH INSISTENCE ON SELF. ALSO, THOSE REVEALING LETTERS. BUT I RESERVE THE LAST WORD. UNTIL THEN, I'M OUT OF HERE.

— Wait! This piece I wrote: "Time to rescue Kerouac from the Beats."

— A FINAL INTERROGATION, THEN: THE OCCASION FOR THIS GAMBIT?

— A televised panel discussion in Toronto. The imported star of the show was Beat-American biographer Ann Charters. I was a last-minute addition flown in from the boonies, a Kerouac-buff whose role was to keep the discussion from degenerating into a love-fest. Some producer had remembered my Quebec City articles.

— PREPARING FOCUSED YOUR THINKING?

— What did "Beat" signify as a literary movement? As a lifestyle? Why the on-going interest in Beat literature? What the Beat legacy? So the questions. Exploring them, I discovered my thesis: Kerouac is BIGGER than Beat.

— LINK THIS DEVELOPMENT TO QUEBEC CITY.

— The Quebec City gathering celebrated Kerouac's French-Canadian roots. It touted *Le Grand Jack*, not as King of the Beats, but as a literary Louis Riel. This is a radically different yet total interpretation: "See what happens when an innocent Canuck ventures forth among the god-less English? They destroy him."

— THIS YOU TOLD THE PANEL?

— Yes, the point being not to urge acceptance of this Québécois interpretation, but merely to have it recognized as a comprehensive alternative to the Beat-American.

— BEAT IS NOT THE ONE AND ONLY. ERGO, KEROUAC'S BIGGER THAN BEAT.

— My fellow panelists greeted my assertion of Kerouac's singular greatness with guffaws of protest. Cries of what about Ginsberg, Ferlinghetti, Gregory Corso? What about William Burroughs?

— THIS, OF COURSE, YOU'D ANTICIPATED.

— It's Beat-American gospel. Stand back, I cried, and look at 20th-century literature written, not just in the United States, but in English. Consider, for example, the mighty Joyce.

— THEN LOOK BACK AT THE BEATS.

— Ginsberg wrote one memorable poem: "Howl", title by Kerouac. Burroughs produced some unforgettable images, notably in *Naked Lunch*, title again by Kerouac. But can anybody take seriously the chanting of *om-om-om* or literature by cut and paste?

— KEROUAC'S WORK, ON THE OTHER HAND?

— I cited *Dr. Sax*, with its stunning mix of fantasy and realism, its prototypical postmodernism. I cited those prophetic classics *On The Road* and *Dharma Bums*; and *Visions of Cody*, with its patches of brilliance; and *Big Sur*, which as a fictional portrait of a suffering alcoholic ranks second only to that masterpiece *Under The Volcano*. Forget the rest of Beat literature, I shouted. This opus alone stands a chance of surviving the millenium.

— BUT SEPARATE KEROUAC FROM THE BEATS?

— How did the man himself put it? "As for the Beat Generation, it's not important, it's a fad. You see, this is silly, it (the B.G.) has nothing to do with the serious artists who started the whole thing just by, you know, writing a poem, writing. It's a fad, just like the Lost Generation."

— WHAT? YOU WANT US TO IGNORE THE BIOGRAPHICAL MATRIX? THE HISTORICAL CONTEXT?

— Not at all. Just re-examine it. In the mid-sixties, on the key issue of psychedelic drugs, for example, and specifically LSD, leaders of the so-called Beat Generation got behind that hubris-driven, would-be messiah Timothy Leary: "Turn on, tune in, drop out."

— THE BEAT GENERATION WENT SURFING.

— Kerouac stood alone against the tidal wave of counter-culture opinion. To Leary's fatuous assertion that LSD was a miracle-drug, he responded: "Walking on water wasn't built in a day." He warned repeatedly against the use of psychedelic drugs and told anybody who'd listen that, since experimenting with psilicybin, he'd never been the same.

— THIS IS TANGENTIAL. KEROUAC'S WORK IS NOTHING BUT BEAT.

— Wrong. It's BIGGER than Beat. Demands more than one context.

— BELONGS TO MORE THAN ONE DISCOURSE?

— Different perspectives reveal different anomalies. The Beat-American emphasis on spontaneous prose, for example, proves a red herring.

— SO YOU DECLARED TO GASPS.

— I cited *The Impromptu Stylistics of Jack Keroauc*, a rigorously logical work, brilliant really, in which critic Rebecca Rosen marches down this well-trod garden path. She winds up ignoring *Dr. Sax* and arguing that *Desolation Angels* is the pinnacle of Kerouac's achievement. Can you believe it?

— THAT MISH-MASH OF MANUSCRIPTS?

— Listen to Kerouac: "It's a spontaneous flow that comes, and nobody could understand what I was talking about when I said you should just open up and let it come out. It's the Holy Ghost that comes through you. You don't have to be a Catholic to know what I mean, and you don't have to be a Catholic for the Holy Ghost to speak through you."

— SAID THE HOLY GHOST AS STRAIGHT MAN, SLIGHTLY TROUBLED: WHAT'S BEHIND THIS CELEBRATION OF SPONTANEOUS PROSE?

— Well may you underline Kerouac's Christian imagery. Yet "spontaneous bop prosody" is touted as profoundly Buddhist. Why?

— WE'VE BEEN HERE BEFORE, BUT AGAIN YOU'RE GOING TO TELL ME.

— Because viewed as Buddhist, spontaneous prose serves to link Kerouac's work with that of Allen Ginsberg. The latter opus needs the former to survive.

— THIS YOU GLEAN FROM THE QUEBECOIS INTER-PRETATION?

— A corollary, merely. I go further. As methodology, as aesthetic philosophy, spontaneous prose is ludicrous, farcical: an embarrassment. Particularly its rejection of revision.

— WRITING ISN'T JAZZ?

— Kerouac did his best work by flying in the face of his wacky philosophizing. He wrote and re-wrote. *Dr. Sax, for example,* he created as a comic book.

— YOU MENTIONED LEGACY.

— Kerouac invented the so-called New Journalism. Check out *Visions of Cody*, the 15-page section called "Joan Rawshanks in the Fog". Written years before Tom Wolfe even dreamed *The Electric Kool-Aid Acid Test*, its detail, its high-energy, hell-bent prose, its mix of inner and outer, subjective and objective, make it a New Journalistic tour-de-force.

— WHAT OF SUBJECTIVE INTENSITY?

— Kerouac showed that walking on water can be built in a hurricane, but only if you're self-lessly honest. He wrote out of the eye of individual experience, and so transformed the autobiographical novel. That's where the Beat-less critical appraisal of Kerouac must begin. With the work.

— ENOUGH PROVOCATIONS. FRANKIE, I'M GONE.

28

Biographer Gerald Nicosia writes that Kerouac's obnoxious megalomania was born in the mid-fifties, but he's being protective. Kerouac always had a tendency to self-aggrandizement. As a boy he imagined himself the world's greatest writer, and at nineteen, when he had the first of his great waking dreams, he saw himself as the hero not of a story but a legend — and, notably, as the author of a book "so golden and purchased with magic that everybody smacks their brows." A couple of years later, when Kerouac cracked up at navy bootcamp, the Yossarian syndrome, a psychiatrist diagnosed him as "a schizoid personality with angel tendencies" — 1940s jargon for megalomania.

The fifties brought only inflation. When Kerouac discovered reincarnation, for example, he produced a list of past lives that included Honoré de Balzac and William Shakespeare, as well as two of the greatest-ever Buddhist saints. He admitted to having been an Indian potboy and an English thief, but this was a born story-teller's ploy, a sop to credibility.

The sixties? More of the same. In San Francisco, recently arrived, Kerouac declared that he'd been present at the crucifixion of Christ. Then, better still, that, no, he couldn't have been, because he would have tried to prevent it. Down the California coast, in Bixby Canyon, Kerouac decided that he'd found Jesus himself, come again to lead his disciples on a march from California to New York and beyond.

Why do I rehearse this history? Because in it I find comfort, even now. And maybe the courage to explore my own angel tendencies, which surfaced late in 1966, when I returned to the Haight knowing I'd been the Near James but penniless and no place to stay and ended up crashing at the Fell Street House.

Two nights after I arrived Ruth the Painter freaked out, began yelling that her home had become a madhouse in which she couldn't paint. She'd signed the lease and wanted everybody to get the hell out — everybody except a beautiful couple and their disturbed four-year-old son, but certainly including me and Oscar and Bonnie Torn, a razor-sharp red-head who'd announced that a guy named Joe Bob was on his way to the Haight from New Orleans. That's what had set Ruth off, the idea of yet another addition to Oscar's ever-changing retinue — always somebody knocking on the door to see the poet-guru.

A fellow named Bernie was visiting when Ruth freaked. An ex-New Yorker who was balding in his late twenties, Bernie sported a green cowboy hat, held down an inside job at the post office and edited a literary magazine. Bernie was publishing Oscar's poem about God laughing seven times — though to me this no longer mattered. He lived in a two-room apartment, Bernie's Bunker, on the second-floor of yet another run-down mansion in the Haight. Said he had room for three people, no problem, and Oscar and Bonnie and I gathered our gear and went with him.

Next day Oscar made up with Ruth the Painter and moved back into the Fell Street House. Bonnie and I stayed with Bernie and the two of them became lovers. As for me, my sex drive was dead — too many things on my mind — and mostly I went for walks. I spent my days rambling, smoking dope, watching for signs, and my nights on a mattress on the living-room floor.

One afternoon, while sitting under a tree in the Panhandle, I spotted Oscar hurrying along Fell Street towards Bernie's Bunker. I took one last toke, then shouted and waved and caught up. He said, "Joe Bob arrived last night."

I'd never seen him so excited.

Mounting the stairs, we heard somebody wailing on a harmonica. Oscar said, "Joe Bob!" and started taking steps two at a time. We burst into the Bunker and almost hit Bernie, who was dancing around the kitchen waving a ladle. He laughed and jerked his green-hatted head, hey, get a load of this, at the guy blowing harp in the corner.

Joe Bob was finishing a bluesy rendition of *When The Saints Come Marching In*, wailing away with his eyes closed. Even so he was strikingly handsome, mid-to-late twenties, well-chiseled features and wavy black hair. On the table in front of him stood a half-empty gallon-jug of cheap red wine. He opened his eyes, surprisingly blue, but Oscar cried, "Don't stop!"

Joe Bob whooped at the sight of his pal and started blowing for real, chuffing and wailing like a freight train. He rocked back and forth, stomping one foot on the floor, and the whole kitchen shook and who cared? Bernie was dancing around clacking spoons. Joe Bob blew a fierce, howling riff and whooped a finale, but Oscar yelled, "Don't stop!" So Joe Bob went at it again.

Oscar was laughing and crying and yelling, "Don't stop! Don't stop!" and finally I couldn't stand it, keeping it all inside. I spotted the wine and yes! Grabbed the bottle, whipped off the top, and with Joe Bob wailing, Bernie banging spoons and Oscar crying, "Don't stop! Don't stop!" I lifted the jug and splashed wine into Joe Bob's black hair, half a glass, splashed it out, and Joe Bob looked up and nodded and kept wailing.

"Appreciated the gesture, man," he said afterwards, when everybody had collapsed and he was drying his hair with a towel. "Appreciated the gesture."

Turned out Joe Bob had been blowing blues harp off and on for ten years. "Picked up my riffs from real old blues men in Nworlins — cats like Jimmy Reed, Howlin' Wolf, Sonny Boy Williamson. Used to hang out after hours in the French Quarter.

I said, "In New Or-leans?"

"No, Nworlins," Joe Bob said, laughing. "Nworlins."

As if to complement his drawl, turn speech into song, Joe Bob had a deep bass voice. Blue eyes, pale skin, curly black hair: Joe Bob was the most beautiful of cats. See him climbing the hill to the Drugstore Café between Oscar and me, green duffle open to the December chill, eight-foot blue scarf whirling around his neck and over his shoulder to hang halfway down his back. This was style. In one hand, dangling from a forefinger, Joe Bob carried his gallon jug of dry red wine. In the other, an old-favorite hardcover: Walt Whitman's *Leaves of Grass*, large-format, illustrated boldly in charcoal.

Oscar was talking Rainer Marie Rilke, droning on about angels and puppets, when Joe Bob cried: "Enough antiquated elegies! You want poetry?" Joe Bob handed me his jug, flipped open his Whitman and began reading aloud, marking the rhythm with his free hand: "Afoot and light-hearted I take to the open road,/ Healthy, free, the world before me,/ The long brown path before me leading wherever I choose." He declaimed the first stanza, really from memory, then snapped the book shut: "Now that's poetry!"

Oscar sniffed: "Talk about antiquated. Whitman was dying when Rilke was born."

"Whitman lives!" Joe Bob whipped out his blues harp, tossed me *Leaves of Grass* and, there on the hill, swung into *When The Saints*. Behind him, in Nworlins, he'd left an ambitious, too-possessive wife and a job as an artist in an advertising agency. Besides his Whitman, Joe Bob carried a single small suitcase: socks and boxer shorts, all neatly folded, two pairs of corduroys, three long-sleeved shirts, a blue turtle-neck sweater, two boxes of colored pencils, three harmonicas in different keys, a hardcover copy of the *I Ching* and the manuscript of an unpublished novel he intended to rewrite.

Women were crazy for Joe Bob. When he wasn't drinking wine, spouting Whitman or blowing blues harp, he "balled chicks" on the mattress in the living room. Balling: I remembered the term from Kerouac. *The Subterraneans*? Occasionally, Joe Bob got orgies going, but mostly I watched from the armchair, declined to participate. Too many things on my mind.

Since returning from Pacific Grove, I'd written home asking when exactly I was born. My mother replied quickly, but already I'd abandoned astrology and resumed vagrant reading. I discovered Meher Baba, avatar of the age: "I was Rama, I was Krishna, I was this one, I was that one — now I am Meher Baba." Dismissed him as a charlatan. Gurdjieff, Ouspensky, the *Bhagavad-Gita*: none of them explained the mysterious force.

I wondered about the *I Ching*, the *Chinese Book of Changes*. In the Haight that book was a Bible. And hadn't Kerouac mentioned it in *Dharma Bums*? I badgered Joe Bob to show me how it worked and finally we sat down in the Hobbit Hole, which was really Bernie's storage room, just down the hall from the Bunker. Joe Bob had cleaned the place, christened it and installed two mattresses. We sat on one each — me smoking grass, him drinking wine.

Joe Bob talked first about how the *I Ching* was an oracle and warned me against consulting it daily, as some people did. He intended to seek its advice only once — on the day he arrived at the Fork in the Road. Until then, he was content to lug it around in his suitcase.

I nodded understanding.

"The idea behind the *Book of Changes*," Joe Bob said, "is that everything's in harmony. Two opposing principals are at work in the universe — male and female, active and passive, creative and destructive. The *I Ching* calls them Yin and Yang."

"Eros and Agape?"

"Oscar's old favorites? Why not? These principals are forces, really, and they push each other back and forth. That's where change comes from — from the interaction between these forces."

"And the name: *Book of Changes*."

"Right. Underneath change, though — and this is the secret — there's order." Joe Bob took another slug of wine. "There's order, only it has nothing to do with cause and effect. Everything's related, see? Everything's in harmony. At any given time, and in any given place, there's only one way things can happen. If I throw a penny into the air and it comes up tails, it's because that's the only way it can possibly come up at that time and place."

"Because everything's in harmony?"

"Exactly. And that's why the *I Ching* can answer questions. It uses the opposites, interprets them, to tap into the encompassing harmony."

Joe Bob began a complicated explanation of how to consult the oracle by tossing pennies into the air and counting how they fall, heads or tails. Only I wasn't listening. What had Charmian Foster said? The same people cropping up in different times, different places.

At the back of my neck, hair tingled. Once I'd been the Near James and here I was, returned to earth. Maybe the other disciples had also returned. Maybe we were gathering to perform some important task. "Joe Bob," I said, when he paused to sip wine, "do you have a favorite disciple?"

"Come again?"

"A favorite among the disciples of Jesus."

He laughed: "Frankie, I don't know about you."

"No, no. Listen, Joe Bob. Peter and James and John. You say everything's in harmony. What about John? You like John?"

"John? Sure. 'In the beginning was the Word, and the Word was with God, and the Word was God.' How's it go? 'In him was life, and the life was the light of men. And the light shineth in the darkness, and the darkness comprehended it not.' Great stuff!"

"That's it, then. You were John!"

"Frankie, what are you talking about?"

"Reincarnation. In a past life, I was James — the Near James. I found out in Pacific Grove. And you were my brother John."

"You mean John, the disciple? I was thinking gospel writer." My face must have spoken because Joe Bob slapped my arm. "John sounds good to me, Frankie. Let's hit the Drugstore. I'll buy you a cheeseburger."

29

On that glorious summer day in 1990, after eating an early lunch in what was once the Drugstore Café, I headed down Masonic into the Panhandle. I swung west through the almost-empty park remembering how dozens of starry-eyed believers would gather here daily to receive food from the Diggers. Where now the psychedelic revolution? I crossed busy Stanyon Street into Golden Gate Park and rambled past Hippie Hill, where with a friend named Misty I'd often sat smoking grass.

I stood a moment — so much I'd forgotten — and checked my map. I followed John F. Kennedy Drive as it wound through the park to the tree-circled Polo Grounds, where one Saturday early in 1967 we'd gathered in the thousands. In my notebook I scribbled: "Half of us, at least, believed a new world was being born. We expected a magical transformation: a miracle. We got the Human Be-In."

The occasion was unprecedented. Woodstock was still two years in the future. This was IT, the largest-ever gathering of The Tribe, more than 20,000 people turning up at the Polo Grounds simply to BE in Golden Gate Park. The Be-In was a counter-culture event — the first with a date attached: January 14, 1967.

Pick up any book about the psychedelic sixties and in it you'll find a paen to the Human Be-In. And rightly. Though at the time, lost in a maze of my own making, I considered it a bust. I remember thinking, as the Be-In wound down around me: "I knew it, I should have left when Oscar did, I should never have waited around."

But all over the Haight I'd seen signs advertising the Be-In and its Beat-Generation stars and so I'd held off, just in case. Now I stood in the trees at the edge of the Polo Grounds sharing a joint with Misty as beautiful people drifted past.

159

I'd arrived early that afternoon, having walked from the Haight, found the field teeming with revellers in robes and costumes, ringing bells and banging tambourines and carrying mirrors and baskets of fruit and banners depicting the holy marijuana leaf. The Diggers were doling out turkey sandwiches at makeshift tables and white-robed acid-heads wandered through the crowd carrying brown paper bags full of LSD. They gave away thousands of tabs donated by the legendary Owsley Stanley: tiny pills called white lighting, the strongest acid yet.

On stage sat the stars of the show: Allen Ginsberg, Lawrence Ferlinghetti, Timothy Leary, Gary Snyder, Lenore Kandel, Michael McClure — everybody but Kerouac. To me that seemed wrong. Where was Jack? Which was why I pocketed and didn't pop a few tabs of white lightning.

Still, I fought my way front and centre and listened while Lenore Kandel read from her recently banned *Love Book*, interested because she'd made a cameo appearance in *Big Sur*. Kandel proclaimed that Love was God of the New Age, and then Timothy Leary was at the microphone, decked out in flowers and beads, daffodil in hand, denouncing fake-prop TV-set America. Drop out of high school, he said. Drop out of college, drop out of grad school, drop out as a junior executive, drop out as a senior executive, drop out and follow me. Finally he sat down on the stage and played patty-cake with a little girl.

The crowd loved it. I was more interested in Gary Snyder, who figures hugely in *Dharma Bums*. The first step, he said, was to detach yourself from the plastic, robot Establishment. He rang a change on Leary: "Drop out, turn on, tune in."

This I'd done. What was the second step? Here was Ginsberg, big black beard and glasses, hollering into the mike, urging us to seek the guru in our hearts and join the psychedelic renaissance. LSD was not the final answer, he said, but a revolutionary catalyst, and everybody who could hear his voice should try it. Every man, woman and child over fourteen should drop acid to induce, once and for all, a collective nervous breakdown in these United States of America.

With this I had no problem. But where was Kerouac? Why wasn't he here? I was still wondering when, as Ginsberg led a Buddhist chant, Misty appeared beside me: "Knew I'd find you at the front."

We moved away from the stage, found a place to sit cross-legged and toke up as rock bands roared on and off stage. Quicksilver Messenger Service, Jefferson Airplane, Big Brother and the Holding Company, The Grateful Dead — later they became huge. Now we lost ourselves in the music. During the Dead's set somebody set off orange flares. A parachutist floated to earth as the sun set and everybody said, "Ahhhhh!"

Was this our promised miracle? This parachutist? Secretly, I'd been hoping still for Kerouac. Why not? Ginsberg was here. Also Snyder, Ferlinghetti, McClure. But as the sun dipped below the horizon and Snyder blew on a conch shell, signalling the end, I had to face it: Kerouac wasn't going to make it. The Human Be-In was a bust.

Ginsberg led a chant to the *Coming Buddha of Love* and urged people to stay and clean up. Hundreds were already picking up garbage. Hundreds more were drifting away home. I stood in the trees with Misty, sharing a joint, wondering how to explain my next move.

Misty I'd met three weeks before at the Diggers' Christmas party. She'd sat down beside me, obviously tripping, and gently touched my face: "You're beautiful, man." She had frizzy, carrot-red hair and no place to stay. I'd taken her home to Bernie's and there she'd remained, more friend than lover since I'd lost interest in sex. Mostly we rambled around the Haight blowing dope.

Misty was three years older than me. She'd studied psychology at Berkeley. The summer before, while hitchhiking late to a class, she'd hopped into a van with three men. They'd driven her out of town and dragged her into some woods. "Please don't hurt me," she'd said. "Don't hurt me and I swear I won't tell."

They'd left her in the bushes, bruised and bleeding. Misty hadn't told. Instead she'd dropped acid. The night she told me this story, I hugged her until morning. But now I had problems of my own. The disciples were gathering in New Orleans. Joe Bob had left on Boxing Day: "See you in Nworlins, Frankie." Oscar had followed the day after New Year's. I didn't know which disciple Oscar had once been, though I wondered about Judas. Anyway, he'd taken a bus out of town. That I couldn't afford.

Now, as the Human Be-In wound down, I told Misty, "If Kerouac had shown up, who knows? But he didn't and the signs point to Nworlins."

"What signs? I don't understand."

"Neither do I, not completely." This business of gathering-disciples was too insane to share, even with Misty. I couldn't quite believe it myself. But, having survived a second tumultuous acid trip a few days back, I clung to it secretly: a thread in the darkness. "I just know I have to go."

"Okay, I'll go with you. I've got a few dollars. I'll buy food, get pots and pans from the Goodwill Store." She looked up at me eagerly, all wet-blue eyes and carrot-red hair. "We'll camp out. You carry, I'll cook."

"I don't know, Misty." I took a last toke, held it, exhaled and popped the roach. "The signs don't say anything about bringing somebody else."

Misty kicked at the grass with a moccasin. "I've got a friend in Los Angeles. We could crash on the way."

"As long as I'm in the right place at the right time," I said, "crash pads will take care of themselves."

Misty had tears in her eyes.

"Okay, okay. Maybe we're meant to visit your friend."

Two days later, early, we rode a city bus to the Great Highway and started hitchhiking. We carried one rucksack, two sleeping bags and a burlap sack containing three tins of spam, a bag of brown rice, a box of quaker oats, half a dozen oranges, an aluminium pot, two bowls, two glasses and some basic utensils. More than I'd bargained for, but I was going with the flow.

By early afternoon we were standing on the highway above Carmel. I was wondering if we were meant to visit Charmian Foster when a big blonde woman, shoulders like a linebacker, picked us up in a station wagon. I told her we were going to Nworlins and she said she'd drive us thirty or forty miles.

Turned out she was going to Los Angeles, but she had several stops to make so she couldn't take us far. Half an hour down the highway she started asking where we wanted out.

This was Big Sur country — nothing but trees, cliffs and sun-dappled ocean. I studied my map. Maybe the woman would change her mind? But no. Instead it was, "Here? What about here?" Finally, on the coast side of the highway, we passed a stone building that looked like an old-fashioned inn but was really a restaurant. Surely, from there, the occasional car would emerge and I said, "Here."

Misty made a face: "Here?"

The strange blonde pulled over and let us out. She squealed her tires as she drove off, left us surrounded by evergreens and silence. The restaurant — which now I know to be the cliff-top "Nepenthe" Kerouac had visited six years before — was a quarter mile back. We waited. Two cars passed going the wrong way. Otherwise, nothing but silence.

I needed a leak, walked down the highway, stepped into some bushes. Standing there, I noticed a dirt road — an old fire road, by the look of it — winding down through some woods towards the ocean. A padlocked gate blocked the entrance and a sign said: "Private: Keep Out."

Misty liked the idea of camping near the ocean but balked when she saw the sign. I tossed my rucksack over the gate and climbed after it: "The fact that we're here is another kind of sign."

Misty shrugged and followed. The fire road wound downhill, thick with pine needles, overgrown with grass. Evergreens shut out the sky. We stopped to rest and heard water running — a stream? The road became two rutted tracks. Misty twisted her ankle. "Let's forget it," she said, wincing. "Go back up and hitch until dark."

"No way, I'm not quitting." I strode ahead. "This road can't go down forever."

Abruptly, I hit level ground. The track became a footpath. I trotted into a clearing, found myself in a valley between two steep hills, almost cliffs. The woods hid the highway. Now the stream ran loud. A few steps more and there it was, tumbling across the path near a circle of rocks — a fire pit. In it lay half a dozen blackened tin cans. Beyond, almost lost in the evergreens, leaned a pine-bough shelter. "Misty! We've found Shangri-la!"

"Incredible," she said, catching up. "How'd you know this place was here?"

Modestly, I shrugged: "Just followed the signs."

We dropped our gear, followed the path along the stream to a grassy knoll and stood in the wind looking out at the ocean. The waves were three feet high. We picked our way down onto the rocky beach, threw off our clothes and waded into the water, freezing cold. Misty climbed onto a rock and stood naked, the wind whipping her hair into a carrot-red mane. Startled at her beauty, unsettled by her womanliness, I plunged into the January ocean.

Back at the shelter I unrolled our sleeping bags and zipped them together, then built a fire. Misty cooked up a pot of rice and spam. We ate and washed the dishes in the stream, then sat and watched the fire burn to ashes. The embers looked like the lights of a city seen from high above. We crawled into our sleeping bags and made love.

Next morning, over porridge, we agreed the ocean was too cold for swimming. I wanted to loaf around camp and read about Taoism and Lao Tzu. But Misty wanted to get back on the road. I said nobody would be guided into Shangri-la one day just to leave the next. But she worried about our trespassing. Grudgingly, I relented.

By the time we'd broken camp the sun was above the trees, the day too hot to be perfect. We started up the path, stopped at the clearing to take a last look around. Might be faster, I realized, to climb one of the hills to the highway. Misty wasn't so sure but yes, yes, I insisted, it'll be faster. And when I started up the easier-looking face, she followed.

At first the slope was no problem: hard ground, long grass, forty-degree angle. Then the grass became sand, shrubs and bushes and the hill almost a cliff. Misty said I was climbing too fast so I took her awkwardly bundled sleeping bag, slung it over my shoulder and pushed on.

164

Gradually, I drew ahead. Soon I forgot everything except the cliff, the sun beating down and the sweat rolling off me. Fifteen minutes up I hit a loose, sandy spot. I scrambled upwards breathing hard and stopped to wipe my face only when the worst was behind me.

Misty called: "Frankie! It's too tough. Let's turn back."

"We're almost there," I hollered. "Can't turn back now."

Again I began beating my way up the cliff. My rucksack was heavy and Misty's bag awkward but I wouldn't quit. Root by root, I clawed my way upwards. Finally I hauled myself over a ledge onto level ground and, puffing, stood up. Before me — why was I surprised? — sat the restaurant we'd passed on the highway. Nepenthe.

Trouble was, a dense thicket stood between me and the restaurant's empty patio — a dense, chest-high thicket of thorn bushes maybe thirty yards deep. I tried going one way, then the other. Finally, I scrambled down the cliff and came up in another spot, working hard. The thicket was waiting.

I tried using my rucksack as a shield, ramming my way forward. Cut my arms, my hands. I flailed at the thicket with my rucksack: *whack! whack! whack!* then stood breathing hard, fists clenched. I could see the restaurant, the patio chairs stacked neatly in piles. The highway was beyond. But I couldn't get through. We'd have to go all the way back down and take the road.

I hollered for Misty. She didn't respond and I yelled again. This time she shouted back, but from strangely far away. Then I spotted her kneeling by the stream, happily waving a washcloth. She'd gone back down without telling me. Here I stood, hot and sweaty from having tried to beat a way through a thicket for both of us, or so I told myself, and Misty was down by the stream.

I grabbed my rucksack and the sleeping-bag bundle and started scrambling down the hillside. This was faster than coming up but not fast enough for me. I flung my rucksack into the air, watched it roll and bounce down the cliff into a clump of bushes. Down I went after it in great, skating strides, sand pouring into my shoes. I reached my pack and flung it again, watched it bounce and bang down the hill, throwing off clouds of dust.

Finally, sweating and furious, I reached the stream. Misty was drying herself on a towel. "Poison oak up there," she said. "Better wash. Here's some soap."

I grunted, waved away the soap and emptied my shoes of sand. I drank from the stream, splashed water over my face and hands, then picked up my rucksack and Misty's sleeping bag. "It's getting late," I said, and led the way, silent, up the fire road.

We dumped our gear at the side of the empty highway. No cars coming either way. Misty wandered down the road and stood tossing stones into the trees. Her arm was surprisingly good. I sat down on my rucksack. In my anger I'd ignored Misty all the way up the fire road, but now I watched her throw stones: frizzy, carrot-red hair, an old workshirt three sizes too big, tired jeans wearing through in the seat. Suddenly I had tears in my eyes. I joined Misty and threw a couple of stones myself. "You wait and see," I said. "Some guy'll come around that corner, take us all the way to Nworlins."

"Frankie, I'm thinking of going back to the Haight." She tossed a last stone. "We've got no money, no food. I haven't seen my friend since college. What if —"

"Go with the flow, Misty. How do you think we found Shangri-la? Nothing can go wrong if we follow the signs."

"All right, let's hitch both ways. Whichever way we get a ride, that's the way we're supposed to go."

"We're supposed to go to Nworlins."

"Maybe not right away. In the Haight I could make a couple of deals. Get some bread together. Then we could leave again."

"The signs are pointing south now."

"Says who? Let's hitch both ways and see."

I looked up and down the highway. If we were in the right place at the right time, it would be impossible to get a ride back to the Haight. Except that fifteen minutes later, when an old white panel truck shuddered to a stop in front of us, it was heading north — back towards San Francisco. The driver said, "Hop in."

He was fifty, maybe fifty-five, wore baggy grey trousers and a crinkled white shirt. Hadn't shaved in three days. "Where you goin?"

"We were going to Nworlins," I said. "First stop Los Angeles."

"Los Angeles?" The driver looked from me to Misty and back again. "You want to go to L.A.?"

"That's where we were going," I said. "Couldn't get a ride."

"Hell, I'll take you to Los Angeles, that's where you want to go. San Francisco, Los Angeles. It's all the same to me."

I raised my eyebrows at Misty but she turned and looked out the window. The choice was mine. "Uh, Los Angeles," I said. "If it's all the same to you, let's go to Los Angeles."

The driver didn't stop. Just slowed down and made a U-turn and again we were heading south. I said, "Fantastic!"

Misty stared out the window. After a few minutes, the driver leaned forward, looked over at Misty. "Sure a lucky fella, have a little lady like her. Hey!" He called around me over the roar of the engine. "What's your name, anyways?"

"Misty."

"Misty? Mine's Hap."

"Mine's Frankie."

"Pleased to meet you. Hey, Misty. You wanna sit in the middle here."

"I'm okay, thanks."

"Suit yourself." Hap sat back in his seat. "Lemme know if you change your mind."

Hap launched into a monologue about the importance of having friends and I admired the scenery: to the right, trails winding along cliff-faces, and to the left, the vast Pacific, its waves splashing white over the brown and black rocks that lined the coast.

Hap was talking about an older guy who'd picked up a couple of hippies. "They all became buddies. Started living together, having good times."

I looked over at Misty but she was leaning against the window, her eyes closed. I couldn't get comfortable, kept crossing and uncrossing my legs. The truck started rattling at sixty miles per hour — Hap demonstrated — and so, at fifty-five, we droned into evening. Headlights came on. I started to nod and Hap nudged me, said I'd be more comfortable by the window. "Misty won't mind sitting in the middle."

"Misty's asleep." I gritted my teeth and willed my eyes to stay open. After another hour Hap pulled into a restaurant, said, "Let's get some grub."

In my pocket I had pennies and dimes — all that remained of our money. "If it's okay with you, we'll wait here."

"What's the matter, no dough?" Hap looked around me at Misty. "If'n I had a little lady like you, Misty, I'd know how to take care of her." He got out on his side of the truck, then stuck his head back in. "Come on, the both of you. It's on me."

Over hamburgers, french fries and coffees all round, Hap talked only to Misty. Wanted to know where she came from, what her parents did — teachers, both — how she'd met me. I went to the washroom. When I came back Misty was telling a story about growing up in Fresno and both she and Hap were laughing. I relaxed a bit, took my time with my coffee.

All night long we drove, Hap at the wheel. Misty dozed fitfully. She was willing to sit in the middle but I was bent on being the Protector. Tried to stay awake, to "yeah" and "uh-huh" Hap into thinking I was following his non-stop monologue, which had two themes: that hippies and old-timers had more in common than I realized, and that I was a lucky fellow to be with a lady like Misty, and if Hap had someone like her, he'd know how to take care of her.

Was this ride never going to end?

Just after midnight the radiator boiled over. Hap carried a can of water in back but we had to sit on the side of the highway until the engine cooled. Twice we left the highway for coffee. The third time, at a truck stop, Hap bought us steak and eggs. Not a bad guy, I decided — if only he'd quit hustling Misty.

The sun was coming up when we reached Los Angeles. But hallelujah! Misty dug out her friend's address. I checked the map, found the street and showed Hap. He knew the area, said he'd take us to the door. Half an hour later, with traffic beginning to build, we pulled up in front of a dilapidated rooming house.

All three of us piled out of the truck. Hap and I stretched our legs while Misty went to the door and rang a bell. She rang three times. Finally the door opened and she went inside. A few minutes later she reappeared, looking glum: "My friend moved out months ago. Didn't leave a forwarding address."

"No forwarding address? Did you check the phone book?"

"Yes and she's not there. I also phoned and asked about new listings." Misty kicked at the sidewalk. "I don't know, Frankie. No money. No place to crash. Maybe we should go to Fresno. Stay with my folks a while."

"Fresno? That's back the other way."

Hap said: "You want to go to Fresno, Misty? No problem."

"Come on, Frankie. We can get some money together, then go to New Orleans."

"But we're halfway to Nworlins now!"

"Have you looked at a map lately? You go ahead if you want, Frankie. I'm going to Fresno."

"Sure, go ahead," Hap said. "I'll take Misty to Fresno, no problem."

I took Misty by the arm and led her down the sidewalk.

Hap stood leaning against the truck.

"Listen, Misty," I said. "You can't go to Fresno with that guy! He's dangerous."

"Hap? He's just a lonely man who needs company."

"Yeah, sure. And those three guys who picked you up in Berkeley were lonely, too."

Misty flushed. "I can't skulk around forever because of one bad experience. If you're so worried, why don't you come with me? We can leave again when we have some money."

"Listen, Misty, the disciples are gathering in Nworlins. I should be there."

"What disciples? What are you talking about?"

"Oh, never mind." It sounded insane, even to me. "Give me a moment, will you?"

Across the street an empty building site was strewn with rubble, overgrown with grass. I walked out into the vacant lot, dug a rusty tin can out of the dirt with my toe and stomped on it. What was Misty trying to do? I shoved my hands into my pockets and jingled the last of our money. Misty and Hap were leaning against the side of the truck, eating popcorn out of a brown paper bag. I couldn't leave Misty alone with this guy. But Fresno? No way the disciples were gathering in Fresno.

Now I understood why Joe Bob carried the *I Ching* everywhere. This was a Fork In The Road. But wait a minute. Maybe I didn't need the *I Ching* to see which way the signs were pointing. Yin and Yang were always active. I fumbled the coins out of my pocket and, in my cupped hands, shook them like dice. There was only one way these coins could fall at this time and place. All I had to do was interpret their meaning. If more coins came up heads, I was supposed to go to Fresno with Misty. If more came up tails, I was meant to leave her with Hap and go on to Nworlins.

I tossed the coins into the air, watched them fall to the ground, bent over and counted: one, two, three heads. And tails? One, two, three. I counted again. Three heads, three tails. Couldn't be right. I kneeled, searched the dirt. Nothing. The signs weren't pointing either way. How could that be? Still on my hands and knees, I looked up at the sky. Choice! I had a choice to make.

Finally I stood, pocketed the coins and looked over at the truck. Misty waved. Hap was standing at her elbow, talking, still talking. Maybe the disciples were gathering in Nworlins. But no way I could leave Misty alone with this guy. I walked back across the lot and climbed into the truck. "Let's go to Fresno."

30

Rain spattered the tower windows and thunder rumbled through the Rockies. I lay in darkness, my jacket an uncomfortable pillow, and savored ironies. Four years before, in November of 1966, when Frankie had rolled into the Haight-Ashbury chasing his larger-than-life Kerouac, a yea-saying Canuck who roared back and forth across the continent with wild-eyed buddies, or else sat cross-legged and alone, seeking enlightenment on mountain-tops like this one, the real me was back in New England, fat and old and red-faced and lonesome, marrying the virgin Saint Stella of the Cross, real name Stavroula Sampatacacus, so she would take care of my newly paralyzed mother.

And two months later? When Ginsberg, Ferlinghetti, Snyder, Leary and the rest were chanting *om sri maitreya* into the setting sun, and Frankie half-heartedly with them, disappointed that I hadn't parachuted as a Human into the Be-In? Why, I was late-night drinking in Lowell, sitting in my old-home-town living room with a Canuck buddy, ridiculing those media darlings the hippies for trying to storm the gates of heaven — later I tempered this judgment — and denouncing Timothy Leary as a fraud and a charlatan, a verdict I never did soften, damning him not only for his Pied-Pipering but for my own psychedelic bummer, a magic-mushroom descent-into-a-maelstrom I barely survived.

From out of nowhere, as if to end this savoring of ironies, came a flash of Frankie's father stumbling as he emerged from La Fin de Monde into the Ste. Thérèse sunshine. That swept me, sobered, back to Jubilation, where between lightning and thunder I counted nine seconds. What was the factor? Six seconds per mile? Again the sky lit up. I counted seven and thunder cracked. I focused on Frankie huddled in bed and chuckled as he rose grumpily to pull on his clothes and dash through the storm.

I crawled out of my bag. In the darkness, by touch, I found a candle. I lit it on third try, as Frankie arrived and began pounding on the underside of the trap door. "Kerouac! Open up!"

"Where have you been?" I helped him into the tower. "I've been watching the light-show for hours."

"The hell you have." With the inside of his arm he wiped his forehead, then jerked his thumb at the candle. "I'd have seen the light."

Frankie sat down at the table-top and flipped open a notebook. I stood beside him and for the next half-hour we watched the storm worsen. Wind howled through the valley and rain smashed the windows in waves. The tower creaked and groaned and Frankie glanced at me in the flickering candle light. Whenever lightning struck he'd scribble a note about where. But mostly, like me, he stared at our reflections in the windows, waiting for flashes to light up the valley and marvelling at the ferocity of the storm.

Again I found myself thinking San Francisco, only this time it was late fall, 1952. My affair with Carolyn Cassady had led to jealousy and reprisal and I was living like a hermit in the Cameo Hotel, corner Third and Howard. I was making $600 a month as a railroad brakeman, living on $17 a week and sending the rest to Mémère. In my room I had nothing but Bibles to read — one left by the Gideons, the other a tiny, hand-sized New Testament I'd stolen from a Fourth Avenue bookstore, the Used Religious Books section, after the owner tried to cheat me in a trade. When too tired to write, I'd lie on my bed and read about Jesus.

Standing now in the tower on Jubilation, I remembered my feeling of being attacked by words, buffeted by ideas and revelations. The Bible itself, I decided, by reflecting an unbroken continuity of poets and prophets through Time, and so making concrete a literary tradition extending over centuries and having a beginning, a middle and an end, a discernible order, the Bible itself proved the existence of God.

To Frankie I said, "I just realized why I found solace in the Bible long after my favorite Zen koans lost their power. It was that

172

unbroken continuity through Time, that unprecedented parade of poets and prophets, seers and saints."

"Hey, why not?" Frankie said as he scribbled a note. "You've already told me you're a masturbating saint, Roman-Catholic variety."

Out popped W. C. Fields: "Close, my boy, but no cigar." Back I came: "I'm still on the road, Frankie — not yet a saint and not exclusively Roman Catholic or even Christian. I sing the crucifix but also the Star of David. I sing the *Tao Te Ching* and the *Tibetan Book of the Dead*, the *Vedas*, the *Koran* and the *Avesta*. I sing alchemy and individuation, Bach and Picasso, Carl Jung and James Joyce. I sing the beatific consciousness and the ananda state in which one enters into immediate relations with the Absolute. Truth is One, Frankie, though saints and sages call it many things."

"You're out of your skull."

"In the One World Church of Yesterday's Tomorrow, which in the Golden Eternity is always with us, myriad are the kinds of saints." Even to myself I sounded like a mad revivalist, but this was my story and I stuck to it. "The Christians among them emerge from the ranks of nuns and priests, seers and monks and prophets. And the Mahayana Buddhist saints, the so-called bodhisattvas, are near relatives — though not Christian."

"Wait! I remember! The Arhat enters into nirvana, but the bodhisattva, whose essence is perfect wisdom, returns to relieve others of suffering and illusion, right?"

"Frankie, you surprise me."

"What disturbs me is the reek of self-righteousness."

"You mean the idea of karma?"

Lightning stabbed a nearby mountain and Frankie scribbled a note. "Where was I? Karma says, 'I'm spiritually advanced enough to seek enlightenment because I've lived wisely during countless past lives. You're a thief and a low-life beggar because you've sinned shamefully.'"

"Smug and self-righteous, no question."

"A second ago you were singing bodhisattvas."

"There's no room in the Golden Eternity, Frankie, for the dogmatism of earth."

"Your Eternity's full of holes."

"So what? Buddhism's designed for a specific audience. Consistent within itself, it's at once a spiritual philosophy and a work of art through Time. It's an elaborate construction, a glorious intellectual edifice."

"Like Christianity, only foreign."

"Which brings us to Timelessness, where consistency doesn't always suffice. Where to achieve sainthood, and so join the great parade, you must prove that others perceive holiness in you.

"No danger of that with Kerouac."

"You think not? Saints are simply heroes who have given themselves to God. Some saints establish an ethical standard: Gandhi, say, or Francis of Assissi. But not all embody a superior morality. Some are great teachers — think of Augustine, of Thomas Aquinas. Others are mystics like Edgar Cayce, Neal Cassady's favorite. Others still are prophets: Nostradamus, Mohammed."

"And wait, let me guess! Jack Kerouac — the Great Walking Saint!"

I sniffed: "I'm registered in that category, yes."

"Why am I listening to this stuff?"

"Better than staring into the void?"

Lightning cracked an eggshell across the sky and thunder exploded overhead. "Now I remember." Frankie scratched a note in his log. "I need all the distractions I can get."

"Don't worry, the tower's grounded. I checked. Even if we're hit directly, the lightning will just go 'psssst' and shoot down the wires into the ground."

"Where were we? Still on the road?"

"These days, many religions and churches simply proclaim their saints — the Eastern Orthodox Church, for example. Other institutions are even less formal. But eventually, a variation on the Roman Catholic process wins out: 'B and C,' we call it."

"Okay, I give up."

174

"Beatification and canonization. It's a tricky business. Part One requires two witnesses: a postulate of the cause, who makes the case for sainthood, and a devil's advocate, who reveals the sinner's underbelly."

"These two characters stand before a tribunal and thrash it out?"

"Metaphorically, yes. But this happens in Heaven, Frankie. It's a matter of record."

"You've spent time on this."

"In my case the postulate of the cause is a biographer — or will be. Some time during the next fifteen years, a man named Gerald Nicosia will publish a biography citing the visions, the miracles, the religious poems. Showing how beat means beatific. He'll sing *Dr. Sax* as the first postmodern novel and make the case for yours truly as a hillbilly scholar and hokey, come-as-you-are saint."

"And the devil's advocate?"

"An English professor from old Stinktown on the Merrimack — a man named Charles Jarvis. In Time he'll testify first. Even as we speak he's scribbling away at his nasty palimpsest, poking around in the dark corners of my sometimes squalid life."

"You're talking masturbation."

"Much worse, I'm afraid. Jarvis will portray me as an obnoxious megalomaniac. He'll ridicule my accomplishments as a football player, claim I owe them to my father. He'll attack my image as a sailor. My visions he'll attribute to my brother, Gerard."

"And from there it gets darker."

"Bigotry. Male chauvinism. Sexual perversity. He'll quote Ginsberg on my love for black panties, garter belts and stockings."

"Now we're getting somewhere."

"Jarvis will be graphic about certain embarrassing homosexual episodes and far from reticent about my drunkenness. He'll weep crocodile tears, lamenting that a bright-eyed Endymion came to such an end, to living out his final days as a loud-mouth booze-hound in fatigue pants, dirty workshirt and hunter's cap."

"But you look great! How —" Frankie slapped his forehead. "What am I saying?"

"Fortunately, Nicosia wins the argument."

"And you're beatified. Presto!"

"Well, three miracles enter into it. But I've described those."

"Ah, the miracles." Frankie rubbed his chin, playing along. "Those you worked during your earthly life-time." He thought he had me. "To count towards beatification, however, miracles must be accomplished after death."

"You amaze me, Frankie. In the Roman Catholic church, yes, that's true. But in the One World Church of Yesterday's Tomorrow, temporal order and the death of the body mean a great deal less."

"I'm glad you didn't say nothing."

"So you should be — because this is where you enter the tapestry."

"I'm not entering anything."

"Frankie, what if I need your help? As ex-King of the Beats, I'm venerated. And I've been beatified. But I've yet to be canonized. I'm still on the road to Great Walking Sainthood. And your hunch isn't far off. I've yet to accomplish my first posthumous miracle."

Before Frankie could respond, lightning clawed its way towards us through the sky. Then the world exploded. The tower shook and we tumbled to the floor. The candle guttered out.

"Frankie, you okay?"

"*Ciboire!*"

"Please, no blasphemy. You want to get hit again?"

"*Câlisse de tabernac d'hostie de saint ciboire de saint sacripant!*"

Still on my hands and knees, but getting into the spirit of Frankie's rebellion, I shouted into the engulfing blackness: "You! Hey, you! I dare you to do that again!" Nothing happened. "*Baptême!*" I added. "*Saint hostie de calvaire!*" Still nothing. I cut loose with my scariest Shadow laugh: "*Mweee heee heee haa haa haa!*"

"Jesus! Enough of that."

"The Shadow knows!"

"Like hell he does. The Shadow said the tower was grounded. That even a direct hit would zip harmlessly into the ground."

"Guess it depends."

"Wait!" Frankie snapped his fingers. "I've got it. This was your posthumous miracle! You've saved our lives!"

"No miracle, Frankie. At best a cut-rate synchronicity. Sometimes I despair of you."

"Do me a favor, Kerouac. Until this storm blows over, no more talk of sainthood."

31

Obviously we can't conduct tests. But alcoholism has a pathology, a series of stages through which it passes. With Kerouac, and this is unusual, we have enough detail to identify those stages. Trace the pathology of the illness."

So Camille declared, autumn of 1989, as we hiked up Tunnel Mountain. Recently she'd been reading around in my Kerouac library, refusing to explain. Now she was talking. A few moments before, as we'd started up the winding path — blessedly empty, the tourist season over — she'd rehearsed her now-familiar rap about alcoholism, which she called Jellinek's Disease.

She'd memorized a book called *Alcoholism: The Genetic Inheritance*, and claimed that the alcoholic inherits an irregular body chemistry. Initially, this "deviant metabolism" induces an unusually high tolerance. But, in the alcoholic, drinking kicks off a chemical process, a chain reaction that leads to the production of an addictive substance in the brain.

Camille could talk in mind-numbing detail about how this heroin-like substance, TIQ, attaches itself to opiate receptors in the brain. "Soon, to function properly, these brain-cell membranes need alcohol. They scream for it. You drink to shut them up. Your TIQ level increases and your cell membranes grow thicker. They scream for more and more alcohol. You drink to avoid withdrawal. So begins the cycle of addiction."

Usually, when Camille began this rap, I tuned her out. But now, as we wound up Tunnel Mountain above the Banff School of Fine Arts, where she taught, I discovered that she'd found a new angle. "The early stages of the disease go unremarked, as with Kerouac, because who worries about an increasing tolerance for alcohol? It's not until the middle stages that radical changes occur and affect behaviour. By then the alcoholic's brain cells are so distorted that they feel comfortable only when alcohol is present."

"This you see in Kerouac?"

Camille nodded: "The key signal is loss of control. With Kerouac I'd point to 1952, when he provided a vivid example. Tragic Saturday in Frisco?"

February 8, 1952. My own fifth birthday. Kerouac had been living with the Cassadys — with Neal, Carolyn and their three children. Staying in the attic of their house on Russian Hill. He had burlap curtains and a paisley bedspread and from his makeshift desk he could hear cable-cars ringing up and down Hyde Street.

Though they weren't yet lovers, Jack was falling in love with Carolyn, and when Neal was out working on the railway, they'd ramble around North Beach and Chinatown. Early in February, 1952, during one of these walks, they planned a quiet dinner to celebrate Neal's birthday, February eighth, just the three of them.

Come the afternoon of the big night, while returning home from his part-time job as a brakeman, Kerouac ducked into "absolutely the wildest bar in America," corner of Third and Howard, for one quick drink. You want the sordid details? They're all in *Visions of Cody* in a description Kerouac wrote first as a letter, never sent, to his writer-friend John Clellon Holmes.

Yes, he got talking with a couple of hookers. But mainly he took that first drink. And then a second and a third, and when he looked up it was nearly midnight and he'd missed Old Neal's party and he telephoned home ("Come on, Neal, let's celebrate your birthday") and precipitated a disaster.

But the loss of control. That's what Camille was underscoring. Kerouac himself, she said, knew why he'd lost control: "That new dedication in *The Town and the City*? The key phrase was 'all because I got drunk.'"

I remembered. In a copy of the novel he'd already given Carolyn, Kerouac now scrawled: "With the deepest apologies I can offer for the fiasco, the foolish tragic Saturday of Neal's birthday, all because I got drunk. Please forgive me, Carolyn, it'll never happen again."

I said, "You've done your homework."

Camille nodded but didn't miss a beat. "Why did Kerouac lose control? Because in February, 1952, not yet thirty, he was entering the middle stages of alcoholism."

We paused at a switchback so I could catch my breath, and as we looked out over Banff townsite, our rented house visible through a stand of evergreens, Camille said: "In the middle stages, any drinking kicks off a chemical reaction. This translates as a physical demand for alcohol — a craving. Once you take that first drink, you can't stop drinking."

She held up a fist and counted her fingers open and closed: "Blackouts, reduced tolerance, extravagant behaviour, guilt and remorse, periods of abstinence, geographic flight, morbid self-pity, unreasonable resentments, hospitalization — I've missed something But they're all middle-stage symptoms. And all were present, through the fifties, in Kerouac."

As we resumed hiking, rounding the corner to the back of Tunnel Mountain, Camille cited specifics. In San Francisco, 1953, while getting ready to ship out as a steward on a vessel bound for Panama, Kerouac went on an all-night binge, downed thirty beers and ten whiskeys and set sail in a shuddering alcoholic void feeling his "nerve-ends being slowly living deathly cut in the center of the gut."

By 1954, Kerouac was admitting in letters that he was "weak for booze," and in 1957, while visiting England, he drank so much that he shocked an old friend from college. Back in New York, more than once he got beaten up in Greenwich Village bars. That same year, after *On the Road* appeared, Kerouac wrote Neal Cassady that he was "drunk all the time — no more wine, just whiskey."

Camille showed no signs of ending this litany: "By 1959, Kerouac often drank until he passed out. That's extravagant, unless —"

"We know Kerouac drank, Camille. But he had reasons. He felt guilty when Neal Cassady was jailed for possession, believed

On The Road had played a role. And look at Mémère. Forever on his case, destroying his friendships, scaring away women — even sending poison pen letters."

"Rationalizations, Frankie. That's the symptom I missed."

"Oh, and the critics! One national magazine said Kerouac was "simply ignorant." Another called him a cut-rate Thomas Wolfe. Then came the heavyweights, jealous of the attention he was getting, everyone from John Updike and Herbert Gold to Kenneth Rexroth and Norman Podhoretz and Truman Capote, with his famous zinger: 'That's not writing, that's typewriting.' You wonder why Kerouac drank?"

"Frankie, you're not listening. All that envious back-stabbing merely gave Kerouac another excuse. By 1959 he was drinking a quart of whiskey a day and having frequent blackouts. That's another key signal."

"Blackouts? Of what?"

"The end of the middle stages. The physical addiction is complete. Now the body needs alcohol. And withdrawal causes distress. Abstinence is no longer possible. Going cold turkey can cause shaking and sweating and even tremors, delusions, hallucinations. Delerium tremens."

"The dread DTs."

"You got it. With Kerouac I'd point to 1960. That's when he reached the end of the middle stages. His breakdown in Bixby Canyon?"

At that I spun out, remembering. As he entered the new decade, Kerouac rallied. He resolved to write a novel about the past three years, to explore his disillusionment. Instead of visiting New York City and its bars, he rambled suburban Northport, gathering himself. Ready to write, he popped the old reliable benzedrine tablets — but then just paced his workroom, his mind roiling, unable to work. He organized files and wrote brooding letters. Between the lines they cried: Help!

From San Francisco, Lawrence Ferlinghetti responded by offering Kerouac the use of his cabin at Bixby Canyon, just down the coast from Monterey. Ferlinghetti had undertaken to publish

Book of Dreams and Kerouac could edit the work at Bixby. Why not? Late in July, Kerouac rode a train to California.

In San Francisco, despite an elaborate plan to avoid old drinking buddies, Kerouac went straight to City Lights Bookstore and then across the alley to Vesuvio's, and so began his California sojourn with a two-day binge. Eventually, down in Bixby Canyon one full-moon Saturday night, he went mad. He describes the experience in *Big Sur*, evokes the full screaming horrors, complete with demons, jibbering voices and visions of hell.

To Camille I said, "You think that was delerium tremens?"

"Believe it. What's amazing, and also revealing, is that the biographers remain baffled by this 'nervous breakdown.' Even Tom Clark, who's usually so clear, fails to spell out the cold-turkey connection, and to link this 'nervous breakdown' with the alcohol withdrawal that caused it."

"Maybe there is no connection. Maybe your theory is nuts."

"Frankie, Kerouac lays it out in *Big Sur*. Having made it to Bixby Canyon, he drank whiskey and sweet red wine until not a drop remained. Remember how he wakes up to the final horrors — and the last bottle gone? He even mentions delerium tremens by name, says it's not a physical pain but a mental anguish."

I was growing tired of this but Camille wouldn't stop. "Late in the novel, Kerouac's alter-ego is stumbling around 'stupefacted, trembling and sweating.' His buddy asks if he wants to go to a nearby restaurant, Nepenthe, for a drink. Our boy says no —"

"And ends up shivering on his cot in the cabin, assaulted by visions of hell and relieved only by the Cross of Jesus. Camille, I know the novel."

"Also: 'trying to squeeze the last red drop out of the rancid port bottle.'"

"So what are you trying to prove?"

"Just that Kerouac suffered from Jellinek's Disease. Bixby marks the end of the middle stages, the beginning of the end."

"Jellinek's, Jellinek's!" For the first time in the hike I strode ahead. "Who gives a damn?"

32

Repentance implies sacrifice. That much the program had right. But the Higher Power business? That bothered me. So I reflected in San Francisco, summer of 1990, as I hiked through Golden Gate Park towards the ocean, pondering the famous twelve steps. One, admit you're powerless. Two, believe only a Higher Power can restore you to sanity. Three, turn over your life to God as you understand him. Four, make a searching and fearless moral inventory.

For "Higher Power" a Jungian might substitute the single word Self. Still, the first seven steps, at least, could be neatly summarized: Christian repentance. And who needed irrationality? I scribbled a note: "Higher Power repentance the central dynamic. But if alcoholism is a disease, what about diabetes? Are diabetics required to make fearless moral inventories?"

Golden Gate Park was bigger than I remembered, more than three miles across, but I contemplated repentance and scribbled notes until I saw the Dutch windmill that heralded Ocean Beach. Then I broke into a trot. I emerged from the park and crossed the four-lane Great Highway, pausing briefly on the steps that led to the beach to stare, remembering, at warning signs painted on the cement wall: "Drownings occur due to heavy surf and severe undertow." And, "PLEASE REMAIN SAFELY ON SHORE — U.S. Park Police 556-7940."

On the beach I removed my shoes and socks and waded into the water up to my knees. I stood in the surf and foam, waves rolling past me, and remembered the last time I'd stood here — what? more than two decades before? — one wild and starless night in 1967.

A night of repentance.

From Fresno I'd returned, alone, a couple of weeks before. Discovered Bernie's Bunker thick with strangers, and even the Hobbit Hole occupied. My third night back, Bernie flipped out like Ruth the Painter before him, stood on his bed in jockey shorts and green cowboy hat yelling that he'd grown tired of working all day at the post office so freeloaders could sit around blowing dope, and everybody but Bonnie Torn could get the hell out.

A few moments later, Bernie announced a second exception — ah, the ethos of the Haight — but I felt compelled to show solidarity with the ousted, most of whom I hardly knew, and kept stuffing gear into my rucksack. I spent that night on a bench in the Panhandle, and subsequent ones at either the Free Frame of Reference, a Digger-run crash pad, or at the Hare Krishna temple next door. Both were elbow-to-elbow sleeping bags and noisy into the wee hours, but better than sleeping in the rain.

At Bernie's, just by being around at meal-time, I'd eaten regularly. Now I discovered the importance of the Diggers. Every day at four o'clock, two or three guys would turn up at the Panhandle in an old Dodge truck. They brought garbage cans, presumably pristine, full of hot cabbage soup. You presented your bowl and they doled it out free, along with chunks of day-old, crusty bread.

One afternoon, as I waited, hungry, at the usual spot, I found myself wondering whether, back there in Los Angeles, I'd made the right choice. Since returning to the Haight I'd seen not a single sign. When I wasn't thinking food, I rambled the streets wondering why this might be. The wrong choice?

A few miles out of Los Angeles, Hap yakking non-stop, I'd let Misty sit in the middle. She and Hap talked while I stared out the window, my mind whirring. Joe Bob had said everything was in harmony — and so predetermined. How, then, could I have made a choice in that vacant lot? If I'd made a real choice, then Joe Bob had been wrong. And I'd been wrong about Joe Bob. That meant the disciples were NOT gathering in Nworlins. Which made sense because the Near James was heading for Fresno.

This satisfied me until I found myself scratching my neck for the third time and realized I was itchy all over: my neck, my arms, my hands, my face. Misty took one look and said, "Poison oak. You'll need cortisone shots. Don't worry, I know a doctor."

Hap pulled into a gas station and I went to the washroom. Hot water eased the itching and I stood patting my face with wet paper towel. What would have happened, I wondered, if I'd left Misty with Hap and made for Nworlins? Instead of being safely on my way to a doctor in Fresno, I'd be crazy with itch on the highway south of Los Angeles. Frantic with poison oak, alone with a few lousy coins in my pocket. I grinned at the queer, puffy face in the mirror. I'd made the right choice.

In Fresno, Hap said goodbye with tears in his eyes. Misty made peace with her parents, high-school teachers both, who'd been worried about her. They let me sleep in their guest room. Somewhere, Misty found money for cortisone shots. After a couple of days, the poison oak disappeared. Misty drove me to the highway in her mother's car. She was thinking about returning to Berkeley: "Maybe they did know something, those academics."

At the highway, when she kissed me goodbye, Misty cried. I realized I'd never see her again. But I didn't let it touch me. I didn't cry until years later, when I began to understand.

Back in the Haight, I reasoned that if, in that vacant lot, I'd made a right choice, then I'd avoided a wrong one. Yin-Yang. Nworlins would have been the wrong choice. But maybe, in that time and place, being who I was, I could not have made the wrong choice. Maybe that was how events were predetermined. You had a choice but, being who you were, there was only one choice you could make. Joe Bob had been right. That meant he was my brother John. And the disciples were gathering, after all, in Nworlins.

Round and round I went until the day the Diggers' travelling soup kitchen failed to arrive at the Panhandle. My stomach aching with hunger, again I found myself wondering whether, back there in Los Angeles, I'd made the right choice. I emptied my shirt pockets looking for change — and turned up a tab of acid. White lightning from the Human Be-In. Discovering this tab now was a sign. To see clearly, I needed another trip.

Evening was falling when I popped.

I walked off the initial rush, which made me feel nauseous, in Golden Gate Park. Next thing I knew, the sky was dark. A light rain was falling. I stood in a circle of blowing palm trees. If the disciples were gathering in Nworlins, what was the Near James doing in the Haight? Maybe Charmian Foster had lied. Maybe I'd never been the Near James. But what about Munsie the barber?

Looking up into the gathering storm, suddenly overwhelmed, I addressed the mysterious force: "Please! I don't know who you are, or what, but I can't take any more of this confusion!" I was crying. I fell to my knees. "Please! I'll go anywhere, I'll do anything, only please, I can't take any more of this, I just can't take it any more!"

Oscar stood leaning against a palm tree, shaking his head. "Don't you remember, Frankie? The Seventeen Scale? You have to die and be born again."

Then he was gone.

I stumbled to my feet and trotted off towards the ocean. Golden Gate Park was alive. I was part of a living tapestry. I couldn't see the whole pattern, but now at least I knew what next. In the distance, and then not so far away, thunder rumbled. I felt I could run forever, no problem. I ran until I saw the Dutch windmill that marked the end of the park, then slowed to a fast walk.

The wind had picked up. The light rain had become a downpour. On the Great Highway, cars were using high beams and windshield wipers. I looked both ways and crossed. A sign said, "Drownings occur due to heavy surf and severe undertow. PLEASE REMAIN SAFELY ON SHORE." No, it didn't apply to me.

On the beach I removed my sweater and workshirt. My T-shirt I pulled halfway over my head, but the rain chilled me and I changed my mind. I took off my boots and socks. Dressed only in jeans and T-shirt, I ran to the water. The ocean was loud and frothing white, spectacular. I stepped into the surf and right back out. Now the pounding rain felt warm. But I had to die and be born again. I stepped into the freezing water and forced myself to stand ankle-deep. I waded out until rolling ocean reached my knees. My feet grew numb.

I forced myself farther still, to where waves crested and toppled, crashed white around my hips. The cold was terrible. I stood hugging myself against the wind, my teeth chattering. At my ankles I felt an undertow. I looked back at the shore but no, I wouldn't quit. Couldn't. A car went by on the highway. Then another. Okay, three more. One. Two and three. I wasn't ready. But I turned and forced myself to walk. Step, step, step into the ocean. Now I was beyond where the waves broke, ocean swelling around my chest.

Lightning crackled across the sky, startled me into running. Despite myself I angled shoreward, until again I was knee-deep, but charging back and forth parallel to the shore. Lightning continued to explode over the city but I stopped and, breathing hard, stood hugging myself. Again I felt an undertow. Again I looked at the beach but CRACK! I had to die. CRACK! I had to die and be born again.

And again I was running, only this time I ran out, straight out into the ocean. The water reached my thighs, CRACK! swelled and rolled around my waist, CRACK! CRACK! I stumbled and pitched forward and finally I was under, tumbling, spinning. I felt the undertow and look, there was the surface, shimmering far above, and no! No! I didn't want to die!

Frantic, I made for the surface. My chest bursting, I broke into the air and managed a breath but now I couldn't touch bottom, the water was over my head. As lightning cracked the sky, I swam desperately for shore. Finally I managed to stand but the waves knocked me down and again I was tumbling, the undertow fierce. Again I fought my way to the surface and got my feet under me and with the lighting cracking overhead I staggered ashore, fell onto the sand and lay panting.

Where were my clothes? I trotted back and forth along the beach in the pounding rain, unable to find them. Maybe the missing clothes were a sign. Maybe, despite myself, I had died back there under water. Maybe I'd died and already I'd been born again, into another world — a world in which my clothes would be out of place. They'd disappeared because they'd mark me as a visitor.

The rain sluiced down in sheets and I started to shiver. No use hunting for my shirt, my boots and socks. They were gone. Up the nearest steps I stumbled and looked both ways. A hundred yards down the highway was a restaurant. I ran towards it through puddles, my jeans going squish, squish, squish. Strangely, I felt great. I'd died back there underwater and already I'd been born again. I couldn't believe how great I felt.

The restaurant looked all-too-familiar: a counter, some stools, a dozen formica tables. But that proved nothing. The back wall boasted mirrors from the waist up. A waitress stood at a sink, her back turned, washing coffee mugs. I stepped to the counter, then remembered I had no money and looked around. Two men, clean-cut sales types, sat at a table in the middle of the restaurant, the only customers.

Did people in this world speak English? I walked over and enunciated clearly: "Could either of you spare a quarter for a coffee?"

One man stared through me. The other looked at my bare feet, then at the footprints I'd left on the floor: "I give only to those who wear shoes."

The first man snickered.

The same old world. I knew it. But did that mean I hadn't died underwater? That I hadn't been born again? I walked to the rear of the restaurant, sat down on a stool and studied my reflection in the mirror. I tried to dry my face with the inside of my arm.

Beside me, in the mirror, the waitress appeared. An older woman, she reminded me of Jessica, once a beautiful Indian princess. "Can I get you something?"

"If you don't mind, I'd like to sit and get warm."

The waitress nodded, started to speak, then decided against it and walked away.

I stared at myself in the mirror. I was dripping wet: my hair, my face, my T-shirt. But I'd stopped shivering. I didn't know anything any more, not for sure. But remembering Jessica had given me an idea. Staring hard at my face in the mirror, I silently addressed the mysterious force: "Please! I don't know who you are, or what, but I need another sign. If I really was the Near James, then please: let me see my face as it was then."

In the mirror, slowly, my face changed. My jaw grew fuller, my nose smaller. The laugh marks around my mouth disappeared. I gazed at myself in the mirror. The face looking back was my own face — but purified, somehow. Perfected. It couldn't be improved and remain mine. There, in the mirror, staring back at me: the Near James. I'd been beautiful. I looked like... an angel.

The waitress appeared in the mirror carrying a cup of coffee. She said, "On the house."

Back came my old face — but I'd seen the truth. Now I knew for sure: the Near James. Whatever I'd got wrong, that I'd got right.

"Why do you look so happy?" the waitress asked. "You're shoeless, soaking wet, shivering with cold. Why so happy?"

The two salesmen were getting up to leave. Without thinking, but loud enough for them to hear, I said, "Because all who don't love will be destroyed."

"Pardon?"

"That's why I'm happy. Nineteen hundred and sixty-seven years we gave them." I gestured towards the departing salesmen. "All those who haven't learned to love will be destroyed!"

33

In San Francisco, 1990, before leaving the Haight-Ashbury to walk through Golden Gate Park to the ocean, I went to a restaurant called Dish, corner Haight and Masonic — once upon a time, the Drugstore Café. I'd saved the Drugstore for end-of-tour — not only because it had been the heart of the Haight, standing-room-only frenzy seven nights a week, but because for me it had been the scene of cathartic weirdness.

Now the place was almost empty: one blue-jeaned waif nursing a coffee, two tourists bent over a map and three exasperated realtors, shirt-and-tied, thrashing out a deal. The waiters and waitresses were late teens, early twenties — probably hadn't been born, I realized, appalled, when last I'd entered these premises.

Structurally, the restaurant was unchanged: distinctive corner entrance, large windows along two walls, high ceilings, overhead fans and four pillars, one of them graced with its original full-length mirror. A collection of fancy plates adorned the walls, tables boasted white linen and potted ferns provided greenery. But the wooden counter at the back of the restaurant and the window in the wall behind it, through which waiters shouted orders — these were as before, when I was nineteen years old and the Drugstore Café was holy.

I ate a sandwich of tomato chunks and alfafa sprouts and scribbled notes. The centre had held. If the Haight had changed dramatically since the sixties, so the district I knew existed only in memory, yet the Drugstore remained recognizably itself. And as I downed a third cup of coffee, again I saw Bernie, driven by whatever it was that made the Haight special, enter the Drugstore late one morning and rush straight to where I stood, at the back near the washrooms.

"Frankie, I've been looking for you." He grabbed my hand and shook it. "I'm vacating the Bunker, going back to New York. But get this: the guy who's subletting the place? He knows nothing about the Hobbit Hole."

"Doesn't realize it goes with the Bunker?"

Bernie nodded, gleeful. Just in case, because the front door was usually open, he'd brought me a key: "A cat could move into the Hobbit Hole, keep a low profile and stay as long as he liked. Nobody'd know the difference."

That afternoon I collected my remaining gear from the Free Frame of Reference and moved into the Hobbit Hole — a gable, really, on the third floor of a Victorian mansion that has long-since been restored. I couldn't stand upright in my new abode, too tall for that, even where the ceiling peaked. But this inconvenience was minor. The Hobbit Hole was a perfect base from which to pursue my quest.

Lately I'd been smoking endless quantities of grass with a newcomer to the Haight. An older guy of twenty-six, Toby had just been discharged from the army and didn't want to talk about Vietnam. He'd driven across the continent in a rattle-trap Chevy that now served as his crashpad. He was clean-shaven, short-black-haired, and some said he was an undercover cop: a narc. I figured he was too straight-looking, and far too heavily into drugs.

"I guess this is fair, man," he'd say as we swung through the Panhandle towards the Hobbit Hole. "I supply the grass and you supply the place to smoke it."

I'd laugh uneasily. I felt guilty about not inviting Toby to crash in the Hobbit Hole, but valued that sanctuary — and my privacy, my solitude — too highly to share it.

By now, with so many old-timers having split, and except for Toby, my only friend was Mitchell, the beautiful cat who lived with Jessica in the upper half of the Fell Street House. More than once Mitchell had turned up in the Panhandle as I waited, spoon and bowl in hand, for the Diggers to arrive with cabbage soup. And invited me home for dinner. Mitchell worked as a waiter in the Café Cantata, an uptown restaurant, and kept urging me to find a job.

"Too distracting, Mitchell. Something BIG is happening here. I've got to figure out what."

Still, I was grateful for the dinners. And delighted one night when I found Mitchell at the Psychedelic Shop, enveloped in incense and sitar music and flipping through the latest San Francisco Oracle. Delighted because back at the Hobbit Hole I had a lid of Toby's grass — he'd needed a place to stash it — and this was my chance to reciprocate.

Mitchell didn't need much convincing. Soon we were sitting cross-legged on a mattress in the Hobbit Hole, passing a joint back and forth. Mitchell, I reflected, was at peace with himself. He knew who he was. Always wore blue jeans, well-washed, a clean sports shirt, a tweedy grey sports jacket. Didn't go in for gaudy. I remembered meeting Mitchell the night I'd seen Jessica's face change. Oscar had declared him an archangel. And when I'd asked Jessica about Duality, she'd laughed and nodded at Mitchell: "He's the wise one here, not me. He's the one you should be asking."

At the time I believed she was being modest. Now, in the Hobbit Hole, I wondered. My last acid trip, that night at the ocean, had awakened me. I realized I'd been side-tracked. I'd been looking for the other disciples, hoping one of them would know why we were here. But I'd been the Near James — one of the Big Three. Which of the other disciples would know more me? Now I was back on track. And knew what to do.

Having lit a third joint, I held my breath and stared hard at Mitchell, silently asking: "Please, I've got to know. If you are the One I'm looking for, then let me see your face as it was then — when I was the Near James."

Suddenly, Mitchell grew a beard. His hair went from black and wavy to brown and curly, much shorter. Mitchell looked older — ancient. His was the wisest face I had ever seen. The change lasted only an instant but that was enough. In a previous life, Mitchell had been Jesus himself — the Son of God.

"Mitchell! It's you!" I averted my eyes, ashamed for some reason to look into the face of my leader. "What can I say?"

"Say about what? Frankie?"

"Can you… can you forgive me?"

"Forgive you for what?"

"For not having known you sooner."

"What are you talking about?"

"Mitchell, I've just recognized you." I looked into his face and again saw the square beard, the quiet wisdom. "I've just seen your face, Mitchell. The one you wore when I was a disciple."

"Frankie, what exactly did you see?"

"You're the one, Mitchell. The reincarnated Jesus. The Son of God."

"We're all sons of God, Frankie. Though sometimes, it's true, I've felt singled out. What exactly did you see?"

Next morning, when the grass wore off, I had trouble believing what I'd seen: Mitchell? The reincarnated Jesus? No way I could tell people. They'd think I'd gone nuts. If it was true, all I had to do was wait. Mitchell would come to full consciousness and reveal our present purpose.

Meanwhile, dope-smoking as usual. Two days after I recognized Mitchell, Toby scored three lids of dynamite Mexican grass: Acapulco Gold. He told me about it, excited, that night at the Drugstore. Why not go to the Hobbit Hole and test it? Why not, indeed? As we swung down Masonic, Toby made his usual joke about how fair it was: he supplied the grass and I supplied the place to smoke it.

"Sometimes I wish it was the other way around."

"No luck finding a room?"

Toby shook his head.

Moved by a new spirit of generosity, determined to be worthy of my recent discovery, I said: "You can crash at the Hobbit Hole, you know. Any time you really need a place."

"You mean that?"

"Well, it's small. And I like being alone. But any time you really need a place, sure."

At the Hobbit Hole, Toby rolled up three or four bombers. From toke one I knew this was no ordinary grass and exhaled saying: "Wow! Is this cut with something?"

Toby laughed: "Don't think so — though it's got a kick." He started rapping about some chemical he'd tried two days before. "Like acid, only better. I'm getting more. If you like, we can drop together."

"Good stuff?"

"Something else, man." Toby shook his head, handed me the joint. "I saw myself as I really am."

"You saw your face change?"

"I'd rather not talk about it, man. Here, have a toke."

For a while we smoked in silence.

Usually, Toby was non-stop talkative. Tonight, for stretches, he stared at the ceiling in silence, distracted, and finally I asked what he was thinking. He said, "About how our actions have consequences."

"What do you mean?"

"Take baseball. If you keep striking out, you get benched. Or again, out in the world, you write bad cheques, you end up in jail. Wouldn't it be great if we could anticipate the consequences of our actions?"

"Sure would."

I passed him the joint but he waved it away: "What about you, Frankie? Do you always foresee the consequences of your actions?"

"Sure." I took another toke.

Toby raised his eyebrows: "You foresee the consequences of your every action?"

"Sure, I do." For an instant I felt uneasy — I didn't know why — but I took another toke and the feeling passed. "Sure, I do. Sure."

Again Toby waved away the joint.

I sucked on it, held my breath and wondered: Was Toby trying to tell me something? What did he mean — that he'd seen himself as he really was? A fellow disciple? I stared hard at Toby and called silently to see his real face.

Expecting nothing special, nothing to compare with my discovery about Mitchell, I was shocked when Toby's short black hair receded at the sides and swept into a "V" down the middle of his forehead. At the top corners, where his hair receded, two tiny horns sprouted. Toby's ears grew pointed. His eyes became round black holes.

The Devil himself.

All this in an instant. I gasped — then caught myself. Toby grinned and held out the joint. I ignored it. Deliberately, not wanting to reveal what I'd discovered, I got my feet under me, scuttled across the Hobbit Hole and ducked out the door.

"Frankie, where you going?"

Down the stairs I stumbled with Toby calling after me: "Hey, man! Hey!" Out the front door I went, walking fast but refusing to panic, refusing to run. I hurried along the Panhandle to the Fell Street House, climbed the back stairs and knocked loudly. Mitchell opened the door. "You won't believe this," I said, "but I've been smoking dope with the Devil himself."

Inside, Mitchell heard me out. Then, unflustered, launched into one of his convoluted sermons. "Mind and matter, spirit and body — there's a division of sorts in death. But for the living, Reality is One." He drew a circle in the air with his hands. "The whole supercedes and contains all polarities, understand?"

"No, I don't."

"Jesus and the Devil, like any pair of opposites, are parts of the same whole." Again the circle. "Two sides of the same coin?"

"Mitchell, the Devil can't be real?"

"The first step towards achieving wholeness is to become conscious of division."

"The old Yin-Yang."

"Yet reality is One." A third time, the circle. "Imagine a twisting line down the middle."

"Mitchell, the Devil himself?"

Round we went for half an hour, maybe more. Still, when he looked at his watch, Mitchell surprised me. He'd worked all day, he explained, and had to meet Jessica next morning, returning by bus from visiting her sister. I said the Devil himself might be waiting at the Hobbit Hole, and Mitchell invited me to spend the night on the couch. He dug out a sleeping bag, insisted he didn't mind and went off to bed.

In the blackness, all lights out, I realized the couch was too short. That I'd never get to sleep. I moved the bag onto the floor, crawled into it and lay in the dark, my mind spinning. Probably the Devil was toking up in the Hobbit Hole. Or else he'd be at the Drugstore Café, stuffing his face. At the thought of food my mouth watered and I realized how hungry I was. Today, again, the Diggers hadn't turned up in the Panhandle.

I crawled out of the sleeping bag and went to the kitchen. The fridge was almost bare: a loaf of bread, a jar of mustard, some dill pickles, a bowl of rice. Dismayed, I thought again of the Drugstore Café, where at least I'd be able to bum some kind of meal.

Trouble was, I realized as I pulled on my jeans, the Devil might be at the Drugstore. But then, so what? Duality made it inevitable. The Son of God was in the Haight, so the Devil had to be here too. Jesus implied Satan — I understood that now. Certainly I had nothing to fear. In fact, as I quietly let myself out the front door, I realized that I found it exciting, the idea of talking with the Devil himself.

Yet, a few moments later, when I walked into the Drugstore and saw Toby sitting alone in a corner, I went cold. I stared at him hard, checking to see whether I'd made a mistake, but no! Again I saw the black "V" of short hair down the forehead. Again the tiny horns. Toby was the Devil himself. No mistake — though again I could scarcely believe my eyes. The Devil himself was sitting quietly in the Drugstore and nobody but me could see who he was.

Toby got up and came over, punched me gently me on the shoulder. "What's the idea, man, splitting like that? You okay?"

"Listen, Toby. I know you're the Devil."

"Come again?"

"I can see that you're the Devil."

"The Devil?" Toby laughed and threw his hands in the air. "Okay, I'm the Devil."

"That's who you saw yourself as, isn't it? The other day."

"Maybe it is. So I'm the Devil. So what?"

"So what? Toby, do you want to die?"

"Who said anything about dying?"

"All who don't love will be destroyed, Toby."

"Man, that grass really kicks in, doesn't it?"

"If you don't want to die, you'll have to change your ways."

"I don't know, man. I think it's too late for that."

"Listen, Toby, maybe you haven't been able to love because you've always felt unloved. If you know that somebody loves you, maybe you'll be able to change your ways."

"Okay, I'm convinced."

"Toby, I love you even if you are the Devil. I know you're the Devil and I love you just the same. So you're saved, don't you see?"

"Sure, man." Toby danced around, waving his hands in the air. "I'm saved! I'm saved!"

A woman walked by carrying a tray full of food and I remembered why I'd come. I looked around. The Drugstore Café was jumping — yet I didn't see anybody I knew well. Only the Devil. I said, "I want to be alone a moment, Toby. Need to think."

"Sure, man." Toby slapped my shoulder. "I understand."

I stood near the counter and watched Toby resume his seat. Sometimes he looked like a regular guy. Other times, like the Devil himself. No way I could ask the Devil to buy me something to eat. I looked around the Drugstore, but nobody I knew had turned up. Well, why not ask Toby? He was saved, wasn't he?

As I approached him, again I saw the short hair, the horns, the black holes. I shook them off: "Toby, I haven't eaten today. Would you buy me something to eat?"

"Hey, man, no problem! You should have said something sooner." Toby led me back to the counter. "What would you like?"

"A hamburger would be great."

Two jumbo cheeseburgers, Toby ordered, with a double order of fries and two chocolate shakes. As we stood waiting for our number to be called, my stomach rumbled. I felt uneasy, waiting with the Devil. But I didn't feel I could walk away. We stood in silence.

Finally, our number. Toby paid the cashier, picked up the tray and led the way back to the corner. My mouth watered at the smell of the food. Toby laid the tray on the table, then turned, thoughtfully, and gestured with his hand: "You know, Frankie, I bet you can just see the evil pouring from my face."

Again I saw the "V," the black holes, the tiny horns: "Yes, I can see you're the Devil."

"That's fair, then." Toby nodded. "You save me and I buy you a meal." He rubbed his chin. "But you know, man... that's almost like... making a bargain... with the...."

He didn't have to finish. In the Hobbit Hole, I'd boasted about foreseeing the consequences of my every action. If I took the food, I'd conclude a bargain with the Devil. And everybody knew the consequences of that: I'd lose my soul.

"Sit down, man," Toby said. "Let's eat."

"No, I don't want it!"

"Come on, Frankie. I was teasing."

"No! You're not saved at all. I'm not making any bargains with you."

"Okay, okay. I understand." The Devil picked up the tray. "But here: if you don't want it, give it to somebody else."

I reached for the tray, then caught myself. I couldn't give away the food unless I admitted it was mine. The instant I did that, I'd completed a bargain. "No! That food's not mine to give away. It's yours and you can do what you want with it because that food has nothing to do with me."

I made for the door, left the Devil calling: "Hey! Hey, man! I was kidding!"

Down Masonic I hurried, again refusing to run. I crossed Page Street into the Panhandle, then stood in the trees and looked up at the night sky. What deviousness! Obviously the Devil had plotted the whole exchange, from before we smoked in the Hobbit Hole, and — oh, Christ! I'd told him he could stay with me any time he really needed a place. I'd been referring to the Hobbit Hole but the Devil would twist my words, argue that my "place" was really my body because that was where my spirit lived. The Devil would come and take over my body. He'd argue that I'd invited him — that he really needed a place to stay.

No! I wheeled and started back the way I'd come. I had to face the Devil, to tell him no, he wasn't welcome to stay with me, not under any circumstances, no matter how badly he needed a place. I swept up Masonic and re-entered the Drugstore. But the Devil wasn't there. I elbowed my way to the counter, but no. I checked the washroom, still no sign.

By now the Drugstore was standing-room-only, the air thick with cigarette smoke. I had to find the Devil and tell him no, he was NOT welcome to crash, not under any circumstances, but as again I pushed through the coffee-only line, a big guy in a jean jacket, looked like a Hell's Angel, said, "Watch where you're going, man," and the whole place went over, the entire Drugstore, everything shifting and suddenly I felt sick. Demons — nothing but demons. And that was it. These people had been able to see the Devil as clearly as I could. But no surprise: they expected him to be here. He was their leader. The Drugstore was headquarters. I was in Hell.

As I made for the door, pushing and shoving, afraid I wouldn't be allowed out, a woman's voice rose out of the din: "Decisions, decisions." At the door, in my panic, I tripped over a foot and sprawled onto the sidewalk. On my hands and knees, hurt but relieved to be outside, I began to breathe normally — then realized that the Devil must have returned to the Hobbit Hole. I'd have to confront him there, because otherwise he'd take over my body and oh, Christ! where was Mitchell? Where was Jesus when I needed him?

Then: wait a minute. Decisions, decisions. Those words were meant for me — a signpost. Why did I have to confront the Devil? If he did come to take over my body, couldn't the Son of God protect me? Except maybe I didn't need the Son of God? Maybe alone I could defeat the Devil? Maybe it was my turn to be Number One son?

As I stood and brushed myself off, my mind racing, I remembered the outskirts of Los Angeles, the coins I'd tossed into the air, and realized I had a choice to make. I looked up at the sky. That meant a right choice and a wrong choice. Obviously, the Son of God was the right choice. Never mind going it alone. If the Devil tried to take over my body, I'd ask the Son of God for help. I started down Masonic towards the Panhandle, and this time I ran, making for the Fell Street House, determined to knock on the door until the Son of God opened.

34

While growing up in Ste. Thérèse, Frankie discovered his father to be two different people. This I learned on Mount Jubilation as I lay in darkness, listening to the approach of a thunder storm. He'd watch his father, Sunday afternoon sober, shuffling around the back yard, his baggy grey pants — ten years old, three sizes too big — held up by a piece of rope. He'd be working on some project. Frankie could always tell if his mother had assigned the job because then it would be something that really had to be done.

Yesterday the temperature had hit seventy degrees and theirs was the only house on the street that still boasted storm windows. The toilet was backing up into the bathtub and the drain had to be dug out. The spring flood had abated and three loads of sand had to be spread around the yard so the man next door couldn't pump water out of his basement onto their property.

Easily distinguished from these projects were those his father devised. Envisaging a halcyon summer of back-yard soirées, for example, his father extended a waist-high platform from the back of the house. Then mounted an immense wooden bar on this rickety structure. That evening, while the family ate supper, a loud crash interrupted the blaring TV. Frankie was first into the yard. There, on the ground, sat the bar, splintered, irreparable, the platform having collapsed under its weight.

Or again, after months of denying it, his father admitted that the backyard shed was an eyesore. In a frenzy he went at it, ripping and tearing and banging, until finally the structure lay in pieces around him. Then he realized, with a shock, that he had no place to keep his tools, his plywood, his old bedsprings. And so, using the materials he'd just torn apart, he knocked together a second shed, put it in the other corner of the yard — and got upset, started yelling and waving his arms, when Frankie told him it looked just like the first.

Sober, Frankie's father was all histrionics and broad gestures. "Clean-up brigade!" he'd cry. "Fall in! Get a move on, there. You're in the Air Force!"

This was when Frankie's mother was working in Coeur d'Aimée as a cleaning lady and his father was in charge of the house. "Twenty minutes to inspection! Get everything out of sight! I don't care what you do with it, just get it out of sight!" And he'd lead the children in a mad dash around the house, sweeping floors and fluffing pillows and tossing toys into baskets.

Or at lunch, Janey would declare that she didn't feel like eating. His father would address the ceiling: "She doesn't feel like eating?" Out he'd dash from behind the kitchen counter, pretending anger. "What's the matter? Beans not good enough for you?"

"I'm not hungry."

"Not hungry? People are starving in China! And you tell me you're not hungry?"

The children would giggle.

"Laugh!" He'd take little runs at them, one arm raised as if to deliver a backhand. "Go on, laugh! The fat of the land! You kids are living on the fat of the land and don't even know it. But you'll find out. The Depression's coming. You'll find out."

The Other Man came at night, after his father went to the hotel. He'd return a different person. Sometimes he'd sit and listen to Sinatra. *Without a song, the road would never end.* Other times he'd roar and slam around the kitchen, cursing and swearing about how it's a jungle out there, dog eat dog but the game is rigged, the fix is in and the little guy stands no chance.

Sometimes the Other Man came Saturday afternoon.

Of all the chores Frankie did, fetching his father from La Fin du Monde was the only one he hated. He'd ride up Avenue des Archanges, park his bicycle against the hotel and step out of the sunshine into the smoke and beer-smell. His father would be sitting in a corner with four or five cronies, talking French. "Ah! *Mon garcon! Viens icitte, Frankie. Assis toi.* Come. Sit down."

Frankie would say no, he couldn't stay. But his father would take his arm and sit him down and offer him up to a circle of laughing, red-faced strangers. As soon as he got a chance, Frankie would tell his father why he'd come. Maybe the sink was blocked. Or the electric pump had broken down and they had no water. "Mum says you've got to come home."

"I'm on my way," his father would say.

But instead of getting up he'd order another round, one for the road. Frankie would try to escape: "See you back at the house."

"Nonsense," his father would say. "I'll just be a minute here. Have a drink. Want a beer? A coke, then. Sure you do. Waiter! *Garçon! Un coke s'il vous plaît.*"

And for the next fifteen or twenty minutes, until his father was ready to leave, Frankie would endure an endless hell of drunken table-talk and din.

Then came the Saturday in 1962, Frankie a hyper-sensitive fifteen, that Uncle Henry arrived unannounced. He'd bought a Rambler and wanted to show it off. Under orders from his mother, Frankie rode his bicycle up the street, parked it beside the hotel and quietly entered. His father was worse than usual. But he didn't realize how much until, after half an hour of entreaties, he finally got him outside.

Bent on getting away, Frankie hopped onto his bicycle. His father wobbled away from in front of the hotel and stumbled, almost fell, sprawled instead across the hood of a parked car.

"You okay?"

"Give me a hand here, son." His father righted himself, but didn't take his hand off the car. "I can't seem to walk straight."

"Sure you can. All you've got to do is try."

His father took a couple of wobbly steps, still holding onto the car. Then he stopped, stood shaking his head.

"God damn it!"

Frankie got off his bike and leaned it against the phone booth. He went over to his father, put his arm around the man and moved him away from in front of the hotel. "I'm just going to get you started."

Father and son walked fifteen or twenty yards along Chemin St. Esprit, then turned down Avenue des Archanges.

It was Labor Day Weekend, the end of summer. The sun was shining, the sky was blue. People were laughing and talking in their front yards, drinking cokes, swinging in hammocks.

Frankie removed his father's arm from his shoulder and stepped away. "Okay, I've got to go back and get my bicycle. You go on ahead."

His father came unsteadily to a halt, stood weaving in the sunshine. "I can't, son. Can't make it alone."

"Sure you can. You've got to!"

His father held out his hand.

"*Calisse!*' Frankie again threw his arm around his father and started him walking. Then, halfway down the street, he saw her: the French girl he loved. Petite, black-haired and laughing, she wore white shorts and a sleeveless sweater. She was out front playing badminton with her brother. Frankie had been worshipping her all summer. Now she spotted him and looked quickly away, pretending not to see. Frankie pushed his father away, hissed at him: "Stand up straight, Dad, for God's sake! Stand up and walk!"

"Can't." His father stood swaying back and forth in the middle of Avenue des Archanges. "Can't make it alone, son."

"You've got to." Frankie started walking briskly down the street. "Come on."

His father didn't move. He rested his chin on his chest. Then, as he stood there in his Hawaiian shirt, swaying back and forth, he started to cry.

"Dad! For God's sake!"

"Can't make it, Frankie." His father reached out his hand. "Can't make it alone."

The girl Frankie loved had stopped playing badminton. She and her brother were staring, wide-eyed. The whole street was watching.

"Dad, I'm leaving now." Frankie took a couple more steps. "Come on, Dad. Please!"

"Go get your mother, Frankie." His father was blubbering. "Get your Uncle Henry. They'll help me."

Frankie turned and started home, then turned again and looked back. His father was standing in the middle of the street, blubbering like a two-year-old.

"Jesus Christ, Dad!"

Frankie whipped out his handerkerchief — always he carried it, just in case — returned and handed it to his father. He helped wipe his nose, his mouth, then draped his father's arm around his shoulder and, head high, looking neither right nor left, moved slowly down the street.

35

Two days after I found myself in Hell, the guy who'd sublet Bernie's Bunker left me a note: "WHOEVER YOU ARE: This storage room, otherwise known as the Hobbit Hole, belongs to my apartment. Vacate it within twenty-four hours or I call the cops."

Again Mitchell urged me to find a job, any job. But this time, having cast him as the reincarnated Jesus, I felt compelled to heed his advice. The Hip Job Co-op, a volunteer, Haight-Street agency, sent me downtown.

— FRANKIE: THE LETTERS.
— I thought you were out of here.
— YOU WERE GOING TO INCLUDE THE LETTERS.
— You didn't say I had to. Just that I could. I've decided against it.
— LET'S CHANGE YOUR MIND.
— Remember *Visions of Cody*? That interminable transcript section called "Frisco: The Tape"? It's boring, right? Irrelevant? Almost ruins the book?
— ARGUABLE IN ITSELF. BUT THE ATTEMPTED ANALOGY IS TIPPED AT THE LINE OF SCRIMMAGE. FAILS TO PRODUCE EVEN A SINGLE POINT.
— They're twenty-five years old, these letters. A quarter of a century. It's like somebody else wrote them.
— YOU DENY A CONTINUITY BETWEEN "FRANKIE THEN" AND "FRANKIE NOW?"
— No way. That's your game. I'm tracking Truth and these letters obscure it.
— AH, TRUTH. DO THE LETTERS HIDE MORE THAN THEY REVEAL? MAYBE YES, MAYBE NO. BUT HERE'S A TRUTH,

FRANKIE: THE IDEA OF PARADING NAKED MAKES YOU BLUSH AND TREMBLE.

— I don't see any reason to take it all off. Just because Kerouac did? That's not good enough.

— KEROUAC SET A STANDARD. BUT FRANKIE THE NARRATOR, WITHOUT WAITING TO HEAR THE REST, GRABBED THE FILE FOLDER OF LETTERS AND BOLTED FOR THE INSIDE DOOR. HE HOPED TO DASH THROUGH THE LIVING ROOM AND INTO THE KITCHEN, WHERE HE'D STUFF THE LETTERS DOWN THE NEWLY INSTALLED GARBURATOR. BEFORE HE'D TAKEN THREE STEPS, HOWEVER, AND DESPITE HIMSELF, FRANKIE LEAPT STRAIGHT INTO THE AIR, DID A BACKWARDS TWISTING SOMERSAULT, TOUGH ENOUGH ON A MIDDLE-AGED MAN THAT THIS ONE FLUNG HIS OLD LETTERS AT THE CEILING, AND LANDED WITH A THUD ON HIS BUTT. MIRACULOUSLY, THE LETTERS DRIFTED SINGLY AND IN PAIRS TO HIS DESKTOP, WHERE THEY FELL INTO A NEAT PILE, CHRONOLOGICALLY ORDERED. RUBBING HIS BUTT, FRANKIE RESUMED HIS SEAT, MUTTERING:

— Sal Paradise never had trouble like this. Neither did Jacky Duluoz. I don't get it.

— NO? THE QUESTION IS THIS: WHAT HAPPENS WHEN YOU SHAKE YOUNG FRANKIE TO HIS FOUNDATIONS? OR AGAIN: WHAT'S LEFT WHEN YOU LAY WASTE HIS DEFENCES? THESE LETTERS, I'M AFRAID. THESE EMBARRASSING BUT OBLIGATORY LETTERS.

March 7, 1967.

Dear Mom:

Sorry I haven't written sooner but lately I've been run off my feet. I've taken a job as a bicycle messenger with Golden Gate Delivery Service and spend eight hours a day pedalling up and down hills. I carry a walkie-talkie — actually strap it around my chest — and make $1.40 an hour (plus $7.50 a week if I work all five days).

I realize that I could have got something better, Mom, but right now this is what I want to do. The job leaves me time to think. I wasn't really working at the post office earlier, as I said I was. I just wrote that so you wouldn't worry. But now you needn't worry so I can tell you the truth.

I'm staying downtown at a hotel called the Cameo. A friend lent me enough money to pay the first week's rent and I'll remain here until I can afford to move. I found a Gideon Bible in the dresser so I've got something to read. Certain recent experiences have given me a new perspective on religion and I've got some catching up to do.

Maybe you could send the Montreal Library the money they're demanding? Tell them I lost the books. You've long since paid back the $25 I lent you before I left home. Figure out what I owe you and I'll pay it back as soon as I can.

That's all for now. I am well and trust that you and the others are too. Write soon and let me know how everyone is doing.

Love,
Frankie

P.S. I almost wrote "Jack." That's what they call me all day on the walkie-talkie. They already had both a Frankie and a Frank. When the dispatcher asked me for another name, out it popped: "Jack."

*

March 25, 1967.

Dear family:

I hope you are all well, as I am. Janey, thanks for your letter. I'm glad to hear you've received a raise and no, I haven't made any girls pregnant lately, ha ha. As for

Thibideau's wedding, I'm afraid I can't make it because I won't be in Ste. Thérèse.

I'm still working as a messenger for Golden Gate Delivery. I've discovered that when my deliveries exceed a certain number, a commission arrangement comes into effect. My *Gazette*-route bicycling is paying off. These past two weeks I've cleared $67 and $68.

The big news is that I've moved into a rooming house on the outskirts of the Haight-Ashbury. There's a kitchen down the hall, so once I get the hang of it I'll be able to cook my own meals. I already make my own lunch, usually peanut butter sandwiches, and bring it to work in a lunch box so I can have chocolate milk to drink (out of a thermos).

My daily routine starts at 6:45, when I get up and do a few stretching exercises. For breakfast I make eggs or pancakes or porridge or toast. Then I put on my uniform — blue pants, shirt and jacket with crest — and ride the city bus to work. I get on my bicycle and pedal like crazy from 9 to 12:30 or so, then take half an hour for lunch. I go again until 5:30, after which I ride home on the bus (15 minutes) and make supper. I do the dishes, take a bath and read until bed time.

Mostly I read the Bible. After a long, long search, and much, much to my amazement, I have discovered that the Bible is the only book that even begins to explain everything that has happened to me. I see now that I was brought here to find this out.

Lately I've been thinking a lot about all of you and I've realized that your problems are my problems. I'm enclosing a money order for $50, which you should use to pay off some of the bills. It's a first instalment. I've decided to stay here in San Francisco, working as a bicycle messenger, until all our bills are paid off.

Please don't try to make me change my mind. Much as I miss you all, every single one of you, this is the way it must be done.

Your loving son and brother,

Jack

*

April 8, 1967.

Dear Mom:

Enclosed is a money order for $100 — instalment number two. You needn't worry, Mom, that I'm doing without anything I need. The question is: what do I really need? And the answer, materially, is food and shelter.

As I have already told you, I eat well. Usually I have pancakes for breakfast — 12 to 14, which I make using three eggs. For lunch I eat three or four sandwiches (meat, cheese or peanut butter), plus half a dozen cookies and an apple or a banana, and drink a thermos of carnation milk mixed with chocolate.

For supper I fry up a pound of meat or fish and have it with potatoes or rice and a small can of vegetables. Sometimes I cook spaghetti. As for shelter, my room is small but the rent is only $10 a week. Besides a bed, I've got a dresser, a small table and a chair — all one person really needs.

Mom, about those clippings you sent, hoping I'd see some job I like and "come home right away." Believe me, I look forward to that. But I will do it only when all our debts are discharged. I've told you this before, but I see you didn't take me seriously. Now I've told you again. If you check the Bible, you'll see that my parents' debts are my debts as well.

I think often of all of you there in Ste. Thérèse. Incredible that you've still got snow on the ground. (All I see here is rain.) Glad to hear you've finished Eddie's room with gyprock. That should warm it up a bit. Also glad that you're finally putting in a water heater. How's Expo coming? Most of the exhibits ready? Please write soon as it's always good to hear from you.

Your loving son,
Jack

P.S. Sorry you find it strange that I sign my letters "Jack." But that's what they call me all day and I've grown used to it. In a funny way "Frankie" is dead.

*

April 25, 1967.

Dear Mom:

Not to worry about me being drafted by the American Army. I have a social security card (needed it to work), but no draft card. I'm not on file with the draft board, so how could they draft me? God's army is the only one I care to join.

I was sorry to hear that Janey is doing so much partying. Why not give her a Bible to read? As for Eddie's long hair: if he wishes to wear it long and the school authorities permit it, then why not? He will, in time, learn that "fitting in" and doing what everybody else does is no way to live.

The apostle Paul wrote, "Doth not even nature itself teach you that if a man have long hair, it is a shame unto him?" In time, Eddie will realize the truth of this -- and then he will get his hair cut.

Enclosed is another money order for $100. I'm glad to hear you're putting the money to good use. But, Mom, you've again said "come home" when I've told you that I'm not coming home until we've paid off our debts. Please note: I did not say, nor have I ever said, "Until I have paid off our debts." I will come home when WE have paid them off — the whole family.

This does not mean that I expect or ask anything of anybody else. If I have to discharge the debts alone, I will do so. I would hope, however, that each of you will remember, when you are buying something you think you need (alcohol, for example), that you will not see me again until that something has been paid for in full.

You asked, Mom, whether I go to church. The answer is no, I don't, because I have found no church that teaches what Jesus taught. Those I have visited appear to be places where people go to show off new clothes. Please note: I do not say categorically that's what they are, for I neither judge nor condemn. I say that's what they appear to be. I see no connection between going to church and following Jesus.

And I hope you believe me when I say that what Jesus taught is true. For he said, "Seek and ye shall find; knock, and it shall be opened unto you." And, "Wheresoever two or more are gathered in my name, there also will I be." And again, "He that loveth me will be loved by my Father, and I will love him, and will manifest myself to him." Jesus manifested himself to me, Mom. So I know what he says is true.

Yes, I too found it amazing. Believe me, I looked everywhere for answers, and when at last I looked to Jesus, there He was. Please remember when you read these words that this is your son and brother talking. Not some phony street corner prophet. I knocked and Jesus opened — and so I know that the Bible is true.

Love,
Jack

P.S. Sorry to hear the lake's flooding. Surely the water won't rise as far as the house? Keep me posted.

*

May 9, 1967.

Dear Mom:
That's terrible news about the flood. The whole back room? I wonder if Thibideau's parents still have that extra rowboat? If the flood get worse, maybe you could borrow that?

At this end I'm doing well at Golden Gate Delivery, clearing roughly $85 a week. I'm starting work now at 8:30

212

and finishing at 6, which explains the difference. One of the guys will soon switch onto a motorcycle and when he does I'll be able to start at 8. Then, with a little luck, and by pushing just a bit harder, I should be able to clear $95 or $100 a week, which would mean I could sock away $65 or $70. Numbers like those soon add up.

I've decided that, as long as you are doing all right in Ste. Thérèse, instead of sending money in dribs and drabs I'll stash it in a bank and send it in larger chunks. That'll save us the cost of countless small money orders. Don't worry about anything, Mom. Just keep paying the bills as best you can. And then, when finally I do come home, they won't exist. All you have to do is believe in me. I've told you I can do it and I will do it.

In answer to your question, yes, I do spend most of my time alone — or at least without the company of other human beings. I get up around 7, eat breakfast and get to Golden Gate Delivery for 8:30 (soon to be 8). I pedal around the downtown core until 6 p.m., delivering letters and small parcels.

Usually I get home around 7 o'clock. I eat supper and prepare the next day's lunch. By the time that's done, it's 7:45. I relax for 15 or 20 minutes, then do some upper-body exercises (push-ups and sit-ups). I do enough lower-body during the day. Around 8:30 I take a 20-minute bath, and then I read the Bible until 10 o'clock, when I turn out the light.

On weekends I take long walks, often through Golden Gate Park, where I read in the sun. I also spend a lot of time at the public library, in the religion section. I do my washing Saturday night and usually shop for groceries on Friday, right after work. Or else Sunday, if I'm too tired.

I did have one friend, a guy named Mitchell, but I thought he was somebody he wasn't and we've drifted apart. I don't mind because nobody is alone when God is with him.

Remember: God so loved the world that He gave his only begotten son, that whosever believes in Him should never perish, but have everlasting life. Jesus told us to love one another as he loved us -- and then laid down his life to show us what he meant. That's what every one of us should be doing, each in his own small way.

Your loving son,
Jack

P.S. Don't worry about my address. Keep my mail coming c/o General Delivery.

*

May 21, 1967.

Dear Mom:

Jack Kerouac's family was once sorely tested by water, as I recall, so I'm relieved that you weren't flooded out. But if the water ruined the linoleum in the back room, you have to replace it. What else can you do? At least the foundation's intact.

I can't tell you how sorry I was to learn that Dad refuses to change his ways. Surely in time he'll realize that drinking isn't going to solve anything, but will only make life worse, both for himself and others. I do hope, however, that you aren't nagging him. That would only aggravate an already bad situation, as I'm sure you know by now. Tell Dad no, I'm not writing any more. Just these letters. That which comes not of faith is sin.

I'm glad you've decided that, except for the flooring, you won't buy anything more on credit. That will be a big help. For my part, I'll continue saving until I've got enough money to pay off the remaining debts. Maybe you could send me a list of what we owe? I've started going into work at 8. The weather has been warming up some — 85 degrees the other day. A little too hot.

Mom, you've once again asked that I reconsider what I'm doing. But Jesus taught that any man who looks back after he has taken up the plow is not fit for the Kingdom of Heaven. Also, he rebuked the Pharisees for teaching that freedom means saying to your parents, "It is a gift by whatsoever thou mightest be profited by me." So, all I'm doing is my duty.

Your loving son,
Jack

P.S. Just received the Expo '67 *Gazette* you mailed ages ago. Thanks for sending it. Having looked it over, though, I honestly can't see what the fuss is all about. Vanity.

*

June 7, 1967.

Dear Mom:
I'm afraid there's not much news at this end, either. In fact I have no news at all. Sorry if I've been "lecturing" lately. I'll try to stop.

I enclose a money order for $50 as you said you were short. Naturally, I'll send money whenever you need it. I would prefer it, though, if you could hang on and meet the payments until I can get enough cash together to pay off everything at once — which I will *certainly* do.

I stress "certainly" because last letter you said "if" a couple of times, as in "if" I am still saving to pay off the bills. Mom, that's the only reason I'm still here in San Francisco: to save enough money to pay off the bills.

Now that I think about it, maybe you could send me details of what you pay each month? Please do this soon, and include the totals outstanding at each place, as I'm anxious to know where we stand.

215

Thanks for sending Thibideau's wedding photo. I'm sure she's a lovely girl. As the apostle Paul wrote, "Better to marry than to burn."

Good news that Eddie is taking over the *Gazette* route. It's a chore, but looking back, I realize I enjoyed those summer bicycle rides, those cold winter walks. Remember when those men stole our boat during the flood? And I went and stole it back, left them stranded?

That's about it for now. Hope everything is going well there, with a minimum of bickering and arguing. I miss you all.

Your loving son,
Jack

*

June 24, 1967.

Dear Mom:

Thanks for the partial list of debts. I'd expected worse. Why, Ogilvy's department store can be discharged in four months. You say we'll never get quit of bills because something new is always cropping up. You forget that once the debt is zero, you'll be able to pay cash for everything you buy — and put money in the bank besides.

The only way we'll succeed, though, is if you (and the rest of the family) stem the tide of new bills until I reverse it. I hope you'll send a more complete list of debts as soon as possible, including details about Household Finance, Uncle Henry and Lobey's Men's Wear.

My address, since that's the third time you've asked, is 1436 Grove Street. Please keep my mail coming to General Delivery, however, as it might get lost if it came here to the house. In an emergency you could call Golden Gate Delivery Service (626-6788). That's it for now. I miss you all very much.

Love,
Jack

*

July 17, 1967.

Dear Mom:

There are several reasons why I couldn't do what I'm now doing from Ste. Thérèse Sur-le-lac or even Montreal.

1. The temptation for me to let bills slide would be much greater and we might never get out of debt.

2. The temptation for you folks to spend money on goods you don't really need (like alcohol) would be much greater. You might say, "Well, with Jack helping, we can afford this little extra" — when you wouldn't really need it.

3. Most important, if I were there the family would lack incentive. If Jesus had NOT gone away, he would have saved nobody. If I were home, Dad would have no reason even to consider going on the wagon.

Believe me, I'm at least as anxious as you are to get the bills paid off. I'd like to move on to doing something else. But this is the only way. So, if you can, please continue meeting the payments without my help — as you've done in the past. Then, in no time at all, we'll be free: no more bills hanging over our heads.

You asked about my future. I have no idea what I'll do, Mom, but "getting ahead" or "becoming a success" are out. I don't worry, however: "Consider the ravens: for they neither sow nor reap, which neither have storehouse nor barn, and God feedeth them: how much more are ye better than the fowls?"

I'm sure that, once we've discharged this debt, God will reveal a new task. Please send a complete financial statement with your next letter.

I was about to close, but remembered something else. How do you make those special muffins? And what about that meatball stew? Can you think of anything else that would be good for supper — quick and easy to prepare and not expensive? I'm getting tired of eating the same meals over and over. I've gleaned a few recipes from package-backs but I know you've got "secret methods." What about those donuts you used to make?

Love to all,
Jack

*

Aug. 12, 1967.

Dear Mom:
From your latest I deduce the following:

Hot water tank	$146
Electric	365
Sewing machine	285
Ogilvy's	60
You did't count the flood repairs, but I guess	500
Lobey's Men's Wear	200
Uncle Henry and Household Finance probably	1,750
GRAND TOTAL	3,306

Don't be discouraged, Mom. The debt isn't that bad. I do wish you'd send me precise figures, though, for the last two items. If I had exact totals and details on the payments (amounts and frequencies) I could make some accurate projections about how long this will take us. Might surprise you.

At this end, I've been working from 8 to 6 for some time now, setting daily delivery records and clearing $110 a week. We haven't had rain for a while and that helps. When it rains I have to wear a wet suit, jacket and pants both, like when I picked tobacco. That slows me down. Also, the streets are treacherous, especially the ones with cable-car tracks.

Yes, I read the Bible nightly. Also, I've been investigating the Protestant Reformation, mainly William Tyndale and Martin Luther. Following Jesus is not just a matter of doing our best, as you recently suggested. As Luther pointed out, our best is simply not good enough and deserves nothing but death and destruction. That's why God sent Jesus into the world. Because alone we can do nothing.

Now, once we believe that Jesus saves us not because we deserve it, or because we're doing our best, but simply because he loves us — why, how can we help loving our fellow man? How can we help changing our ways?

Write soon and let me know how you're doing.

Your loving son,
Jack

*

Aug. 24, 1967.
Dear Mom:

Enclosed is a money order for $1,000.

I'd intended to save until I could pay off the bills in one shot. After thinking about it, though, I decided instalments of $1,000 would be best. For one thing, we'll save money by reducing the interest payments on what we owe.

I don't want you to say, or even to think, that my paying off the bills is anything but a duty. As the Bible says, "He who does not provide for his own, and especially for those of his own household, has denied the faith, and is worse than an unbeliever."

You said in your last letter, Mom, that God doesn't want us to suffer. That's true. But I'm not suffering. Everything I do, I do of my own free will — for God has set me free. I act, not because I must, but because I'm grateful for the gifts God has given all of us.

Mom, I hope now you'll stop worrying. We'll pay off the bills. If I were alone, it's true, I might not be able to finish. But nobody is alone when God is with him. It is not me who will pay off the bills, but God, who is working through me. And God can never fail.

So please don't fret. This is only the first $1,000.

I hope everyone there is well.

Write soon, Mom.

Love,

Jack

36

T O FRANKIE THE NARRATOR, WHO WAS STILL FUMING, I PUT A NO-HARD-FEELINGS QUESTION:
— WASN'T 1967 THE YEAR THAT TENS OF THOUSANDS OF YOUNG PEOPLE DESCENDED ON SAN FRANCISCO WEARING FLOWERS IN THEIR HAIR?
— In a word, yes.
— OUR BOY TURNED HIS BACK ON THE SUMMER OF LOVE?
— I got out, yes, just before the Haight turned into a nightmare wonderland of would-be pimps, big-time dope dealers and baffled fourteen-year-olds looking for love.
— THOUGH EVERY COUPLE OF WEEKS YOU'D VISIT TO MARVEL AT THE THRONGS OF BEAUTIFUL PEOPLE AND THE GAWKING TOURISTS AND CONGRATULATE YOURSELF ON HAVING MADE YOUR ESCAPE.
— Do you mind?
— BACK IN HARNESS. OKAY, I'M GONE.

Two days after I found myself in Hell, as I say, the guy who'd sublet Bernie's Bunker left me a note: "WHOEVER YOU ARE: This storage room, otherwise known as the Hobbit Hole, belongs to my apartment. Vacate it within twenty-four hours or I call the cops."

Again Mitchell urged me to find a job. Now, having cast him as the Reincarnated Jesus, I felt compelled to heed his advice. The Hip Job Co-op, a store-front agency, sent me downtown to Golden Gate Delivery Service, which was perenially short-staffed. The dispatcher hired me on the spot.

On the strength of this job, I borrowed twenty-five dollars from Mitchell and, to save on bus fare, rented a stop-gap room at a downtown hotel — a fleabag called the Cameo.

The night before I moved, I spotted Toby out front of the Psychedelic Shop, turned and walked the other way.

"Frankie! Wait up!"

"Get out of my life, Toby. I know who you are."

"Okay, okay. Just answer one question: What did you do with the grass I left at the Hobbit Hole? The Acapulco Gold?"

"I flushed it down the toilet."

"Three lids? You're putting me on."

"No, I'm not. I know you're the Devil, Toby. Anything to do with you is Evil."

I left him on Haight Street, one hand over his eyes, shaking his head, muttering. Never saw him again. Now I wonder if his superiors pulled him out of the Haight. Maybe he quit and later became an agronomist?

Newly installed at the Cameo, frightened and disoriented and lost to an evolving archetype, a pattern of initiation whose details were mine to create, I spent my days pedalling a one-speed bicycle around the San Francisco streets. Nights I was too beat to do anything but read. Curious about my past life as the Near James — just how important had I been? — I began perusing a Gideon Bible I found in my hotel room.

Six weeks of immersion was all it took: Mitchell wasn't the reincarnated Jesus. God had used Mitchell to lead me to the real Son of God. The mysterious force had been God the Father driving me to repentance and baptism — to die and be born again. The Devil had turned up to steal the baptismal gift of the Holy Ghost — a gift evidenced by my vision of myself as angel. And Jesus had manifested himself to save me from the predatory Devil.

For the first time since I'd popped acid, everything made sense. And one Sunday afternoon, fresh from John's account of the crucifixion, I fell to my knees in the Cameo Hotel and said the Lord's Prayer for the first time since childhood.

Had I once been the Near James? This no longer mattered —
though the Bible, I noted, didn't rule it out — because there
remained the spectacular style of my salvation, starting with the
storm-tossed baptism. Obviously, I'd been chosen to perform
some important task. God would show me what it was. All I had
to do was wait.

Meanwhile, living at the Cameo meant always eating out.
This was expensive. Three weeks, it had taken me, to repay
Mitchell's loan. I needed a place where I could cook. I searched
the Haight but beautiful people were arriving from all over the
continent, many with flowers in their hair. No way I could
re-enter the communal life, not now. And vacant rooms didn't
exist.

I broadened my search area. Finally, one Saturday afternoon,
half a mile from the Haight, I spotted a room-for-rent sign. Rang
the bell but nobody answered. Three times I left and returned
and at last a big woman answered the door. She ran a blacks-only
rooming house, didn't want trouble and showed me a window-
less cell — by far the lesser of two rooms, I learned later, then
vacant. Perfect, I insisted. I'd take it. No, I didn't mind sharing
kitchen and bathroom.

Next day, though it took me weeks to realize it, I became the
only white person not in the rooming house, but the neighborhood. And so I remained for the next several months — months
that, I note in retrospect, produced not a single race-related
incident. True, I didn't go looking for trouble. But six nights a
week I ate in the kitchen and one of the roomers became almost a
friend. This was a woman named Lurline, who hummed bluesy
tunes while she cooked supper for her live-in boyfriend. A
couple of times she bent over in front of me and her dress fell
open and I'd leave the kitchen to avoid temptation.

But the only real problem at the house was a dock worker
called Big Man. This giant stevedore lived at the end of the hall
and invariably greeted me with a too-hard slap on the back. All
the roomers feared Big Man. Lurline said he had a mean streak.
Just before I'd arrived, when another roomer accused him of

stealing food from the fridge, Big Man threw him down the stairs and broke his leg.

One night Big Man brought home a woman. Two o'clock in the morning, they started shouting about money. Big Man told her to get out. She said not until he paid what he owed her. I heard a crash, then slapping. I was still screwing up my courage to intervene when, crying and cursing, the woman burst out of Big Man's room. She stumbled past my door and down the stairs, then stood outside on the sidewalk yelling that Ernest was a liar and a cheat. Finally Big Man exploded out of his room, charged down the stairs and chased her into the night.

Briefly, I considered moving.

But cheaper rooms didn't exist. Besides, I had other things on my mind. Somehow, I had to emulate Jesus, who'd sacrificed himself to save the world. A life-time ago, when I'd left Montreal, my mother had wanted me to stay and help out financially. The money worries, I knew, were a symptom. The real problem was my father's drinking.

Gradually, I developed a plan. I'd lay my life on the line, as Jesus had done, by remaining in San Francisco until the family was out of debt. If my father loved me, he'd quit drinking. It was simply a matter of will power. I imagined myself returning home to a debt-free family headed by a tea-totaller.

But see me zipping around San Francisco on a heavy-duty, one-speed bicycle, a walkie-talkie strapped to my chest, resplendent in a blue uniform: light blue shirt, dark blue slacks and matching jacket, a crest on the back proclaiming "Golden Gate Delivery Service." Up Bush, down California, swing along Montgomery to Market, down Sixth onto Mission, up Seventh, out to Van Ness and then back all the way to Sansome, up Washington, whatever the weather, round and round and round.

A messenger had to respect the cable-car tracks, especially on rainy days. California Street was the worst, and three or four times I caught a bicycle tire and crashed to the pavement. Parked cars were another hazard. Once, while whizzing along Montgomery, I glanced over my shoulder as a driver opened his door and smash! sent me sprawling into the middle of the street, helpless in the path of a monster truck. At the last possible instant the driver swerved, honking furiously, and missed me.

I took a five-minute break, then went back at it.

Three months into the job, the dispatcher began loud-hailing me as the best messenger in the history of Golden Gate Delivery Service. My secret? Non-stop revision. Like my fellow messengers, I now knew every back alley and shortcut in the downtown core. But often a messenger would have ten or twelve deliveries in his basket and three more to collect. As I pedalled I'd work out the most efficient order in which to make stops, and I'd keep changing that order as I received new calls, save myself a minute here, a minute there. Those minutes translated into more deliveries — and so dollars.

Even so it took me five months to sock away $1,000. I mailed off the money order, then waited. My mother was strangely slow to respond. When she did write, her letter of thanks was more troubled than thrilled. She worried about me constantly, she said, and again urged me to return home. My father had no intention of giving up drinking and felt I was trying to blackmail him. That was the word he'd used. Blackmail.

That night in bed, as I read and re-read my mother's letter, I remembered a night I'd forgotten. I was fourteen, fifteen at most. My father was working in Montreal, selling shoes in a department store, and when I woke to the creak of the kitchen door I automatically checked the clock. Quarter to twelve. No trains due: he'd stopped off at La Fin Du Monde.

My father stumbled into the house and shut the door behind him. He kicked off his boots, threw his coat on the couch: "Maggie, I'm hungry. What have we got to eat?"

My mother told him to keep his voice down, he'd wake the kids. That his supper was in the oven where it always was at this time of night. Having retrieved the food and eaten a bit, my father threw down his fork and yelled that his meal was cold: "Guy slaves away at work all day, he's got a right to a hot meal. Get out here and make me something to eat."

"Make it yourself," my mother responded. "What do you think I am? A bloody servant?"

The usual exchange. I pulled my pillow over my head but it did no good. And tonight the battle took a twist: "To hell with this," my father said. "I'm going back to the hotel. Give me ten bucks."

"You're not going back to the hotel. You've had enough drink for one night."

"That thirty dollars I gave you yesterday — where is it?"

"That money's for bills. The milkman, the baker, the grocer — I can't look anybody in the face any more. Have to send Frankie to the store so we can buy a can of beans. If we don't pay something this week, we won't be able to — Maurice! Get out of that!"

My father had stomped into their bedroom and was opening drawers, banging them shut. "I've had enough shit, Maggie. Where's that money?"

"I've already told you. There is no money for drink. Get out of my dresser. And shut up that talk. The kids can hear every word you say."

"Let them hear! I'm the king around here! I'm the king of this fucking castle and I'll say what I please. I'm warning you, Maggie. I want that money and I'm going to fucking get it."

"Over my dead body, you will."

"All right." My father was back in the kitchen. "All right, if that's the way you want it." Slamming around among the utensils.

"Drink, drink, drink!" My mother had followed. "Don't you see what you're doing? You're destroying yourself with drink."

"See this, Maggie? See this? Now, where's that fucking money?"

"Put that down, you bloody fool."

"Where's that money, Maggie? Tell me or I'll kill you! I'll fucking kill you!"

This was the worst yet. Out of bed I leapt and ran into the kitchen. My father stood in the middle of the room, hunched over, swaying, still in his white shirt, his tie askew. In his right hand he had a butcher knife.

"Frankie! Go back to bed!" My mother was in her night gown, her black hair loose to her shoulders. "Right this minute."

"I won't." I edged around my father, the linoleum cold against my bare feet. Went and stood beside my mother. "Not until he goes."

"Mommy! Mommy!" Janey came running out of the girls' room. "Mommy, are you all right?"

"Now look what you've done." My mother took Janey in her arms. "You'll have the whole house up in a minute. You kids go back to bed. Come on, Janey."

I said, "I'm not going back to bed."

The butcher knife gleamed. My father swayed, almost fell over, caught himself. He stank of beer. "Okay, smart guy." He laid the knife on the counter. "You've been asking for it." He put up his fists. "Now you're going to get it." He swung at the air in front of my face. "Come on, smart guy. What's a matter?"

"Maurice! For the love of God!"

My father looked huge — far bigger than I'd ever seen him. His knuckles were white, his eyes bloodshot.

"What's a matter, smart guy?" He took another wild swing. "What's a matter? No moxie?" He put one fist behind his back and shook the other in my face. "Look! Look, smart guy! One hand! I'll take you with one hand!"

My mouth was dry. I couldn't breathe. I clenched my fists but didn't move.

"Or no! No!" My father fell to his knees, still with one hand behind his back. "Look! Look, smart guy, I'll take you like this."

Janey started to cry.

"What's a matter, smart guy? No moxie?"

I took a half-step. "Get up."

My mother grabbed me by the arm. "Maurice, have you gone mad? Picking a fight with your own son?"

"He's got no moxie." My father was still on his knees, one fist in the air. "No fucking moxie." He banged his fist on the floor. "Me! I'm the one who had the moxie! I'm the one who had the talent." He banged again. "Never had a chance. Fifteen years old! Fifteen years old it was out to work in a glove factory!"

Both fists at once, hunched over, banging, punctuating his words. "I'm the one had the talent!" *Blam!* "But it was out to work!" *Blam!* "Out to work in the glove factory." He switched to open palms, kept slamming them on the floor. *Blam! Blam!* "Never got a break." *Blam! Blam!* "Never had a chance." *Blam! Blam! Blam!*

My father started to cry. I stood over him glaring, clenching and unclenching my fists. He kept pounding the floor and blubbering, repeating the same empty phrases. Finally, still crying and sporadically banging, but just one hand, he rolled over onto his side and, to my surprise, fell into a deep sleep.

My mother put Janey to bed.

I picked up the butcher knife and marvelled at its gleaming in the kitchen light. My mother returned to the kitchen, took the knife and put it away in the drawer. She looked down at my father, sprawled on the floor, snoring. "It's drink that does it," she said. "Drink makes him this way."

She knelt, untied my father's shoes and pulled them off. "Help me lift him onto the couch."

"Let's just leave him there."

"Take his arms, Frankie."

I helped her swing my father onto the couch, then kissed her goodnight and went back to bed. For a while I could hear my mother moving around the kitchen, cleaning up the mess. Finally, she, too, went to bed.

Now, in San Francisco, as I lay in my tiny room poring over my mother's letter, I felt that long-ago night in my stomach. How could I have imagined my father would stop drinking? Instead, he'd accused me of blackmail. So be it, then. If my father wouldn't stop drinking, I'd pay off the bills by myself. I'd do it alone.

But for seven, eight months I'd been working like a slave and living like a hermit. And I'd sent home only $1,000. Ahead of me stretched eighteen more months, maybe twenty-four, as arid and lonely as the past six.

Trouble was, I'd sworn in the name of Jesus that I wouldn't return to Ste. Thérèse until we'd paid off all the bills. Round and round I went, and finally I drifted off to sleep knowing there was no way out....

I found myself on a cement terrace, looked up and saw Jack Kerouac descending a broad spiral staircase. I ran up the steps and shook his hand: "I've missed you more than you can know."

Kerouac shadow-boxed at me, laughing, then threw his arms around me and thumped me on the back. Together we came down the stairs. We walked to the edge of the terrace, which was encircled by a balustrade and overlooked a great city.

Night was falling. Clusters of people stared up at the sky, obviously waiting for something. Suddenly a sleek, ultramodern train, shining silver with blue stripes, glided through the sky towards us, silently laying tracks as it came. Directly overhead, the train made a U-turn, then glided back the way it had come and disappeared into the distance.

Seconds, this took, while everyone watched, and then the train was gone but its tracks were left hanging in the sky. Everybody could see where it had passed. I found this amazing, but nobody else cared so I thought, it's nothing, and turned away.

Kerouac tugged at the sleeve of my jacket — I was wearing my messenger's uniform -- and pointed at the tracks: "Look, Frankie. It made tracks and left them behind."

I nodded: "You think it means something?"

"Fearful sights and great signs."

The phrase sounded vaguely familiar. But it didn't makes sense. "What are you on, Jack?"

"Nothing but Jesus."

"Jesus?" Suddenly I was all ears. "What do you mean, Jesus?"

"The Shadow knows, Frankie." Kerouac punched my shoulder, then turned, strode to the spiral staircase and started to climb. Troubled, I watched him disappear into a mist, then moved to the edge of the terrace. I stood looking out over the balustrade at the skyline of the city, frowning: What had Kerouac been trying to tell me?

Thock! Before my eyes, a tall building disappeared. *Thock! Thock!* Two more were gone — sucked down into the earth like carrots in a Bugs Bunny cartoon. *Thock! Thock!* Then *whisk!* A new building. *Whisk! Whisk!* New buildings popped out of the ground to replace the old ones. *Whisk! Whisk!* These buildings were bigger, more numerous, more beautiful. *Whisk! Whisk! Whisk!*

As the city grew, drawing nearer, I turned to the people around me and pointed at the shooting buildings: "Fearful sights and great signs." As I spoke I recognized the phrase. It came from the Bible. Fearful sights and great signs would precede the end of the world. That's what Kerouac had been trying to tell me. A silent sky train laying its own tracks. Buildings shooting up and down. These were the fearful sights, the great signs. This was the end of the world.

I began pleading with those around me, pointing at the tracks in the sky and the shooting buildings, saying, "Fearful sights and great signs!" But people turned their backs and walked away. Nobody understood what I was talking about. Suddenly I knew what we had to do. "Give glory to God," I said. "Give glory to God!"

But nobody paid any attention.

Now came a tingling sensation, my whole body buzzing, and I understood that the Holy Ghost had come upon me, breathing me full of authority, so now I was no longer pleading but speaking loudly, assertively, telling people: "Give glory to God!" Then it wasn't me speaking at all, but the Holy Ghost speaking through me, enunciating clearly, using my voice to command people: "Give glory to God! Give glory to God!"

People ignored this. Panicking, confused by the rocketing buildings, they charged back and forth across the terrace. And even as we spoke, the Holy Ghost and I, the buildings grew bigger and more beautiful, *thock! thock! whisk! whisk! whisk!* until *WHISK!* one glorious building exploded out of the earth and filled the sky.

It glowed beige and beautiful and strangely old-fashioned, ancient even, with a roof that sloped upwards from two sides then broke into a pinnacle. A giant clock dominated the face of this peak and as I read the time — what? not two minutes to twelve? — the beautiful building cracked loudly and slowly crumbled to the ground, smoke billowing.

Then the other buildings, magnificent skyscrapers, started tumbling, smashing into each other, *crack! crack!* and as people cried, "Earthquake! Earthquake!" I felt myself swung up off the terrace and returned, as if dangling from a rope that had to be tested. Now I was shouting, or the Holy Ghost was shouting through me in a loud voice, enunciating clearly: "Give glory to God! Give glory to God!"

Black smoke billowed over the terrace and everything was chaos as the city crumbled, people screaming and running but not knowing what to do. I kept telling them, shouting: "Give glory to God! Give glory to God!"

But nobody paid any attention and again I was swung up off the terrace, only this time I wasn't returned and tears rolled down my cheeks as slowly I was reeled up into the sky, as if by a giant winch, still holding out my arms and shouting, "Give glory to God! Give glory to God!"

And even as I swung upwards, the loud voice and my voice were one, but suddenly my own voice stopped and the loud voice said once more, this time to me, enunciating clearly, commanding me: "GIVE GLORY TO GOD!"

I awoke sitting upright in my bed, trembling, with the loud voice, the voice of the Holy Ghost, ringing around me, commanding me clearly: "GIVE GLORY TO GOD!"

I sat a moment, stunned, then switched on my lamp and looked at the clock. Quarter to five. I climbed out of bed, sat down at the small table in my room and, at the top of a blank sheet of paper, wrote: "A VISION OF THE END OF THE WORLD."

By the time I'd finished describing my experience, the clock said half-past six. Time to get ready for work. I ate breakfast as usual, but then, instead of donning my uniform, I pulled on my jeans and a workshirt. I folded my blue shirt and trousers, my jacket with the Golden Gate Delivery crest, stuffed them all into a brown paper bag, then carried this bag downtown to the office.

The dispatcher couldn't believe I was quitting. "What do you mean you had a vision? Jack, have you been doing drugs? Listen, we'll put you on a motorcycle. Think of it: your own motorcycle."

On my way home I rented a typewriter.

For the next ten days, I sat hunched over the tiny table in my room, pounding away, writing and rewriting a testament I called *What God Has Done For Me*. Sometimes, when I thought of taking this out into the streets, the mortification involved, I'd weep and pound my pillow. Then I'd remind myself that I had a responsibility. The end of the world was at hand. God had chosen me to deliver the news. I imagined myself glorified, looking like the angel I'd seen in the mirror at the ocean, a latter-days prophet sitting, if not at the right hand of Jesus, then surely at his left.

WHAT GOD HAS DONE FOR ME

I didn't believe in God and I wasn't looking for him. In fact, I was gone far the other way. But God was looking for me, and although I didn't deserve it, He took me and showed me the Truth.

For my part I kicked and fought against Him as hard as I could. I just didn't want to hear about Jesus. But God was merciful and finally He did so many things that I couldn't deny the Truth any longer.

These are the things God has done for me — and I haven't deserved a single one.

GOD BAPTIZED ME   page 2
GOD MANIFESTED JESUS TO ME   5
GOD SAVED ME FROM THE DEVIL.   7
GOD SHOWED ME THAT THIS IS
     THE END OF THE WORLD   12

Before God did these things, I didn't believe in Jesus. But now I know that Jesus is true. Whoever believes these things also believes in Jesus, and whoever believes in Jesus knows these things are true....

37

The morning after the lightning storm, I awoke in the tower to find a slow-motion river of grey-white clouds churning through the valley. It tumbled past Jubilation just below the tower, spraying the windows with foggy wisps. I'd been contemplating Frankie's vision of the end of the world and what it implied, so the river became a rough sea and I stood alone on a ship's bridge, a captain navigating the difficult passage between the clashing rocks of Scylla and Charybdis.

A vision sweeps you through those rocks, I realized. That's the magic of it. For a time you sail boldly in the sunshine of conviction. No more confusion, no more angst, no more existential keening. In their place, transcendent innocence. Surely nothing is more beautiful than manifest commitment to spiritual truth, however partial that truth, however childish its expression?

For months after my fainting vision of the Golden Eternity, I fancied myself a special, solitary angel, a messenger sent to tell people or show them by example that they were living the wrong way. A writer friend once suggested that a man is Beat when he wagers the sum of his resources on a single number. Make that Beatific, I thought as I considered my all-time favorite Frankie — the one who plunged into the streets of San Francisco with a stack of pamphlets under his arm.

But the morning sun was burning holes in the cloud cover. As the valley floor became visible, the illusion of rolling seas faded. And I abandoned ship.

For breakfast Frankie cooked buckwheat pancakes. We washed them down with coffee, then checked the tower for burn marks. Found nothing. It was as if the lightning storm had never happened — except that, with fire hazard at its peak, Frankie had to climb into the tower and stay there.

This would be my last full day on Jubilation. After cleaning the breakfast dishes, I packed a lunch, shouted *au revoir* and followed a trail around the back of the mountain. For over an hour I climbed, emerging from the dwindling forest onto an almost vertical desert of shale and scree and giant boulders.

Eventually I arrived, as Frankie had said I would, at a mossy plateau radiant with alpine flowers. Far below, in a dark green valley, an ice-blue lake fed into a river that meandered past, brazenly turquoise. Snow-capped mountains rolled away to the horizon, and as I ate my peanut-butter sandwiches I remembered looking north from Desolation Peak, seeing clouds of hope drifting in the sky above Canada, and thought how right it was that in the spring of 1967, while Frankie was in San Francisco, transforming himself into Saint Jack of the Sixteen-Page Pamphlet, I made my final trip to his native city.

I'd recently unearthed some notes I'd written seventeen years earlier, plans for a novel about French Canadians in America. *The Vanity of St. Louis*, as I called it, would focus on my own ancestors. It would open in *la belle province*, then move south to the dark mill towns of New England. To do the requisite research, I'd applied for a Guggenheim Fellowship, said I wanted to visit Quebec. I didn't get the grant but never forgot the project and was brooding over it in Lowell when a film crew arrived from Montreal — half a dozen guys wearing beards and granny glasses and black leather coats.

They were shooting a TV documentary about New England Canucks and including footage from bars like The Three Copper Men and Nicky's, my brother-in-law's place. No way they could have missed me, a celebrity writer roaring around in red flannel shirt and green workman's pants, talking homespun French to anybody who'd listen or else falling to my knees to warble Sinatra: "I guess I'll have to dream the rest...."

My performance earned me an invitation to appear on a TV talk-show called *Le Sel de la Semaine*. I had misgivings, of course. A couple of years before, in France, people had laughed at the way I spoke French. But in Montreal, I told myself, I'd be a prodigal returning home. I didn't realize that *la belle province* was still emerging from *Le Grand Noirceur*. That I'd be visiting a Quebec that was clinging to Europe, not celebrating North America — a Quebec in which *bien parler c'est se respecter*, and where a Parisian accent was still *o la la*.

My brother-in-law Nicky drove me to Montreal.

At the studio they sat me down with a supercilious talk-show host in front of an audience, turned on the lights and rolled 'em. *M'sieur Chose*, as I called the host, Mister Something-or-other, wore shirt and tie and shiny suit, while I was decked out in too-short corduroy slacks, tired desert boots and a sports shirt open at the neck, a white T-shirt underneath.

The worst of it was that, every time I spoke, the studio bubbled with laughter. At first I didn't understand it. Then I realized that these sophisticated Montrealers were laughing at my old-style French, learned from Mémère — at my *pataraffes* and *chalivaris*, the language recognizable but definitely not *à la mode*. I was not a returning prodigal but a faintly embarrassing curiosity.

That night, with Nicky and a couple of would-be poets, I started drinking at *Taverne de Trappeur*. We moved to the Jazz Club and then the Black Bottom, one of Frankie's old-favorite bars, and ended up at a brothel where I listened to Billie Holiday on the juke box and paid three times to take a woman upstairs and never went. Eventually I passed out under a table.

I never did get around to writing *The Vanity of St. Louis*, and this I regretted even as I sat on Mount Jubilation, smelling the alpine flowers and looking out at the white-capped Canadian Rockies.

Later that afternoon, having retraced my steps, I approached the lookout through the trees and heard Frankie using his two-way radio, a note of urgency in his voice: "Jubilation Lookout calling Saskatchewan River Crossing... Jubilation Lookout to Saskatchewan River Crossing."

He waited a moment, then tried again. "Jubilation Lookout calling the Crossing. Come in, please."

I shouted from the ground. "What's up?"

Frankie stuck his head out the open window.

"Smoke! Come take a look."

I scrambled up the ladder. Frankie helped me into the tower, handed me the binoculars and pointed: "Look down there. Near the highway. The rock cut."

Black smoke was billowing skywards. "I don't remember lightning striking there."

"I don't, either. Maybe it hit while we were cursing in the dark. Who cares? We've got ourselves a forest fire."

"I don't know, Frankie." I peered again through the glasses. "The smoke's oddly close to the highway."

"Jubilation Lookout calling Saskatchewan River Crossing. Jubilation Lookout calling the Crossing. Come in please."

"Mobile Unit here. Go ahead, Jubilation."

"Smoke! I see black smoke near the rock cut."

No response.

Frankie said, "Mobile Unit, do you read me? We've got a fire to fight!"

"We read you, Jubilation. Where's the smoke?"

"About three miles south of the station. Just off the highway near the rock cut."

Another silence.

"This is Jubilation Lookout. We've got a fire blazing. Do you read me?"

"Jubilation, we're parked at the rock cut south of the station. Along with a big yellow garbage truck. Can you see us?"

I handed Frankie the binoculars: "There's something yellow down there, just right of the cut."

Frankie peered through the glasses, then returned to the radio. "Mobile Unit, I do see yellow in the trees. And lots of smoke."

"The fire is under control, Jubilation. The driver of the garbage truck put it here. His load caught fire and he dumped it."

"He dumped a fire on the side of the highway?"

"That's right, Jubilation. In a clearing here. The forest is safe."

Frankie hesitated, then said, "Okay, Mobile Unit. Saw black smoke and thought I'd better check."

"Thanks, Jubilation." There was laughter in the warden's voice. "Mobile Unit clear."

"Jubilation clear." Frankie slumped in his chair and covered his eyes. "I've done it again!"

"The smoke was real enough."

"But I leapt to the wrong conclusion."

I swung into Sinatra: "Dream, when you're feeling blue/ Dream, that's the thing to do."

Frankie got to his feet, faced the open window and howled: "*Aaaagggghhhhh!*"

"Just watch the smoke rings rise in the air/ You'll find your share of memories there."

"*Aaaagggghhhh! Aaaagggghhhh!*"

"Dream, when the day is through/ Dream, your dreams might come true/ Things never are as bad as they seem/ So dream, dream, dream."

Unable to resist the magic of Sinatra, Frankie joined in on the last two lines. Then he howled out the window once more: "*Aaaaaagggghhhhh!*"

I glanced at my watch. "Almost dinner time. What do you say we have some cider?"

"Don't you remember? We finished it last night."

"No, I've got one more jug. Found it in my pack this morning."

Frankie just looked at me.

Leaving the window open, just in case the warden radioed, we climbed down out of the tower. Frankie went and sat on his favorite grey stump while I fetched the cider and glasses. I returned triumphant and, as I poured drinks, Frankie said, "You know, I could have sworn you checked that pack last night."

I handed him his glass: "A toast, then! To miraculous discoveries."

We drank.

Then Frankie said: "You know this fantasy of yours, Kerouac and the miracles? I've been thinking and I still don't understand your game."

"Let's suppose, Frankie, that a posthumous miracle needs verification."

"I knew you weren't finished."

"A miracle-worker needs an articulate witness who has the courage to testify." I joined Frankie on the stump. "My first challenge, obviously, was to find that only right messenger."

"Will I never learn to shut my mouth?"

"A welter of would-be writers, veterans of the rucksack revolution, were clamoring for the job, none of them consciously. I had to narrow the field. How can I explain this? It's like running variables through a computer."

"What? You mean punch cards?"

"Oh, right, we're 1970. Frankie, I came up with a short list of candidates."

"Wait. Let me guess. My name was on it."

"Not because you're a genius."

"Hey, I admire you, too."

"It's a matter of correspondences. But my information was sketchy. I was seeing through a glass darkly, couldn't make out all the signs."

"Not more signs."

"I had to focus on each prospect in turn. One guy was turning acid-freak. Another had given himself to artificial intelligence."

Frankie tried Sinatra: "Dream, when you're feeling blue/ Dream, that's the thing to do."

I grinned but persevered. "Others were tougher to eliminate. One French Canadian in particular. Victor-Levy Beaulieu?"

"Beaulieu? The name's familiar."

"He's written two or three books. Next year he'll write one about me."

"That's rich!" Frankie slapped his thigh. "Tell me, Kerouac, do you like next year's book?"

"Not much. Too sloppy. Beaulieu will have me visiting France three years early. He'll say I wrote *Big Sur* when I was barely thirty. He'll call Mardou Fox a prostitute. And he'll refuse to correct even what he discovers to be false, and instead warn readers to distrust his chronology."

"But that's a logical extension of the spontaneous method."

"It's a cop-out. Sheer laziness, really — though Beaulieu will defend it as creative freedom. He'll contend that I never achieved greatness because I clung to literal truth, recreating only what I'd experienced."

"An interesting idea."

"Wildly off-base. Look again at *Dr. Sax*. Sure, I wrote about Beaulieu Street — see what gave me pause? But also I created Snake Castle and Count Condu and the Master of Earthly Evil."

"So what does this guy get right?"

"He understands, despite himself, how profoundly French-Canadian I am. And how this influenced my life, mandating my relationship with Mémère and even my blood-brotherhood with Neal Cassady."

"I've never thought of Kerouac as profoundly French-Canadian. Slightly, maybe."

"That's why I'm glad Beaulieu's around. But he wants to see me as the end of something — the end of Quebec out-there — rather than as the continuation of something else. His angry politics was a flashing sign that read only in French. I knew he wasn't you when I turned to religion. Beaulieu rejects Beat saintliness."

"So do I."

"Ah, but Frankie, you're open to magic. No way Beaulieu could have heard me out."

"I'm having trouble myself."

"I hated to forsake Beaulieu, the French-Canadian connection so right. But then I realized that a variation might turn up in a Montrealer whose mother tongue was English. I focused next on you. And the signs flashed an inclusive yes."

"What do you mean, signs?"

"Parallels, portents, premonitions — knots in the twisted rope of shared fate. The tangled ancestry, the alcoholic father. The bizarre presence of Sinatra. Finally, here you were on Jubilation, floundering. I knew I'd found you."

"I'm not floundering."

"Twenty-three and tractionless. Writer's block. God is dead."

"God IS dead!"

"You've driven away the woman you love."

"I didn't drive Camille away. Who knows? Maybe we'll get back together."

"Better hurry, Frankie. And prepare to grovel."

"Okay, how do you do it? Having read my manuscript, you extrapolate?"

"Frankie, I've never read your manuscript."

"So what are you? A mind reader?"

"Not exactly. When you enter the body you accept limitations. But I get rushes, flashes."

"And you want me to believe you're Jack Kerouac, returned from the dead?"

"What if I do?"

"That you're a miracle worker on the road to great walking sainthood?"

I nodded vigorously.

Frankie knocked back the last of his cider. Shaking his head, he got to his feet and placed his empty glass on the stump beside me: "Mister, I don't know who you are or what. But I do know you're out of your mind."

"I need your help."

Frankie wheeled and strode away, calling over his shoulder: "I've left madness behind, pal. You've got the wrong guy."

38

"Those clips from 1959? *The Steve Allen Show?*" Camille brushed her blowing hair from in front of her face. "Kerouac looked like a movie star. Alert, intense, his face so expressive and alive. A young Tony Curtis with intelligence. Or maybe James Dean."

Grudgingly, I offered: "Salvador Dali declared him more beautiful than Brando."

"Perfect!" Camille clapped her hands. "Now, compare that Kerouac with the one who appears on *Firing Line* just nine years later."

A few nights before, Camille had rented a film biography that includes footage from both TV shows: the Antonelli classic I reviewed in 1986. Now we sat at the back of Tunnel Mountain on our favorite slab of grey rock, behind and below where the fire tower once stood, looking out at the Bow River winding away through a broad valley.

"He looks like a beer-swilling logger," she said. "He's fat, he's slovenly. The man looks coarse. Vulgar. Nobody would compare him with the early Brando."

"Kerouac was drunk at that shoot," I said. But as I spoke I remembered a third videotape, one Camille hadn't seen. Montreal, 1967: *Le Sel de la Semaine*. Kerouac didn't get drunk until after the show. On tape he's sober. But no denying the physical degeneration. The face is puffy, the features thick. The change is appalling. As I stared out at the turquoise river rolling away against the mountains, I decided not to mention this. "He was drunk when he arrived for the *Firing Line* interview," I said. "You're not being fair."

"And you're hiding something. No matter. The deterioration of the final, chronic stages is not just physical but mental and social. You yourself have argued that *Big Sur* is Kerouac's last great novel. What was it you said about Ferlinghetti?"

"That his beef with that book is purely personal. 'A tired old novel,' he calls it. But the language, the intensity, the powers of observation — *Big Sur* is one of the greatest novels Kerouac ever wrote."

"Now I remember: It's a portrait of the artist as a middle-aged drunk."

"As such, it's second only to *Under The Volcano*."

"Okay, Kerouac wrote *Bug Sur* late in 1961. Managed to pull himself together. Then what?"

"Then nothing, Camille, as obviously you know. *Satori in Paris* is embarrassing — a pathetic attempt to rationalize an alcoholic fiasco.

"That was 1965. Kerouac swilled cognac while he wrote."

"*Vanity of Duluoz* is slightly better."

"But only because he wrote sober. 1967. Don't you see, Frankie? These later novels show how far Kerouac fell. They reflect mental deterioration."

Camille was scaring me. Now that I thought about it, the loss of creative power was ominous. *Vanity of Duluoz* boasts nothing like the vitality, the sparkling immediacy of Kerouac's finest work. Talk about tired. But was that a measure of alcoholic damage? I shook off the thought: "With *Vanity of Duluoz*, Kerouac returned to his adolescence. To territory he'd already explored. The material was stale, that's all. And what about *Pic*? It has moments. And he finished that later."

"Frankie, you know perfectly well that *Pic* was a rewrite of something ancient. And that, in fashioning an abrupt, awkward ending to make a sale, Kerouac let himself be guided by Stella and Mémère — neither of whom had a track record as a fiction editor."

Caught out, I chuckled.

But also I made a mental note, because for the first time I glimpsed Kerouac's Great Cycle, a creative eruption that lasted ten years from *On The Road*, first draft, to *Big Sur*. Before and after, I saw mere bookends: *The Town and the City*, *Vanity of Duluoz*. One written before Kerouac found his voice, the other after he lost it to alcoholism.

"Laugh if you want, Frankie. But after 1962, by your own witness, Kerouac was just another scribbling drunk. That's mental decline. And we haven't even touched on the social."

"Sorry. I'm not used to you talking Kerouac."

"Get used to it. Socially, the man was still functioning in 1960. Still part of the literary scene. He wrote Ferlinghetti and crossed the continent. Then came the Bixby Canyon heebie-jeebies."

"Which you see as a final turning point."

Camille nodded. "The beginning of the end. He pulled himself together to write *Big Sur*. But by 1962, fat and forty in Orlando, Florida, *Le Grand Jack* was into the Big Slide."

"So he skidded out. Everybody knows that."

"Social disintegration is typical of the late-stages alcoholic. Not everybody knows that. Withdrawal and isolation are symptoms of a disease."

Unsettled, I batted my hand in the air, waving her away.

Camille refused to quit. "Look, in the autumn of 1962, Kerouac visited John Clellon Holmes in New England. Supposedly, he was house-hunting."

"I know, I know. He spent a week sitting around the living room listening to jazz and smoking camels. Killed a quart of cognac a day."

"Also talked non-stop. Claimed to be Christ, Satan, assorted holy men, an Indian chief, a universal genius. For the last three days he didn't shave or bathe, just stumbled around in a T-shirt and pajama bottoms. Finally, Holmes had to bring him a glass of brandy to get him out of bed. Can you imagine?"

Only too well. Kerouac finished the trip with a twenty-day bar crawl that left him best friends with an ex-jailbird claiming to be an Indian chief. "So the guy went on a drunk," I said. "Big deal."

"That's just one example, Frankie. All through the sixties, Kerouac bounced up and down the East coast like a yo-yo: Florida, New England, Florida, New England."

"He kept hoping that if he found the right place, maybe he could quit drinking, turn his life around. You can't blame a guy for that."

"The geographic cure, they call it, Frankie. It's a cure that doesn't exist."

"You're not going to stop, are you?"

"The horror stories keep coming. You want social deterioration? Back in Florida, drunk on cognac and Irish whiskey, Kerouac called old friends long-distance at any time of the night or day."

"The phone bills were insane."

"Hopelessly drunk and filled with self-pity, he'd babble for hours, crying and caterwauling, telling the same stories over and over."

Camille focused on Kerouac in Florida, described another bout of delerium tremens: "Most drunks survive only two."

Then she plunged into the binges at the Wild Boar, surprising me with how much she knew. College kids would drink and carouse with Kerouac in shifts, thrilled to hang out with somebody famous, even if he had become a paunchy drunk who needed a shave and wore lumberjack shirts and blue serge pants with their bottoms rolled up and a safety pin in the ass, and roared around spouting haiku, quoting Shakespeare and doing lousy Sinatra imitations.

Kerouac would knock back beer and wine and whiskey, whatever he could lay hands on, and gloried in "belly-busting" — charging across the floor at a competitor to bang bellies — until finally he gave himself a hernia and had to strap a Kennedy half-dollar over his navel.

But Camille had reached 1968, Kerouac's Boston interlude. A journalist visited and found him drinking alone morning until night, fourteen boilermakers an hour. "You know what Nicosia wrote?"

"You're going to remind me."

"He figured Kerouac was striving 'to dramatize his situation, sacrificing whatever life was left in him to make a visible statement about the undeserved plight of American writers.' Can you believe that?"

"You memorized it. That I can't believe."

"Kerouac wasn't dramatizing anything. He was an alcoholic in the final stage of his disease — a stage that ends in death."

"Uncle, uncle!" I got to my feet. "The sun's going down."

"That brings us full circle, anyway. Back to the physical." Camille rose and brushed herself off. "An alcoholic develops varicose veins. The liver's holding out? Those veins burst and he bleeds to death."

I shielded my eyes and the mountain opposite, much of it covered in evergreens, looked like the face of a giant Greek god seen in profile, a god staring defiantly skyward, beetle-browed, full-bearded. And as I followed the direction of its stare, and looked into the darkening sky, I saw Kerouac at age forty-seven, sitting in a shadowy living room in St. Petersburg, Florida, watching television and drinking beer out of a can.

October, 1969. Kerouac is still recovering from a savage beating. One month before, at The Cactus Bar — the toughest, meanest, black man's bar in St. Pete — Kerouac had started talking "nigger talk." Someone took offence, dragged him outside and beat him senseless. He woke up in jail with cracked ribs, two black eyes and a broken nose.

Now, one eye on *The Galloping Gourmet*, Kerouac scribbles notes for yet another childhood novel: *The Spotlight Print*. He has just eaten a can of tuna. He feels sick. He rushes to the bathroom, kneels over the toilet bowl and vomits blood. "Stella!" he calls. "Stella!!"

To Camille I said, "Enough already. Please."

"That's how Kerouac died. Despite twenty-six blood transfusions. Hemorrhaging esophageal varices."

"He'd suffered a bad beating."

"The beating had nothing to do with it. The veins that rupture are buried deep in the abdomen. Kerouac's death was medically inevitable. The classic death of the alcoholic."

"Why are you doing this to me?"

I spun away down the trail, but Camille called after me: "Frankie, don't you know?"

39

One San Francisco night in 1990, with Camille lounging in the jacuzzi-jetted bathtub, recovering from Fisherman's Wharf, and the children playing Yahtzee, not fighting, I went for a walk. Drifted down Post towards Union Square, passed a cigar store and a couple of bars, not much promise, then turned up Powell Street, letting it happen. A doorman in a Beefeater costume — red jacket, white britches, broad-brimmed hat — stepped into the street and hollered, "Taxi!" Twigged my memory. I'd arrived, found what I hadn't realized I was seeking and climbed the steps into the lobby of the Sir Francis Drake Hotel.

In the elevator, a red star marked the twenty-first floor. Things were flooding back. I stepped out into the Starlite Roof, found San Francisco laid out before me and thought yes! This is what it means: that a view takes away your breath. It was early yet, not yet eight o'clock, and the place was empty. I strolled around comparing vistas and settled on a table with a south-facing window. I ordered a virgin caesar, non-alcoholic, wasn't even tempted, and stared out at the checkerboard office towers, windows light and dark, and the streaming headlights of cars rolling in from the airport. Directly below, tidy and precise, Union Square looked like a giant board game.

A jazz trio went to work playing big band standards. As the music washed over me, I thought of my father, dead now for over a decade, and realized I'd never thanked him. My eyes stung as I remembered him sitting here in the Starlite Roof, trying desperately to relate, to reach me, even to the point of describing a religious experience of his own.

But I'm getting ahead of my story.

Having written and rewritten *What God Has Done For Me*, I brought my double-spaced, sixteen-page typescript to a printing outfit. I paid in advance, roughly two hundred dollars, and made sure I was home two days later when a truck arrived with sixteen thousand bundled pages. Three days I spent collating and stapling. The morning I finished, I mailed my mother a copy of *What God Has Done For Me*. Then picked up thirty copies of my sixteen-page testament, as many as I could comfortably carry, and headed downtown.

For the next three weeks, Monday through Saturday, I made this trek twice a day, leaving home at eleven-fifteen and four o'clock to catch the rush-hour pedestrian traffic. See me short-haired and clean-shaven, dressed in blue jeans, white shirt and a tweedy grey sports jacket gone in the elbows, stationed at whatever busy intersection, Sixth and Market or Bush and Montgomery, handing *What God Has Done For Me* to anybody who'd take it. Afterwards, walking home, I'd find six or eight copies on the sidewalk or in the gutter. These I'd retrieve and, if not badly damaged, hand out again next day.

Reactions? Bicycle messengers, old competitors, took to waving as they wheeled past. Second time she saw me, a receptionist at an office where I'd frequently delivered envelopes shook her head sadly: "What a disappointment you've turned out to be." An older woman, tears in her eyes, took my arm and told me she believed — but even I could see she was disturbed.

I remember an energetic, white-haired man with an intelligent face. He stopped and debated me three times, three different intersections.

"Why are you throwing yourself away like this?"

"What I've written is true."

"You mean you believe it's true."

"What I believe and truth itself coincide."

"You should be attending university."

"If you believed *What God Has Done For Me*, you'd know there's no time."

"You're projecting."

"This is the end of the world."

Having given away all of my pamphlets but three, and with the world lingering strangely, I gravitated to the public library. I'd bring my lunch, spend whole days poking around in the religion section. I tried using the *Book of Daniel* to calculate how many months remained, but soon abandoned that. Having explored the Protestant Reformation, and been especially taken with the martyr William Tyndale, I turned to later theologians like Karl Barth and Teilhard de Chardin. But their Christianity, compared with that of Tyndale, who was burned at the stake for heresy, lay dead on the page.

What was I supposed to do next? Make and distribute more copies of *What God Has Done For Me*? Go elsewhere and repeat my performance. See me gloomily wrestling with these questions one grey afternoon as I made my way home from the library. What I needed, I thought as I crossed a vacant lot and swung onto Grove Street, what I badly needed was another sign from God.

Half a block from my rooming house, I noticed a man sitting on the front steps — a white man. I hadn't seen another white man in this neighborhood since I'd arrived. This one wore a brown sports jacket, a white shirt open at the neck. I kept walking, then stopped. The man stood up. It couldn't be. It simply could not be.

I spun on my heel. I took two steps, then wheeled again. Felt as if someone had kicked me in the stomach. Gasping for breath, doubled over, I grabbed the nearest railing. This was impossible. My father was home in Ste. Thérèse, boozing and running up bills. He couldn't be here in San Francisco. Yet here he was, trotting along the sidewalk towards me, re-naming me: "Frankie! Frankie, are you all right?"

Stunned, breathless, unable to speak, I lowered myself onto the nearest steps. This couldn't be happening. I sat shaking my head as my father shook my shoulder: "Are you all right, Frankie? Are you okay?"

Talk about shock. Nothing, but nothing, could have shaken me more than to discover my father in San Francisco. The moment I found him on the front steps of the rooming house — a reality impossible to assimilate — my elaborate Christianity was doomed to destruction.

I pulled myself together, invited my father into the house. He sat on the single chair in my room, a flesh-and-blood apparition, while I lay, shocked, on the bed. My father, afraid to travel by airplane, described his train ride, coach-class, across the continent from Montreal. He showed me photographs of Ste. Thérèse — of the house, my siblings, my mother.

"I wanted you to put that thousand dollars against the bills," I blurted. "Not spend it on a train ticket."

"Your mother and I talked it over. We thought seeing you was more important."

"When did you decide that?"

"A couple of weeks ago. After we received your story."

"Why did YOU come instead of her?"

"I wanted to come. She didn't want to travel alone. One of us had to say with the kids."

"What about your job?"

"They gave me a leave of absence." My father glanced at his watch, stood and filled the room. "Look, why don't I go back to my hotel, get cleaned up. Give you a moment to think. We can meet for supper."

This I welcomed.

My father gone, I stretched out on my bed and closed my eyes. I could see my parents sitting in the kitchen at Ste. Thérèse. They didn't believe the end of the world was at hand. They thought I'd gone nuts. But hadn't the Bible warned me? No man is a prophet in his own land. How could they believe? Probably my father would try to talk me into returning home. His visit was a last temptation, a final test. I steeled myself.

The next three days I spent rambling around San Francisco with my father. We rode cable cars, shopped in Chinatown, ate lobster at Fisherman's Wharf. For eight months I'd been buried, playing the urban hermit, and the city's vitality knocked me out. But of course! Again the Bible came to my rescue: "They did eat, they drank, they married wives and were given in marriage, until the day that Noah entered the ark, and the flood came and destroyed them all."

Alone at night, shaken despite my denial, I reviewed the experiences that had led me to this moment: the storm-tossed baptism, the manifestation of Jesus, the temptation by the devil, the vision of the end. No getting around it. I'd seen what I'd seen, and what I'd seen proved that now was the end of the world.

My father listened patiently, but preferred to reminisce about his boyhood. Strolling along the Embarcadero in the sunshine, he recalled how the Great Depression had forced him to quit school at fifteen. "For years I'd been working part-time, selling *Gazettes* outside Windsor Station, the bulldog edition, ten o'clock at night: 'Paper mister?' Then the Depression hit. My father was laid off. I got a full-time job in a shoe factory, worked ten hours a day. Seventeen dollars a week, they paid me."

"And glad you were to get it. Dad, I know all that. None of it matters any more. Didn't you read *What God Has Done For Me*?"

"I read it, son." My father lit a cigarette. "I'm just not sure what it means."

"This is the end of the world."

My father threw his arm around my shoulder. "Come on, Frankie, let's get a coffee."

So it went. I wanted to talk apocalypse and my father wanted to talk anything but. The following afternoon, having led him through Golden Gate Park to Ocean Beach, we stood in the sand and I said: "This is it. This is where I was baptized."

"Don't move." My father was looking at me through the lens of his camera. "Great shot. Perfect." He removed the camera from his neck. "Here, Frankie, take one of me against the ocean."

My father removed his shoes and stepped into the water up to his ankles. "Commemorate my visit."

"Dad, there's no point commemorating anything. This is the end of the world, remember?"

"Don't shoot directly into the sun."

That night, his second last in San Francisco, my father insisted on taking me to the Starlite Roof. He'd discovered it the night before, after I'd gone home. Couldn't get over the view. We sat drinking Cokes — a gesture on his part — and my father said he'd once had a religious experience. "Not a major one, like yours. But I remember it vividly. Never told anybody, not even your mother."

He'd gone into Montreal to apply for a sales job and found it taken. On his way home, he stopped off in Coeur d'Aimée for a couple of beers. Missed the last bus and had to walk the two miles. Early autumn, this was, the night chilly but not freezing cold. "I was feeling low," he said, "down on myself. As I was passing the monastery — you know, on the hill? — I sensed a … a presence. I looked up at the sky, all bright with stars, and I swear I heard a voice say, 'Your father is with you, my son. Be at peace.'"

"'Your father is with you?'"

He nodded, took out his cigarettes. "Two days later, I got a phone call. The first guy hadn't worked out. The sales job was mine if I wanted it." He finished lighting up and shook out his match. "Right away, I thought of that voice."

"And you didn't tell anybody."

"Sounded ridiculous."

"What about Christian responsibility?"

"I thought the experience was private. Something between me and God."

Half an hour later, from a telephone booth near Union Square, we called my mother in Ste. Thérèse. My father, who'd phoned earlier, said a few words, then handed me the receiver. I hadn't heard my mother's voice in more than a year. Suddenly she was next door. Everybody was well. But then: "You're coming home with your father?"

"Mom, I've got work to do here."

"You can get a job in Montreal and help out if you want."

"Mom, I'm not doing that any more. Don't you understand? This is the end of the world."

"You were going to be a writer."

"That doesn't mean anything, Mom. Didn't you read *What God Has Done For Me*?"

"I read it, Frankie."

"You've got to believe, Mom. Do you understand? You've got to believe so you'll be saved."

My mother said nothing.

"Mom?" I pressed the receiver tight against my ear. "Mom? Are you there?"

"Yes."

"Mom, please don't cry! As long as you believe in Jesus, everything will be all right."

"Frankie, I want you to come home."

"Mom, please!" I too started to cry. "You've got to believe so you'll be saved. Tell me you believe, Mom. Tell me you believe."

"I believe in you, Frankie. But I want you to come home."

"Not in me, Mom. Not in — " But I was crying too hard to continue.

"Here, son, take this."

I traded the telephone for a handkerchief.

My father said goodbye for both of us, then led the way to a restaurant, where we sat in a booth drinking coffee. Hearing my mother's voice had upset me more than I'd expected. My father was saying something about having reserved a second train ticket. "We can pick it up tomorrow."

"What are you talking about?"

"Train leaves next day. That'll give you time to pack, say any goodbyes."

"Dad, I'm not going home. I've got work to do."

"What work?"

"My Father's work."

"Frankie, I'm your father. And I think you've been here long enough. Too long. You got involved with the wrong bunch, took some bad drugs. What you need — "

"This has nothing to do with drugs. I'll never deny the things I've seen. Pretend I didn't see them."

"I'm not asking you to deny anything. But maybe a change of scene — "

"Dad, it's all in the Bible. 'No man, having put his hand to the plow and looking back, is fit for the kingdom of God.'"

"I've made mistakes, Frankie." My father looked down at the table. When he looked up again, he had tears in his eyes. "All I can say is … I love you."

"I love you, too. But Jesus said: 'He that loves father or mother more than me is not worthy of me.'"

"Frankie, I'm asking you to come home."

"This is a last temptation. I'm not going anywhere. That's final."

Two days later, my father gone, I tried to resume my routine. I visited the religion section of the public library, brought my lunch. Discovered I couldn't concentrate. Started taking walks, endless walks. My father was gone, but he'd left me awash in memories. I'd colored him bad, but now I remembered how, once or twice a year, with Uncle Henry visiting, he'd hang a white sheet in the front room, dig out his projector and show the black-and-white movies he'd made as a young man.

Fifteen years old, my father had donned a bib and bonnet, climbed into a baby carriage and bounced down the side of Mount Royal, making like one of the Three Stooges. Almost got killed. Two years later, he started writing scripts, creating his own roles. Goodbye slapstick, hello gangsterism. I remembered his masterpiece, a twenty-minute feature called *Retribution*, my father starring as a smooth-talking hoodlum who masterminds a heist, double-crosses his cronies and ends up plunging to his death from a train bridge.

I remembered his love of literature. How one Sunday afternoon, when I complained that I had nothing to do, my father bounced up out of his arm chair. "Nothing to do? By jingo, I'll give you something to do!"

He hitched up his baggy pants and made for the front porch. My mother looked up from ironing: "You're not digging out those old books."

He waved his arm and kept going. We could hear him rummaging in his bookcase, knocking over knick-knacks, ex-claiming. Eventually he emerged carrying half a dozen dog-eared volumes. Sat down on the couch and waved me over beside him. "Here, you son of a gun. *The Grapes of Wrath*. What a story."

"Maurice, he's fourteen, remember?"

"Doesn't matter. Look, Frankie, *Martin Eden*. You've read *Call of The Wild*? Same author — Jack London. Here, take it. Or look! *You Can't Go Home Again!*"

He opened the novel, stood up and started reading aloud, waving his arms. My mother said, "Maurice, please!" Finally, he snapped the book shut. "Ever heard anything like that? I'll tell the world you haven't. Here! Take it! Take Thomas Wolfe and read. Don't tell me you've got nothing to do."

All this, during the past year, I'd forgotten. Again the night of the butcher knife came back. But now I remembered, as well, that next day at lunch, my father tried to apologize. He mumbled something about drinking, what it does, how it makes people say things they don't mean. I'd stood up, without a word, and left the table.

Also, for the first time, I remembered another night, when my father brought a friend home from La Fin Du Monde, a guy named Allen. They sat at the kitchen table quaffing beer, laughing and talking. From my bed I could hear every word. Allen had published short stories in an adventure magazine.

My father went to the front porch and dug out one of the stories he'd written in Halifax, during the war, came back and began reading aloud. It was a funny story about a private on latrine duty who tries to pass himself off as a major.

Allen guffawed and pounded the table.

From her bed, my mother yelled, "Keep the noise down, Maurice. People are trying to sleep."

My father kept reading.

When he'd finished, Allen applauded, said the story was hilarious and wrote down the name of a magazine editor.

"Just a minute," my father said, pushing back his chair. "Stay right where you are."

I thought he was going to dig out another story, but no: he pulled open the curtain in my doorway. "Frankie! Frankie, wake up." I pretended to sleep and he shook me. "Frankie, there's someone I'd like you to meet."

Suddenly my mother was in the bedroom as well. "Maurice! What do you think you're doing?"

"What? I'm talking to Frankie."

"Frankie has to get up at five o'clock to deliver *Gazettes*. Get out of here and leave him alone. Haven't you got any sense?"

"All right, all right." My father straightened up. "He's my son, too, you know."

"Up all hours of the night, drinking and carrying on. Keeping the whole house awake."

My father left the bedroom: "Calm down, Maggie."

"I won't calm down." My mother jerked the curtain shut and followed him into the kitchen. "No consideration for anybody but yourself."

"Okay, Maggie, go back to bed."

"Drink, drink, drink. That's all you know how to do. I'm sick to death of it."

Allen pushed back his chair. "Maybe I'd better be on my way."

"No, no," my father said. "No rush."

"You and your drunken-bum friends." My mother went into her bedroom but kept yelling. "Good-for-nothing alcoholics, the lot of you. No-good drunken bums."

She started to cry.

"It's getting late," Allen said. "I really do have to go. We'll get together another night."

"I wanted you to meet my son."

"Next time, Maurice."

But there never was a next time.

My father never did send away any stories. And in San Francisco, as I sat in the autumn sunshine on the steps of the public library, remembering, I wondered: had I judged my father too harshly? And what of my mother? I kept hearing her sob-choked voice, saying she wanted me home.

I'd withstood that last temptation.

But the world refused to end and still no new sign. What was I supposed to do? Resume my old job, save like mad and produce another thousand copies of *What God Has Done For Me*? That didn't sound right. If God wanted more people to read my pamphlet, all He had to do was make *The Chronicle* run it on page one. Maybe I'd finished with San Francisco. Maybe I was supposed to shake the dust off my feet, go elsewhere and do it all again. But where? New Orleans?

Wait a minute. Maybe my father's visit wasn't a last temptation, after all. Slowly I got to my feet. Maybe it was a sign indicating Montreal. And Ste. Thérèse. I looked up at the sky and scudding clouds took the shape of a pointing hand — but, no: I needed serious confirmation.

I'd go to the bank, that was it. See how much money I had left. Then I'd visit the bus depot. I started down the steps. If I had enough for a bus ticket home, that would be confirmation. If I didn't, that would mean I wasn't supposed to go — not yet, anyway.

Vaguely, I knew that roughly three hundred dollars remained. More than enough, surely. At the bottom of the stairs I broke into a trot. Ste. Thérèse! I was going home to Ste. Thérèse.

40

My last morning on Mount Jubilation I awoke strangely early and didn't know why. The sky was still grey. I huddled deeper into my bag, determined to re-enter sleep. Then came a light brushing, a tapping sound, at the west window. Incredulous, I began to understand. Snow? In early September?

On my feet, still disbelieving, I looked out. Giant snowflakes were falling like petals, but so thickly that I couldn't see twenty feet. A fragment from Joyce danced through my agitated mind, that bit about snowflakes falling faintly through the universe on the living and the dead.

That led me to marvel yet again at Frankie's post-Christian revival — the perfect rejoinder to my alcoholic decline. And I flashed to the previous year, the night after I died in St. Petersburg, and realized that in Montreal, fully himself again, Frankie dreamed he saw me waving to him, signalling, and understood that I wanted him back on the road.

Now here we were on Jubilation. I stood watching snow fall as the morning slowly brightened. Cloud-split sun-beams turned the giant, tumbling flakes a million shades of pink and red and I recognized my own last sign: a shower of roses from Saint Thérèse.

I pulled on my hiking boots and climbed out of the tower. The snow, soft and powdery, lay two inches thick on the ground. Squirrels and chipmunks had criss-crossed the path to the cabin. Mounting the front steps, I cried, "Frankie!" Thumped on the door. "It's show-time."

"I'm up! Come on in."

I stomped the snow off my feet and entered the cabin. Frankie, fully dressed but bootless, stood hunched over the wood stove lighting matches.

I said, "Have you looked outside?"

He fanned a spark to no avail. "Not yet. What's to see?"

"Would you believe snow faintly falling?"

Frankie glanced at my wet boots and stepped to the window. "I don't believe it! The warden said it wouldn't snow until Labor Day."

"It's a message from Saint Thérèse."

"Fantastic! Even if it melts, the snow has already reduced the fire hazard to zero. There's no point keeping me here."

"I thought you liked it here."

"I do, I do." Frankie was pacing back and forth, rubbing his hands together. "But I've got places to go, people to see."

"Take your readings," I said. "Talk to the warden. I'll make breakfast."

Frankie pulled on his boots, grabbed his jacket and disappeared out the door. To make breakfast I went into overdrive. Within minutes I had the woodstove crackling and breakfast on the table.

Frankie came through the door stamping his feet and talking: "They weren't expecting this so they have no horses at the Crossing. But they'll ride up to collect me and my gear within the next couple of days." He shucked off his jacket and flung it on the bed. "I'll have just enough time to burn the garbage and clean up. Bring some wood inside, maybe cover the rest with plastic sheeting."

"Breakfast is served," I said, whipping paper napkins off the plates.

"Bacon and scrambled eggs?" Frankie sat down at the table. "Where'd you get the bacon?"

I sat down beside him. "Had it in my pack."

"But it must be bad."

I reached over, took half a package of bacon from the counter behind the woodstove and handed it to him.

"Still frozen. How the —"

"Magic is alive." I started to eat. "Dig in. Your breakfast's getting cold."

"You must have brought a special cooler."

After breakfast I packed my rucksack, rearranged the top layer and tightened the straps. Then I made another pot of coffee. When Frankie finished the dishes he sat down with me at the table: "Listen, I'm feeling bad about blowing up yesterday. I've enjoyed your Kerouac fantasy. I just can't get into it, that's all."

"Not to worry, Frankie." From a side pocket of my rucksack, almost as an afterthought, I pulled a dog-eared copy of *Ulysses*. "Here, I want you to have this. Old Joyce is the father of us all."

Frankie took the book: "I don't know what to say."

"That's professional development." I pulled on my jacket. "Leaves only magic and human relations."

"Come again?"

I dragged my rucksack across the floor: "Help me get this outside."

Frankie held the door while I swung my pack onto the porch. The snow had stopped falling, but covered the dark green branches of the trees and lay an inch thick along the rails of the log fence.

We stood a moment, enjoying the transformation. Then I swung my rucksack onto one shoulder and together we went down the steps and out the front gate. We both knew that we had to sit one last time on the old grey stump. I dropped my rucksack at the foot of the tower while Frankie brushed off the stump and sat down. As I joined him, he said, "Magic and human relations?"

"The last shall be first," I said. "Just look at this day!" I waved my arm to take in the sunshine, the sky now cloudless and blue, the whipped-cream mountain peaks. "This calls for champagne."

"I'd settle for applejack."

"Why settle when you can have bubbly?" I reached around behind the stump, produced a bottle of chilled Mumm's and two champagne glasses: "*Voîlà!*"

Frankie gaped: "How the — "

I wedged the glasses between us on the stump, popped the cork and poured. Handing Frankie a glass, I said, "Be sure there's champagne in it."

Still speechless, he stared at me, hard.

"Emotional honesty," I said.

"Sleight of hand," Frankie said. "Cooled the bottle in the snow. But you're best I've ever seen. Ever work as a magician?"

"Here's to human relations." I picked up the other glass and grinned. "To Camille."

Tentatively, Frankie drank the toast. "What about Camille?"

"Frankie, with women you're sliding. You're back to where you were before your stint as Saint Jack of the Sixteen-Page Pamphlet."

"Here we go."

"You were rolling down the highway and women were gas stations, remember? 'Check your oil, sir?' In San Francisco, you got spun around and found yourself bouncing through uncharted territory, a desert of dirt roads and sand dunes. You didn't get your bearings until Camille."

"So what about Camille?"

"Well, we could start with the night you tried to whip off a quickie with Barbara."

"Okay, so you've talked with her."

"She forgave you. Now you — "

"I don't want to discuss it."

"Nobody's perfect, Frankie. If San Francisco taught you nothing else..."

"I said I don't want to discuss it."

"Prepare to grovel, Frankie." I downed the last of my champagne, stood and carefully set the glass on the stump. "Maybe she'll give you another chance."

"You're not leaving yet?" He stood up.

"Can't ignore the proprieties."

Together we strolled to the tower, but as I bent to retrieve my rucksack, Frankie grabbed me from behind, locked me into a half-nelson. "You're not going anywhere," he said, twisting my right arm up behind my back. "Not until you tell me how you know so much about me."

"You sure you want to do this? I was once Black Mask Champeen of my neighborhood."

He twisted my arm higher. "Who the hell are you?"

I gave him an elbow and we fell to the ground in a tangle. Frankie was quicker than I'd expected, stronger than he looked, and we rolled around in the snow at the foot of the tower. Finally, I let him flip me over onto my belly. He straddled me, bent my left arm high and folded a knee over the hold. "All right, who are you?"

"I'm Jack Kerouac."

"I said, who are you!"

"Jean-Louis François Alexandre Lebris de Kerouac?"

"Listen, wise guy, how do you know so much about me?"

"Angels are like that."

"You've got an agenda."

"Yes! I want your confession."

"You're holding out on me. Who the hell are you?"

"I'm your brother, your father, your son."

"Cut the crap."

"Your ghost, your angel, your shadow. Frankie, I'm your Doctor Sax."

He twisted my arm higher still.

"You fool! I'm your Self!" In a single impossible motion, I tossed Frankie into the air and sprang to my feet. He landed on his butt, astonished, and I helped him up.

"That was quite a move," he said.

"Black Mask Champeen."

"You're not going to tell me who you are."

I laughed and shook my head and he interpreted this as a "no." I brushed myself off and retrieved my rucksack and this time Frankie insisted on helping me adjust it.

We faced each other and I held out my hand. "Angels can grant wishes, you know."

Frankie shook my hand and grinned. "I don't believe in angels. But I enjoyed our duets. Maybe you'll leave me your voice?"

"You've got your own. But if you think you can survive cheap shots, you're welcome to my point of view."

"That should come in handy. Sorry about the rough stuff."

"It's been real, Frankie."

"Be careful going down."

"I'm not going down." I strode over to the tower and started to climb. "I'm going up."

"Want to take a last look around? Why didn't you say so? Leave your pack here."

I kept climbing.

When I reached the platform, I shoved my rucksack through the trap door and clambered after it. Frankie started up the ladder. By the time he joined me in the office, I had my pack on my back and the north window open.

"I didn't want to do this, Frankie, but you've left me no choice." I pulled a red rose out of his shirt pocket and fixed it in his wild black hair, then laughed at the look on his face. "Take care of yourself."

Quickly, then, I stepped onto the chair and out the open window into thin air — or so it would have looked to Frankie. In truth I stepped onto a dirt road that wound past the tower and rolled away over the mountains, up, up and away.

In my best W. C. Fields voice, I said, "Magic is alive, my boy." Then, in my own voice: "All you have to do is believe in your Self."

I wheeled and strode away up the road.

I hadn't gone twenty paces when Frankie hollered: "Kerouac! Jack Kerouac!"

I turned and did a little jig. "So you do know my full name."

"Jack, wait for me!" Frankie started to climb out the window. "I want to come with you."

"Frankie, no! You've got work to do."

He stopped: "I need you, Jack!"

"I'm with you."

"Jack, don't go! I — I love you."

One last time I drew on Sinatra, broke into song: "S'wonderful/ s'marvellous/ that you should care for me."

Frankie laughed despite himself and I watched understanding settle into his face as he perched there on the window sill, my rose glowing red in his wild dark hair. I saw his pride and foolishness fall away and recognized the angel he'd found in the mirror by the ocean, the boy who took his heart into the streets of San Francisco.

262

I waved once more, and this time, tentatively, Frankie waved back. Finally I turned, hefted my rucksack higher and, madly whistling *When The Saints*, strode away over the mountains.

41

Alcoholic beverages compare to psychedelic drugs as conventional weapons to nuclear ones. The drugs aren't addictive but they're faster. Same with the archetypal morality play that ensues as, under massive assault, the Self fights to survive. My failure to appreciate this led to my cold-sweat dilemma in Vesuvio's bar in 1990.

This I realize only now, as I stare at my tube in the back room of our house. Outside, the sun shines, birds chirp at a feeder and melted snow streams off the roof into rain barrels. Having opened my window, I can hear Camille and the children chatting as they build a last-chance snowman. Spring is stripping white blankets from the mountains to expose slate-grey rock, beautiful but rugged. Here in the Rockies, spring is a season of Timeless Truth.

Make that Relative. Already, in Time, the would-be prophet I was, Saint Jack of the Sixteen-Page Pamphlet, is nearer the King of the Beats than me. Young Frankie is a quarter century distant as I write, but just twelve years from 1955, when Kerouac shouted "Go, go, go" at the San Francisco poetry reading that kicked off the Beat Generation frenzy.

But 1967. Home from San Francisco, I confronted a world of extraordinary vitality. Faced with people and places I'd known from my previous life, and whose on-going existence, half-forgotten, spoke volumes, I hunted an intellectual escape hatch. Discovered the evangelical notion of separating faith from experience. Maybe I could insist on the reality of the things I'd experienced while leaving open their interpretation?

A postmodern moment.

My elaborate Christianity collapsed around me. Out of the rubble I walked naked and, with nothing better do do, set to work

264

rebuilding. I renewed friendships, revisited old haunts, re-read favorite authors. Only second time around, barely into my twenties, I did it faster.

Also, I met Camille. Another story.

By early 1970 I was back on the road. That summer found me on Mount Jubiliation, Kerouac-wrestling, a Rocky Mountain fire lookout haunted still by the psychedelic nightmare of the Haight. Unable to assimilate the archetypal experience because I refused to recognize myself in the boy who'd walked out into the streets of San Francisco carrying a sixteen-page pamphlet.

Ancient history, now.

Having lost Camille, I came down from the mountain. Found her again. Swore to do better. And began a second descent into the maelstrom, this one more gradual than the first. Not a psychedelic plunge but an alcoholic slide, a relentless slipping down a grassy slope until suddenly I was over the edge and in water over my head and thrashing, tumbling, caught in the vortex of addiction.

Camille tried to reach me.

But even my father's death, of alcohol-related cirrhosis, I used as another excuse to drink. The details are banal. As the home-front struggle escalated, I stashed bottles of whiskey in cold-air ventilator shafts and down the tank of the toilet. One bottle I hid under the hood of the station wagon, strapped it into the container that holds washer fluid and ran a tube out of it. While driving, I'd pull over to investigate a non-existent rattle, raise high the hood and take a couple of secret belts.

Not long after Camille began advancing Kerouac theories, I smashed the car into a stone wall that encircles Banff Hot Springs. Walked away with minor cuts and bruises, but Camille said that's it. Sprung a full-scale Intervention. I arrived home one afternoon to find all our friends and most of my colleagues in the living room — even my boss, the publisher of *The Rocky Mountain Miracle*.

They all agreed I was an alcoholic and that I needed help. Reminded me of the night I stumbled "home" into the wrong house. Of the afternoon I ordered our most important advertiser out of the office. Of the blackout I experienced after speaking to a local writers' group. They wanted to send me to a rehab-centre in Saskatchewan.

"I'll cut back my drinking," I said. "But I'm not an alcoholic. I'm not going off to any clinic."

Two friends wavered.

Camille cried: "Frankie, look what happened to Jack Kerouac!"

"If Kerouac had wanted," I said, "he could have cut back."

"Kerouac was an alcoholic, Frankie. Once started drinking, he couldn't control it — not any more than you can control diarrhea."

"Says you."

"Says most of the serious literature. Kerouac needed help to break free of his addiction. But back in the Sixties, nobody knew how to give it to him."

"He didn't have to go to any clinic."

"If he was going to live he did."

In the end I played along. Five weeks, two of them ugly, I stayed at the clinic. I listened to mumbo-jumbo about spiritual awakening and steps to recovery and came home dry but un-repentant. I wasn't an alcoholic, not like some I'd met. I still had a job. I'd never slept in the gutter.

By the time we visited San Francisco to celebrate my sobriety, and I found myself in Vesuvio's facing the Jack Kerouac Special, I hadn't touched a drop for six months. From the other end of the bar, a black-haired stranger tipped an imaginary hat. I returned the gesture and was about to send back the Special when resentment swept me.

Why shouldn't I have a drink? Hadn't I proven — not to Camille, perhaps, but to any impartial observer — that I was no ordinary alcoholic? That I could control my drinking? This was my chance to prove it.

A sniff told me the Special packed wallop. My whole body shuddered. As I reached for the glass, my hand trembling, I glanced again at the stranger. And found myself looking at Kerouac. For an instant, I stared. The stranger became himself again. He got to his feet and lurched my way, threw his arm around my shoulder.

"Don't I remember you from Quebec City?" He slurred his words. "That Kerouac conference?"

His face was puffy, his eyes bloodshot. His breath stank.

"I don't think so."

"You're the wild man from the mountains!"

"No, not me." I felt disgusted, yet also envious. Drunk out of his skull, this guy didn't give a damn. "Thanks," I said, pushing the Special his way, "but no thanks."

"It was you, all right. You've gone smarmy. Holier-than-thou."

"I just don't feel like drinking."

"That's a Jack Kerouac Special!"

"Look, I appreciate the gesture, really."

"You can control it, you know." He pushed the chimney glass at me. "One drink won't hurt."

Then the weirdness took over and I spun out in freeze-frame slow motion, back to that moment in the Haight more than two decades before, when I'd returned to the Drugstore Café to confront the Devil, found myself in Hell and stumbled out the door while a woman exclaimed, "Decisions, decisions!"

"No! I can't do it alone!"

So, in Vesuvio's, I shouted into the face of the black-haired stranger. "Don't you understand? I'm an alcoholic."

For the first time, I meant it. One drink wouldn't kill me, but set me back it would. Already I was on my feet. I wanted to see Camille. Having slapped two dollars onto the bar, and with the black-haired stranger gaping, I tumbled out of Vesuvio's into the sunshine and and broke into a run along Jack Kerouac Alley.

I swung right onto Columbus, my camera bag flapping, and for an instant saw myself from above — just another nameless tourist lost in the memory lanes of San Francisco. And as I danced through the pedestrian traffic, making for Post, for Camille and the children, I had a vision of myself at home in the Rockies, a flash-forward to this room where I've spent an endless winter saying goodbye to Kerouac and the boy I once was, and I imagined myself ending this long farewell with my mad dash through the streets of the city.

Only now, as I begin what I realize will become my closing sentence, ambivalent about reaching that final full stop — though anxious, even aching, to plunge outside and join my family at that evolving last-chance snowman — I think of the summer I spent on Mount Jubilation, about the promises I made to Jack Kerouac and myself, and I feel absolved, exonerated, and again I see the falling snow that freed me to seek Camille, the snow faintly falling on me and my father and the Great Walking Saint, who waved and disappeared over the mountains like a ghost, and I recognize with a shock that I, too, am a ghost, swinging away over the mountains, that I exist only by the grace of you who read these lines, and I remember that, *ciboire!* the last word belongs to someone else:

A BEGINNING, PERHAPS.